RED TIDE

by

PEG BRANTLEY

To Victoria —
Enjoy!

RED

TIDE

BY

Peg Brantley (signature)

PEG BRANTLEY

BARK

PUBLISHING LLC

2012

RED TIDE
Copyright © 2012 by Peg Brantley

ISBN: 978-0-9853638-1-9

Published in the United States of America by Bark Publishing, LLC

Cover Design by Patty G. Henderson at Boulevard Photografica, www.boulevardphotografica.yolasite.com

To my mom, who loved and believed in me even when she wasn't here. Happy birthday, Mom.

To my dad and my sister who showed me it could happen.

And to my husband, the Love of My Life, who has waited patiently for the done-done version.

"And all the waters that were in the river were turned to blood. The fish that were in the river died, the river stank and the Egyptians could not drink of the water of the river..."

Exodus 7:20-21
New King James Version

CHAPTER ONE

Sometimes the dead shouldn't stay buried.

Jamie Taylor ducked under an aspen branch. Sometimes the dead needed to be unearthed, exposed, examined, and prayed over.

And sometimes, mulchy, worm-filled graves were not meant to be their final resting places. Places where secrets remained hidden, held fast to rotted flesh and dry bones.

"Never," Jamie said. "People are not meant to be buried in unmarked, unremembered tombs. Not as long as I have anything to say about it." She and Gretchen had begun their search in earnest when the golden retriever alerted next to a mountain laurel. There, Jamie found a small, fragile piece of stained cloth. She marked it with a utility flag so the crime lab tech could photograph and bag the bit of evidence, and then she moved on with her dog, spirits high with the promise they'd find what they were looking for soon.

Hours later, physical exhaustion gave way to punchiness, and her certainty flagged to a dull depression. Jamie signaled to Gretchen with a light tug on the lead. "Time for a break." The golden gave her a look that said, "Not yet," but Jamie knew Gretchen would go until she could go no further.

1

"I need some water, my sweet. And you're getting some even if you don't consider it a priority."

Jamie hiked a few feet up and behind the ground they'd already covered and settled onto a flat rock, her supply pack at her feet. She dug out water for the two of them and surveyed the field they'd been searching since early that morning.

Field... more like prairie. She and one other handler were searching a hundred acres of high country meadow. Beautiful. Until you were forced to navigate the rough and rocky terrain hidden beneath the grasses.

They were looking for the body of a forty-two year old woman, missing for over a year. Her husband, finally drunk enough to tell his dirty little secret to a woman he'd met in a bar, said no one would ever find the body. The woman, after thinking about it for a while, became sufficiently terrorized to go to the authorities.

Analeise Reardon deserves a proper burial. She deserves to be prayed over by people who love her. Her parents, and her three children, deserve to have some closure. "And her damned husband deserves to have his arms cut off at his elbows and stuffed up his ass for starters," she mumbled.

Painful memories of Jamie's mother's murder flooded her thoughts and her breaths grew shallow and quick. Her ribs compressed until they felt like strong, bony fingers squeezing inside her chest. Her vision blurred, and instinct—born of deliberate practice—forced her to shake her head to shatter the tension. She pulled a breath deep into her lungs, then forced air out. *Inhale. Calm.*

This wasn't the first time Jamie and her dogs had participated in a search for a body as a result of someone who had decided divorce cost too much time, money and trouble. It also wouldn't be the last. People never failed to disappoint her.

2

Jamie's gaze travelled the edge of the field and she found a visual she might never have seen as part of the original search plan. Even Gretchen, working the established scent cone pattern, might not have picked up something that far out of the search area.

"C'mon girl. We've got a grave to find." She stowed the water and tucked her supply pack out of the way on her back. Her soil probe slipped easily from its holder, a sort of magic wand to use on her quest. Gretchen gave her a look that in a teenager would have involved rolled eyes and stood, ready to get back to work.

Jamie keyed a number into her cell. "It's me. I've got an anomaly. Grasses." She recorded her present coordinates on the handheld GPS she'd splurged on last summer and began the hike over to the area she'd spotted where the grass grew lush in comparison to nearby vegetation.

The path she took brought her back to the primary search area, then up again, almost fifty yards. Sure enough, a small area of prairie grass was growing thicker and darker and higher than anything else around it. Before she could sink her probe all the way into the earth to create the first breathing hole, Gretchen dropped to the ground. Full alert.

Nearby the song of a meadowlark filled the mountain air.

Sometimes, with a little help, the dead don't stay buried.

CHAPTER TWO

Gray walls, gray ceiling and floor, poured concrete table and chairs—all blended together to eliminate any visual stimulation. Colorado's Supermax prison facility didn't waste any funds on interior design. The lack of color made the stink of sweat and urine seem touchable. Assistant Special Agent in Charge Nicholas Grant hated it here.

He dry-swallowed two oxycontin tablets, his sixth and seventh of the day, no longer certain his back condition bore any relevance to his need for what he euphemistically referred to as "pain management." Now however, wasn't the time to consider his motivation for popping the pills. It hadn't been the time for close to two years but he didn't want to think about that either. He tapped the amber plastic bottle in his pocket, assured by its presence and the control it represented.

The semi-public area was eerily quiet compared to other parts of the penitentiary. But rather than tranquility, the air spiked with anger, resentment and distrust. No one left here the same as when they came in. No one. Not even him.

Prior to his arrival, the prison authorities had checked out and cleared the wall-mounted camera and recording equipment. No extra feeds to an unauthorized receiver were in place and everything tested in working order. So far technology had chronicled his failures on this case. Maybe today it would record a success.

Before beginning the interview, Nick was glad to have somewhere to go to complete his mental preparation and give his subject time to stew. Inmates measure their freedom, such as it is, in inches. *When the guards brought Leopold Bonzer into the interview room and secured him to the cuff rings, his incarcerated ass would be about as mobile as a sick snail on a slow day.*

Nick wandered back up to the security screening area in between two of the guard towers and settled on the corner of an unoccupied but cluttered desk that was already piled with stacks of forms, folders that looked like they had been pulled from a filing cabinet and dumped, unopened sleeves of Styrofoam cups, two canisters of powder for hot chocolate and a few old *People* magazines.

Nick worked to stay on good terms with all of the guards in this part of the prison. Over the years he'd popped in and out enough times to know about births and deaths, marriages and divorces. He knew which guards were die-hard Bronco fans, which ones followed the Rockies and even one who secretly pulled for the Redwings.

"Thanks for getting me the contact request list for Bonzer so fast." Nick fist-bumped the guard. "You'd think after all this time even the tabloid reporters would know they can't have access to inmates here." Sensational stories sold papers. And a serial killer who admitted to murdering fourteen people was pretty sensational. A serial killer who wouldn't give up the location of thirteen of those bodies and to whom no other members of the media had access was especially prime.

The tenth anniversary of the sentencing for Leopold

Bonzer loomed a little over three months away. It had been Bonzer's bad luck to get caught red-handed. He'd killed a postal worker vacationing at Maroon Bells, and then got stopped on his way to dispose of the body. The murder of a federal employee on public land received the attention of the FBI, and Nick had smelled more blood from his very first meeting with the suspect. He hadn't quit in ten years. *Be damned if I'll quit now.*

Slow to give up, the supermarket rags had continued to cook the Bonzer story at a slow spin, like a pig on a spit. They fanned the flames just enough to get a little sizzle, especially on the anniversary of his sentencing, but never so much that the story had dropped into the flames and smoldered away to an ashy memory.

The guard nodded and looked at Nick. "Some guys, their families try to get in to see 'em even when they know they can't. Bonzer's family, if he's got one, is smart enough to have cut him loose. Your guy is almost as big a media draw as our resident terrorists in H-Unit." The prison guard leaned back in his chair and used a toothpick to dig out what Nick assumed were remnants from his lunch. The man sucked some spit, then motioned to one of the camera images with the tiny wooden pointer. "They're loading him in now, Agent. What's your plan this time?"

Nick tensed his jaw. *Is that a smirk? A dig at my lack of success over the last ten years? Professional, not personal, right? Don't let this guy get to you. He's a friggin' security guard for crying out loud. Besides, he has a point.* He shrugged. "Wish I had a plan. Nothing's worked so far. He's looking for some kind of deal in exchange for details on the bodies but I've got nothing to offer. He doesn't even want to try to negotiate his way to a different facility. Claims he's happy here."

"I'd help you if I could. You're different from the other feds we're expected to work with, and if I could think of

6

something to get you what you need, I'd do it. So would most of the staff here. You want to help those families, not just move your own career a rung up the ladder. And it's pretty clear the Bonzer case is more of a career killer."

A sudden wave of doubt poured over Nick. His success rate at the bureau put him near the top, but the one criticism he'd endured review after review was that he might be too soft. His superiors claimed he got too involved in his cases and failed to maintain enough professional detachment. *But if you don't care, why put your life in jeopardy in the first place?* The day he developed "professional detachment" would be the day he would know he needed to get out.

Nicholas Grant thought about the parents and other family members who had lost loved ones at the hands of Leopold Bonzer. Even with his confession to their brutal murders, there would always be one huge loose end for thirteen families. The lack of a body always fosters impossible images and irrational ideas in the minds of a mom or dad, a lover or friend. Until he could give them irrefutable proof, unquestionable evidence that a life had ended, hope would push to the surface.

CHAPTER THREE

"Well, if it isn't Agent Grant." The clean-shaven man wore his wrinkled prison uniform as if it were a thousand-dollar suit.

"Hard to believe I surprised you, Bonzer, seeing as how I'm the only visitor you get other than your legal team. And how long has it been since they were here?" Nick set two frosty cans of soda pop on the table in front of him. He opened the top on one, then purposefully sat so he could cross his legs while Bonzer's ankles remained shackled.

The inmate swung his head to the side, arched his neck and rolled his shoulders, flexing as much as his confinement with his wrists in the table restraints allowed.

A stretching snail. "Feeling confined, Bonzer?"

Bonzer fixed Nick with a glare. He took a breath. Released it. Another breath. Release. "You know I like my privacy." His right eye twitched and the fingers on his right hand fiddled.

"How big is the window in your *private* cell?" Nick took a long swig from his can, his gaze not leaving Bonzer's face.

"A perfect four feet."

"That's four feet *wide*. How high is it?"

"I told you. I like my privacy."

"Four friggin' inches, that's how high. See much of the world from your room at this hotel?" Nick popped the top on the other can and shoved it across the table, then called the guard in to release Bonzer's hands from the restraints.

"Go to hell!" Bonzer took the can. Held it in front of him, temptation warring with pride. His eye continued to twitch.

When Nick went through his training he heard stories about Supermax prison, but he'd seen some pretty tough correctional institutions in his time and figured the stories for so much hype. His first visit here to meet with Leopold Bonzer almost ten years ago had opened his eyes.

Supermax, officially known as the United States Penitentiary Administrative Maximum Facility—or ADX— housed some of the worst criminals the Bureau of Prisons offered. The Alcatraz of the Rockies remained the most restrictive and punitive federal prison in the United States. Mafia family members, terrorists—homegrown and otherwise—drug kingpins, white supremacists and gang leaders all resided within its walls. Even a few serial killers, including a physician who got off on poisoning people, made Fremont County, Colorado their home.

Most of the cells were furnished with a desk, a stool and a bed, all poured concrete. If a prisoner attempted to plug his toilet for whatever reason it would automatically shut off. Showers were available in each cell, but they ran on a timer to prevent flooding. If a prisoner earned a few privileges he might have a polished steel mirror bolted to the wall, an electric light, a radio, and a black-and-white television that broadcast recreational, educational and religious programming. Other than the mirror, each privileged item was remotely controlled so the inmate never actually came into contact with them.

Even though people often compared Supermax to Alcatraz, its namesake never imagined the security this prison would boast, nestled in a valley at the foot of the Rocky Mountains. A multitude of motion detectors, cameras placed in every conceivable location, fourteen hundred remote-controlled steel doors, twelve-foot-high fences topped with razor-wire, laser beams, pressure pads and attack dogs all made Supermax one of the most secure facilities in the United States.

Nick believed the attack dogs were the real dissuaders. Dogs were predators. Carnivores. At their core they lived to rip open flesh and devour warm, raw meat. Other prisons might have them, but he could only imagine the extra genetic encoding the dogs at this prison must have.

"Heard the dogs barking lately?" The words were flippant, casual, but Leopold Bonzer had been badly mauled by a dog as a child. He'd endured seven surgeries: one to save his life and six more to give him a reason to live. Nick could relate.

The usual venom glinted from Bonzer's eyes, but Nick saw something else in them too. Something new flickered behind the mask. There'd been a shift of some kind. He would wait and think this development through before he chose the direction this interview would take. And maybe in the meantime Leopold Bonzer would give him some kind of clue. If he did, it would be the first.

Nick sat back, sipped his cold drink and considered his options. Two minutes of quiet might feel like two hours to a restrained prisoner alone in a room with a fed even if that prisoner spent hour after hour alone. Nick thought, *Maybe especially if that prisoner spent hour after hour alone.* Nick reached into his pocket and pulled out a pair of fingernail clippers. He didn't really need a manicure, but it would give him something to do while he waited. Weapons weren't allowed into the interior of the prison, but clippers still passed the innocuous test.

He pretended not to notice Bonzer trying to twist on his seat, or hear him sucking air between his teeth or even when he hocked a wad of spit and who-knows-what onto the floor near the door. Instead he focused on getting just the right shape on his pinky.

When Leopold Bonzer's face reddened, then emptied of color almost as quickly, Nick slowly closed his fingernail clippers, rubbed them free of smudges and tucked them back in his pocket. For the first time in a very long eight minutes, he looked directly at Leopold Bonzer.

Bonzer narrowed his eyes then arched his back a fraction of an inch. "I might want to talk about relocating."

Nick nodded but said nothing. Instead he leaned forward, put both elbows on the table and rested his chin in his hands.

Bonzer said, "I might be ready to give you what you want... for the right *hotel*."

A million questions played through Nick's head, but he didn't dare interrupt the process. "I'm listening," Nick said.

"Not today. Next week." Bonzer's eyes brittled with intensity. You get me the paperwork so I can look at it... let me see you sign it in front of me. I'll want confirmation from my legal team that it's a done deal. Then I'll talk."

Chapter Four

Jamie kicked the door closed. She hurried to the kitchen to drop her grocery bags on the counter before all of her handpicked, fresh ingredients for dinner landed in a heap on the floor. She scolded herself for the zillionth time for trying to carry everything in one trip, knowing the next time would be the same. She tugged off her jacket and threw it over a chair along with her purse. She looked at her dogs. "Are you guys hungry? I bet your bowls are empty." Three hopeful faces and twelve padded feet followed her to the pantry where she kept the dog food.

"Dad left a message."

A coiled spring released in Jamie's chest while she processed the fact that someone was in her home. Survival instincts collided with voice recognition. The voice belonged to Jax.

Jamie's sister Jackie, whom everyone called Jax, worked as the Medical Examiner for Aspen Falls. Smart and pretty, she'd surprised everyone when she married Phil Sussman. Phil's life seemed to have peaked back in high school where he quarterbacked the Aspen Falls Wildcats. Marrying Jax had been a definite step up for him and the way he controlled his wife's life, including her income, remained a definite bone of contention with Jamie. But Jax swore she was happy, and Jamie's own failed marriage didn't give her a lot of room to preach.

Jamie waited for her sister to make her way to the kitchen from the front of the house.

The dog chow that had popped across the hardwood floor when she'd jumped nanoseconds before disappeared down hungry throats. She set the bag down and shook her head, then continued to fill the three bowls. *Dad? Dad called?*

Gretchen, Socks (short for Socrates, but it also happened to describe his markings), and McKenzie all tucked into their dinner.

"Jeez, Jax. You're early. I didn't see your car. Dad called? When? Where is he?"

"He said he left a message for you too. Have you checked?" Jax pulled her jacket off and went to hang it in the coat closet. Her sister's ritual would involve lashing her shoulder bag to the hanger in an exact manner then shoving it all into the small space.

Jamie began unloading the grocery sacks. "I just walked in. I worked a little longer at the bank to make up for the time I took off yesterday for the search. I'll check my voice mail later. What did he say?"

"Oh, yum. We are gonna feast tonight. What are you making?"

"I have a new recipe for sea bass we're going to try." Jamie enjoyed the thought of preparing dinner for her sister and her two best friends, Ciara and Ellen. Jax had one night a week free, thanks to Phil and his dogged management of her schedule, and the sisters always spent it together.

The braised fennel and shallots, along with the chardonnay and costly saffron the recipe called for, promised some good dining. She would make the fish broth from scratch the first time around, then test it with a purchased premade broth to see whether the difference

13

would be worth the bother. Often the commercial product won over the homemade.

They hadn't heard from their dad for six months. Whatever message Bryce Taylor may have left—even the usual "I'm fine, sorry I missed you, not sure where I'm headed next" crap—ranked as important because it served as the only connection they shared with him. It was tenuous, but they'd learned to take what they were offered.

Jamie sucked in a breath and steeled her heart. "What did he say?" she asked again.

Jax shrugged. "Just said he was fine... and close. Both to Aspen Falls and to finding Mom's murderer."

Jamie froze, two leeks held like weapons ready for battle. She backed up a step. Blinked. "Ten years. It's been ten years since he left." The words clawed out of her dry throat.

Jax thrust a glass half-full of water toward her. Jamie pushed her younger sister's hand away and set the leeks on the counter. She walked to the rough-hewn china cabinet and opened a cupboard. Right now, she didn't want to add even a splash of water to the glass of scotch she was pouring.

Ellen scraped food off the last dish into a pail. "I know you compost, Jamie, but don't you think you're going a bit overboard?" She handed the cleared plate to Jax to rinse before putting it in the dishwasher. Ellen Grimes taught third grade and remained the only one of the four women who'd never been married.

Jamie was stunned the first time she'd seen Ellen in front of her class. The blonde, slightly pudgy, sometimes confused-sounding girl Jamie had known for years was a dynamo in the classroom. She played equal parts mom, coach, disciplinarian and best friend to her kids. Ellen became a different person within those four walls, and there was an electric connection between her and her students.

"That pail isn't for my compost pile. Garbage disposal needs to be fixed," Jamie said.

"Garbage disposal, cracked fireplace grate, iffy oven door... you have officially achieved money-pit status." Ellen grabbed a new bottle of cabernet and took it over to the elaborate wine bottle opener mounted on the far end of the island.

"Those things are cosmetic, at least compared to the new roof, plumbing and electrical repairs I've made over the last five years." Jamie pulled some clean wine glasses out of the china cabinet. Cooking a wonderful meal, sitting down to a table surrounded with the most important people in her life to share that meal, and discussing the issue of her dad—and his obsession—with her sister and friends mellowed her mood. "But you're right. It has eaten away at my savings. If I didn't love it so much I'd sell it."

Jax pulled off the apron tied loosely around her waist and laid it on the counter. "Everyone needs a hobby. Nice you can afford it."

"That sounded a little snarky. What's up?" Jamie pressed a lid on the plastic container, which was not even close to being filled with leftovers, and put it in the refrigerator.

Jax narrowed her eyes and shook her head.

"Ladies, I have laid a fire. And before you all crazed, Jamie, I laid it carefully, taking due note of the weak points in the grate." Ciara struck a come-hither pose and the three women jostled past her, almost ignoring her strident, shifting hips and batting eyelashes. Almost.

Ellen brought up the rear. "You know what they say about a butterfly at the equator sending ripples through the air simply by fluttering its wings? Ciara is about to personally be responsible for a typhoon in the West Indies." She hip-bumped the beautiful model before taking her seat in front of the fire.

Ciara Burke was drop-dead gorgeous. Smoky gray eyes and café au lait skin gave her an exotic appeal that perfectly matched her attitude. Although she would never admit it, she worked hard at "effortless." Married three times, her current single status fit her like a glove, or perhaps a really skimpy, form-fitting body glove. On top of her game with men—several men—she smiled a lot, and often commented that having a suspended driver's license served her well. Available and unavailable males were only too willing to escort her wherever she wanted to go.

Gretchen and Socks sprawled butt-to-butt in front of the warm blaze, effectively forcing their human counterparts to find their own spots. Gretchen's face seemed stuck to the area rug that lay on top of the wood floor, but Socks held his head high, alert and watching every move, especially moves that involved food.

"I love fires that use real wood. In Denver last week everywhere I went I saw gas fireplaces. Makes me totally appreciate an older home even if it is a money pit." Jamie curled up on the floor with an oversized pillow next to her to lean on. McKenzie, her sweet, twelve-pound, fluffy white bichon, snuggled against her ribs.

Ellen poured wine into the four glasses. "So how do you two really feel about hearing from your dad today?" She placed the empty bottle on the plank coffee table.

"You mean after six months of hearing nothing from him?" Jamie punched the pillow and shoved it under her body. The comfortable bichon elicited a groan to make sure everyone knew the sacrifice and adjustments he had to make to resettle once again into Jamie's side.

"Dad's been close to Colorado before." Jax stuck a socked toe into Jamie's ribs. "He's about due to come

16

home for a shower and a shave."

Jamie rolled onto her back and pulled McKenzie on top of her stomach. She ran her hands over his fluffy white fur and moved her gaze to the flickering flames, not responding to her sister's defense of their father. She'd heard it all before.

Ciara pulled up one of the afghans Star Taylor had crocheted before her abduction and murder. "He never forgave himself, you know." She nestled the soft woven yarn right under her chin.

Jax pulled her hair out of its ponytail. "By the time we missed Mom he'd already buried her. Dad couldn't have done anything to save her." She massaged her scalp.

"Headache?" Jamie asked from the floor.

"Mmmhmm."

Ciara tossed the afghan to the side, sat on the edge of her chair and began pulling on her shoes. "I've got an early morning shoot in Aspen and really need to get some rest." She looked pointedly at Ellen. "You ready?"

After the two left, Jamie sat on the couch and waited for Jax to say something. Gretchen's loud snores and the pop and hiss of the fire were the only sounds in the room. Finally Jamie said, "Are you going to tell me what's bothering you? It isn't Dad."

"I hate this." Jax pulled her knees up to her chin and wrapped her arms around her legs.

"Talk to me."

"You mentioned not seeing my car earlier, remember?" The words left Jax's mouth in a quiet rush.

"Yeah, you didn't answer me."

"I used Dad's call to get you to move on... to avoid answering you." Jax touched her forehead to her knees, her face hidden from view. When she pulled her head up again her cheeks were wet with tears.

Jamie's brow furrowed. "Damn. I knew it."

17

CHAPTER FIVE

The guard signaled for Nick to pull his car to the side of the road. When he did, the ADX vehicle pulled up behind him but the driver made no move to get out. *No doubt confirming my plates.* He watched in the rearview mirror as the SUV behind him backed up then pulled forward into the road. It came up next to his car and stopped. The passenger side window slid down. Nick pressed the button on his door, waited for the guard to speak.

"I need to see some identification."

"I've been cleared to—"

"Sir, I need to see some identification."

Nick thumbed his credentials open and held the wallet through the adjoined windows. The guard studied it carefully. He glanced twice at Nick, then nodded.

"Agent Grant, you need to remain where you are until I give you the go-ahead."

"What's going on?"

"I can't say, Sir." The window rose.

The only way Nick could leave his car in an emergency would be through the passenger side into a ditch. Uncomfortable, he pulled out his cell, prepared to find out why he was being detained.

No signal. *Something's up.* He'd always been able to use his phone on the Supermax property. For some reason they were jamming cellular signals. The sound of crazed barking from somewhere in the barren field off to the right seeped through the sealed doors of his car. Nick's memories took over. The wild clamor drowned out the hum of the air conditioner that pumped cool air onto sweat that appeared without fanfare on his forehead *Dogs.* The throaty brays and fierce barks signaled a hunt. *But not for a rabbit.*

Nick sat back in his car seat, closed his eyes, and attempted to gain control over the nausea rising in his throat. Tears mingled with the sweat running down his face. He wasn't a seven-year-old kid anymore. Suddenly they were at his door, pounding at it to gain access, to rip his throat out, eat him alive.

"Agent! Agent Grant!" The guard's meaty fist shook the glass and left oily prints behind. The ADX vehicle had moved. It was in the road ahead of him.

Nick wiped his face with his handkerchief. He took a moment to catch his breath, then rolled his window down.

"You're cleared to go," the guard said. "You all right?"

"Sorry. Late night. I'm fine." He put the window up and proceeded toward the main entrance of the prison.

Briefcase in hand, forms awaiting execution, he strode into the facility. A hum of intense activity hung in the air like some kind of weird ectoplasm. Definitely a busier day than usual at Supermax.

"Agent Grant," the young guard greeted him with an odd look on his face. "I... we... didn't someone—"

"I'll talk to Agent Grant." The warden walked up to Nick and extended his hand. "Good to see you, Nicholas. It's been a while."

"That it has, Warden Henderson," Nick said.

He put one arm behind Nick's back as if to guide him

along. "Associate Warden Cunningham is in my office. Please join us."

Cunningham was in charge of programs within the prison, including medical services and educational opportunities. Nick tried not to think of the potential implications as the two walked down the hall leading to the administrative area of the facility.

The warden's office was well appointed but not ostentatious. Cunningham was standing at a bank of windows overlooking the arid grounds, his back to the room. Another man, seated in front of the desk, was dressed in casual clothes, a contrast to the suits worn by both of the prison officials and Nick. He focused on his iPhone, his thumbs flying over the keys. It seemed cellular service was up and running again.

"FBI Agent Grant, you know Associate Warden Cunningham," the warden made the quick introduction. The two men nodded and met for a brief handshake in the middle of the room, and the warden gestured toward the man seated in front of the desk. "This is David Parker, our chaplain."

Nick hesitated a brief moment before shaking the chaplain's outstretched hand. He'd seen prison chaplains before, but this guy looked like he belonged in a Starbuck's somewhere sipping an iced latte. Definitely not standard BoP issue.

The chaplain held up his iPhone. "Please excuse my brief rudeness." He shrugged. "When the signal became available again, I took the opportunity to try to catch up on a few messages."

"Nicholas, please have a seat," the warden said.

"That's okay, I'll stand. I've got the papers for Leopold Bonzer's transfer and I want to get started with my interview. It might take a while to get all of the details we need from him."

20

"We've had quite an interesting day, Agent," the warden said.

"I know. I saw the dogs."

"Yes, an attempted escape. Rare for someone to even try at this facility. Word gets around, you know. But still, we house very intelligent criminals, and sometimes one thinks he can beat any system."

"You caught him then?"

"Oh yes. Within minutes." The warden's mouth ticked up at one corner.

The associate warden moved to stand behind the desk next to Warden Henderson. "That wasn't our only point of interest today, Agent Grant."

Nick raised an eyebrow.

The warden folded his hands. "There's no good way to tell you this—"

"Tell it to me straight."

"Leopold Bonzer is dead."

CHAPTER SIX

"Dead? How?" Nick choked the words out.

Associate Warden Cunningham explained. "He's being autopsied, but since he didn't have any other prisoner contact we're assuming he died from natural causes. He's dealt with heart issues for the last few years."

A cell phone rang and everyone except Nick paused to check. It didn't matter who might be calling him. He didn't want to talk to anyone.

"I need to take this call," the warden said. "Please excuse me." He exited his office in three quick strides.

Ten years, Nick thought. *Ten long years of dealing with a narcissistic serial killer and losing to him each time we met. Failure. Utter defeat. Dammit!* The last seven had been on his own time and up until a moment ago he was going to obtain information that would help bring closure to several families. *So many people muddling through life with unanswered questions.* Rather than being a hero, he would have to call each of the families personally and let them know they would never have the answers to their questions. He forced himself to speak. "He seemed fine last week. Did something happen?" Denial and anger had no place on the job but he was having a difficult time keeping them under control.

Cunningham shook his head. "Agent Grant—Nick—it was only a matter of time. Bonzer knew he didn't have long to live. That's why he wanted to make a deal. He didn't want to die in here."

The chaplain said, "There may have even been a part of him that wanted to come clean with everything he knew, everything he'd been keeping from the authorities and the families, before he died." He obviously didn't believe his own words any more than Nick believed them.

"Did he have anything written down? Any notes?" If Leopold Bonzer had written anything down the prison officials would have made certain the paper would be in Nick's hands right now, but he had to ask.

Cunningham seemed to understand the profound impact of the prisoner's death. "I'm sorry. He left very few personal effects. They've been boxed but they're still in his cell."

Nick looked at David Parker. "How about you, Chaplain? Did he ever tell you anything that might help?"

Parker's eyes turned sad and haunted. Starbuck's and iPhones suddenly seemed incongruous to him. Nick found himself setting next to a man emanating a strong spirituality. Man of God took the place of Texting Man. This one looked a lot more real.

"My job is to fight for the souls of these men. One way I do that is to hear their confessions. It's a step in the process, if you will. And the process of saving souls is something only a man who has their trust can even begin to do. As you might assume, Agent Grant, I hear a lot of confessions. Even if Leopold Bonzer chose to confess everything to me, I could not break that trust. A prison is a very small place—even one that keeps their prisoners isolated. I could not risk losing the souls I've worked so hard to gain. But please, Agent Grant, that trust also works between us. Believe me, if the prisoner confessed to

23

anyone, it wasn't me."

Nick sat back in his chair. Each man in the room had a job to do, a job they each did well. Each had a calling. But none of that did anything to help the families of thirteen murder victims. He had failed them. *My failure. No one else's.*

The warden returned and took his chair. He pulled out a folder lying on his desk and put it on top of some other paperwork, a signal for the meeting to draw to a close.

"We have another prisoner to prepare for, and the press will be all over this one." The light from the window hit the warden's face, illuminating both his pallor and his wrinkles. His was a face that reflected stoicism even as it acknowledged defeat in ever hoping to see the good in men. There would never be an available room at this particular inn for too many days.

Nick needed to get some closure of his own. He stood. "Warden, I'd like to examine whatever personal effects Bonzer left and I'd like to see his cell. Would that be possible at this time?" Even though Nick could throw his FBI weight around to get what he wanted, he preferred respecting other people's turf.

"Now would not only be the best time, Agent, but the only time. The incoming prisoner will be assigned to the deceased's space. Chaplain Parker, would you mind escorting Agent Grant to Leopold Bonzer's cell? When he's finished reviewing the personal effects, dispose of them as you wish. There is no immediate family."

Through the halls leading to the center of Supermax where the prisoners were housed, Nick and the chaplain passed through security posts and remote-controlled steel doors opening, then closing in their wake. Some clanking, an occasional muted outburst, and a little mumbling accompanied them along the route. The prison used sensory deprivation not only as a punishment, but as a means of control. Unfortunately, Nick's sense of smell wasn't as deprived as much as he would have wished.

"What do you hope to find, Agent?"

"I wish I knew."

Nick sat on the poured concrete bunk. The bedding had already been removed. When Leopold Bonzer died, his body had released its fluids and the smell of defecation remained strong.

Nick Grant closed his eyes for a moment and listened to the clamor of tortured souls around him. Imagined himself confined to this space, hearing these sounds, inhaling these smells, twenty-three hours a day for the rest of his life. *Cabin fever would have nothing on this nightmare. A man would need to be able to turn to someplace else in his mind in order to remain sane, or some version of sane. Where was that place for Leopold Bonzer?*

A cardboard box contained the worldly possessions of a man who, at one time, had made a decent living selling real estate, and who later confessed to killing thirteen people. It was almost empty. A tube of toothpaste, shampoo, deodorant, a comb, and the few personal effects Bonzer had possessed when he entered prison were all he'd left behind to show he'd spent time on this earth. His clothing and shoes were prison issue, and the paperback novel he'd been reading when he died had come from the prison library. Those items were in a separate box on the floor near the double steel doors to the cell. Material possessions didn't prove a person's value by any stretch, but somehow this void went hand-in-hand with the holes Leopold Bonzer had drilled into the lives of so many.

Nick moved the cardboard box filled with the pathetic detritus out of his way, pushed back onto the bed, leaned against the wall, and looked around. Most of the prison cells Nick had seen in other institutions were filled with graffiti and grime, bodily discharges of all kinds, and food that would never be eaten. No sign of the usual spit, semen, boogers or blood appeared in this cell. The prison staff took care of a lot of the body-fluids graffiti buildup by rotating inmates at least once a week, and prisoners were required to leave their residences lacking as much DNA as possible. Leopold Bonzer had cared about his environment and taken as much control as anyone could have in an ADX facility.

Nick wondered, *Where might a man like Bonzer hide something of an intensely personal nature? A secret?* It would have to be easily accessible, both for his own pleasure as well as the frequent moves within the prison. *This cell holds his secret... I just know it.*

There were no family photographs, presumably because no family existed, and no books or other allowable tokens sent from anyone beyond these walls, even though a cult of groupies on the outside lived for anything to do with Bonzer. No doubt they'd sent items over the years, but the subject of their adoration hadn't kept them, at least openly.

The toilet was stainless steel and designed to flush an entire bed sheet without clogging. And based on the cleanliness of the rest of the cell, the toilet wasn't a likely place for Bonzer to hide something precious. The automatic shower shared space with the toilet. Nothing there either.

The prisoner had earned some privileges for good behavior over the years, and enjoyed the black and white television, radio and electric light. Because of the remote control situation they were subject to revocation, but at the time of his death he enjoyed whatever limited use inmates could access.

Nick pulled the box toward him and retrieved the

Personal Property Inventory forms, one form for the initial intake and one for each transfer. He looked them over and checked them against the items remanded to the small cardboard container. Everything matched from one list to the next. What Bonzer had been arrested with and what he'd moved through the system with had been consistent. But one item didn't match the contents of the box.

A photograph. One photograph. A completely legitimate, allowable personal item. It wasn't in the cell, and it wasn't in the box. *A photograph of whom or what? Why hide it?*

Of course it was possible, even probable, that the photograph had somehow been destroyed since the last time the Personal Property form required completion. But Nick had known Leopold Bonzer. The serial killer lived a careful, meticulous, deliberate life. Unless he chose to destroy his property, it existed somewhere in this seven-foot by twelve-foot concrete cave.

Nick got off the bed and went to examine the radio and television just a step away. They were solid pieces of plastic, leaving him with zilch. Someone could slide a picture between the television and the wall, but it would not be well hidden and removing it would be next to impossible.

He looked at the stainless steel mirror bolted tight to the wall, ran his fingers around the piece of polished metal. Nothing. Frustrated, he made a fist and smacked his hand against the mirror.

Agent Grant immediately regretted the outburst and tugged the sleeve of his jacket down to wipe off the impression his fist had left on the mirror. *Well, who should I tell first? The Archers have been waiting the longest.* Liam Archer had recently suffered a heart attack. *Maybe I should talk to Susan Archer first so she can—* He pulled his hand away and stared.

The tiniest bit of a corner of glossy photo paper had slipped past the bottom edge of the mirror. The old, worn layers of paper were beginning to pull apart. Leopold Bonzer's secret was about to be exposed.

Nick pulled on one of the latex gloves he carried in his pocket out of habit and put his fingers gently on the corner of the photo and tugged. It didn't move. If he pulled harder he might damage it. He pulled out his clippers, slipped the nail file under the edge of the mirror and applied a little leverage. The photograph slipped into his hand.

At first he didn't understand what he was seeing. The photograph wasn't of a person or a celebration or an event. It was a field, bordered on at least on three sides by thick trees. He flipped it over, hoping for some handwriting that would identify the picture. Nothing. Then it came to him. *A picture of the burial ground.*

CHAPTER SEVEN

He turned off the lantern. There was plenty of light from the moon. The last trip from the car had left him a little out of breath, but he rested for a few minutes and strength surged back into his body, his muscles, his mind.

Shovel in hand he placed his work boot on the blade and pushed, then pried the dark, moist earth up and piled it neatly to the side. Push, pry, pile. The repetition relaxed him. Push, pry, pile. The sound of the blade of the shovel cutting through the soil empowered him, approved his ambition.

After about thirty minutes of steady work he stabbed the shovel into the dirt. He tugged his damp shirt away from his back, then from his chest, rolled his shoulders and stretched his legs. After a break for a piss and some water he grabbed the shovel again.

Lucky with this one... more loam than rocks, and no goddamn clay. He bent and stood, bent and stood. After another hour and a half, he tossed the shovel up, then followed it. His biceps were smoking hot.

He bent over the rolled-up plastic tarp and untied the knot in the rope that bound it. It was a good rope. The best the hardware store sold. He coiled it and set it near the lantern. He placed the plastic tarp at the rim of the hole and gripped the hemmed edge as far apart as possible, almost reaching the corners. He hefted the bright blue tarp and backed up a step. Two. There was a satisfying thump and the plastic sheet became weightless. He'd hose it down later.

The loose, rich soil behaved, as usual, a lot better going in than coming out. The cool mountain air sifted through the fabric of his shirt. The moon, high overhead, fell behind a bank of clouds and the familiar became foreign. He wondered whether someone was watching him just as he had watched someone else twenty years ago. He shrugged off the notion, but his senses remained on high alert long after he'd transferred the last shovel full of dirt from one pile to the other.

He tamped the top of the grave, a scar in the middle of a sea of grass. After the first snow it wouldn't matter. *Hell, if I work things right it won't matter in a few weeks.*

Back at his luxury SUV, his equipment stowed in the rear, he took a moment to review his ambition. *A worthy ambition indeed*, he thought. *An achievement worth pursuit.*

He had all the money he would ever need thanks to the deaths of the old couple who had taken pity on a small boy and raised him as their own. He held a respected position in the community and he'd achieved a level of prestige among his colleagues.

What he didn't enjoy—had never enjoyed—was any tiny bit of human emotion. He had dedicated his life to achieve one real tear, one genuine twinge, one moment of honest compassion, true and pure.

CHAPTER EIGHT

Jamie was sitting in her boss's glassed-in office, the closed door muting the sounds of the bank behind her. The note on her desk when she walked in this morning said he wanted to see her immediately. Her stomach had curled into itself when she'd read it, and she still felt anxious.

"You know you're one of the best loan officers this bank has ever had. You're fair and honest with our customers, and you're not a prima donna to work with." Gabe Ahrens looked resolute and Jamie waited for the but.

She needed this job. Almost every penny she made went toward her monthly living expenses, home repairs and equipment for her Search and Rescue passion. Her savings account, such as it was, existed only to have accessible money for the house, so she drew it down the moment she had enough in the account for the next big project. And now Jax's ongoing financial trouble meant Jamie might need to help her sister again. Buying Jax out of the family home had put only a tiny bandage over the gaping wound of her sister's money problems. The funds had stretched only so far.

Gabe tore a piece of paper out of his tablet, looked at it, then pushed it across the desk toward her.

Jamie picked it up. It was a list of names and dollar amounts. "What's this?"

"Those are loans that went to our competitors over the last few months because you weren't in the bank. You were out with one of your dogs tracking who knows what where."

"How did you—"

"It's a small town, Jamie. All of these people tried you first, then moved on. Don't get me wrong; I respect that you believe what you do on your searches is important. I do. And I agreed from the very beginning to offer you as much flexibility as we could, but this is a lot of money. The board is going to want some answers. I need someone who can give a hundred percent to the bank, at least during banking hours, and I'd like it to be you."

"You know this job is important to me, Gabe, but my S&R life is too."

"I need to know you're with me on this, Jamie."

Thoughts filled her mind as she scrambled for a solution. "What about getting someone part-time?"

"You mean part-time on-call? Unless you can schedule the need for your searches to happen only on certain days, a part-time loan officer won't work." Gabe pulled the list of loans the bank had lost away from her and tucked it into a folder.

She thought about the garbage disposal and the fireplace grate and the outside steps that would soon need replacing. The home she loved. The home her parents built together. The home her father had poured not only savings into, but had physically been involved in creating. The home her mom had decorated and baked in and where she had loved them and been loved. They had been happy there before her mom was lost to murder and her dad to revenge. *Keep it together, Jamie. Keep it whole.*

And what if one of her dogs got hurt? And then there's

Jax. There's always Jax.

"I'm sorry. I'll try to be in the bank more often."

Gabe shook his head. "I need more than a try. I need a commitment."

Jamie found herself in an impossible situation that required an impossible decision that could go only one way. Indescribable loss flooded Jamie's heart with mourning and anxiety and grief. She would have to turn her back on the one thing that gave her the greatest opportunity to affect lives in a positive way if she wanted to continue to pay her bills and eat.

She sighed. "You have my commitment. I'll be here."

CHAPTER NINE

"Will you need us for anything else tonight, Nick?" His housekeeper was framed and backlit in the doorway of his study.

"I'm good, Felicity. Thanks. Enjoy your evening."

"Remember, Jerome and I will be gone for the weekend but your meals are all in the fridge. Oh, and Jerome wanted me to be sure to tell you the roadster has been repaired and will be delivered next week."

"You two spoil me."

"We don't spoil you nearly as well as a good woman would."

Even though he couldn't see Felicity's face, he sensed her wink. At least she hadn't set him up with another blind date while they were gone. This was the second time the couple had moved with him. First from Virginia to Denver, and finally to Aspen Falls two months ago.

"Goodnight and goodbye. Have fun in Moab, and thank Jerome for me."

Nick sunk deep into the soft leather club chair and closed his eyes. After authenticating the age of the photograph he'd found in the serial killer's cell and confirming that the only latents were Leopold Bonzer's, they'd put a team of surveyors to work to help locate the burial site. That had been two weeks ago. An FBI desk jockey named Arnold Abner, an agent he'd worked with before, was heading up that part of the investigation and reporting to Nick. So far the process of elimination marked their only progress with Nick personally investigating each of the possible locations.

Four of the six sites they'd checked out so far were in the opposite direction Leopold Bonzer had been driving when he got caught. The terrain fit but geographically they didn't make sense unless Bonzer had changed his dumping ground. The fifth location lay in the right direction but was too close to town. His chances of getting caught somewhere that close would have been too high, and he hadn't been caught for a very long time.

The thought that the sixth site might be the one made Nick ill. Government survey maps and photographs from fifteen years ago showed a promising location. One that kids now used as a ball field. Again, it was a little too close to town. As bad as Nick wanted to find the bodies of the thirteen people, he didn't want them to be buried beneath the sod Little League games were played on. Fortunately or unfortunately, they'd cleared Rocky Crevice Park just this afternoon. Back to square one.

He kicked his slippers off and stretched his feet toward the flickering flames in the stone fireplace. Nick loved a fire. He shoved the sleeves of his sweater up each arm, then reached for his glass of scotch. He hoped the liquor would take the pain away. Some pain even the oxy couldn't touch. Vivaldi's *Autumn* suffused the air around him. The music worked its own magic touch on his nerves.

Loneliness had become a physical ache, but Vivaldi smoothed it out and it faded a little with each note that soaked into his brain. His Uncle Gage always said, "If whatever is bothering you is out of your control, let it go, and then let it go some more." He didn't believe he'd always be alone and he could change his status tonight with a phone call, but he didn't have the energy. *Or the heart... or something.* Still, the weekend hours stretched ahead of him like a dusty country road.

Nick's cell phone buzzed on the table next to his glass. The caller ID looked familiar. *Damn.* He picked up the phone. "Mr. Archer, how are you this evening?"

"Susan and I were wondering how that last site turned out. I told her I'd call...."

"I'm sorry. I planned to get in touch with you tomorrow." Nick would never get used to giving someone bad news. Liam and Susan Archer never pushed and never blamed.

"It's not the place," Nick said. "That doesn't mean we won't come up with a positive hit soon. Elimination is part of the process. We're bound to be getting close."

"Nick, I know you believe the photograph is the place where our Amy is buried, but couldn't it simply be a picture of a place Bonzer liked? Or maybe it's just a cruel joke he saved for ten years before—" Liam stopped talking and Nick heard him blow his nose.

"Mr. Archer—"

"Liam."

"Liam, I have one of the best clearance rates in the bureau. I'm good at what I do and you know I am. This case, Amy's case, is not going to be the one that ruins my record. It's been a rough ten years, especially for you and Susan and for the other families, but have I ever once misled you? Have I ever once said one thing and it turned out to be something different?"

"No." Liam Archer pushed his answer through the phone like mist, but without hesitation.

Nick winced at the childlike trust the one-word acknowledgement evoked, and the exhaustion and frailty and failing hope that bled from its source.

"Then trust me. We'll find her."

36

Liam Archer cleared his throat. "I'll let Susan know. And thanks."

"Any time Mr. Archer."

Nick put the phone back on the table and slipped his feet into his slippers. Some days his job didn't live up to its billing. He searched the bookcase for something to read. Tonight he needed distraction until he could no longer keep his eyes open. He finally selected one of his favorite Hillerman's. He never minded re-reading a good book.

He snagged his cell phone to pop it in its charger and it rang in his hand. *So late... so tired... I am so over this day.* He considered letting it go to voice mail. The caller's name on the screen however, nixed that idea. He answered. "Grant."

"We've got another site, Nick. I've got a feeling this one is it. It meets every criteria you're looking for."

After getting a few particulars from Arnold, Nick felt better than he had for two weeks. He knew this could come up negative. Still, the place sounded right. It was about fifteen miles out of Aspen Falls in the right direction, remote but accessible. He wanted everyone out there as soon as possible.

"Call the sheriff's office and get me a team of searchers out there tomorrow at dawn. Make sure they're experienced and know what they're looking for," Nick said.

"You want dogs?"

"Yeah. Dogs too."

CHAPTER TEN

"Why can't you cook like your sister?" Phil Sussman reached for the bottle of red wine on the table, refilled his glass, then set it back down, ignoring the empty glass in front of his wife.

Jamie grabbed the bottle and poured the rest between Jax and Ellen. Her grip tightened a little on the glass bottle when she considered what a satisfying sound it would make as it met the side of her brother-in-law's head.

"And I heard you say earlier why Ciara isn't here tonight, but I didn't catch it. Where is that hot mama?" Phil waggled his eyebrows.

"She's at a shoot in Colorado Springs this weekend." Ellen speared the last bite of beef tenderloin on her plate a little harder than she needed to and swirled it around to gather up as much of the demi-glace as she could.

"That's too bad. I could use a beautiful woman to look at right about now. It would top off a perfect meal."

Before Jamie could say what she really wanted to say, Jax stood up. "Let me help you clear these things, Jamie."

Ellen stood as well. "Yeah, me too." She stretched for the empty serving platter that the focaccia had been on and grabbed the oil cruet.

Phil tossed a gold lighter on the table, then reached

inside his jacket, which was hanging over the back of his chair.

"Not in my house, Phil. Not now, not ever. I've told you before, if you want to smoke you need to step outside."

"I'm just getting my gear together, Sergeant. Get off your high horse."

When the three women were in the kitchen, tension lessened for at least two of them. Jamie rolled her shoulders. Phil never changed. His stripes just got more bold.

Jax launched into her regular defensive posture. "He's going through a difficult time."

"And none of the rest of us are?" Jamie asked. "You let him get away with things you wouldn't hesitate a minute to call us on."

"He tries so hard, Jamie. Let up a little, okay? I love him." Jax piled the dishes next to the sink.

Those three words froze Jamie in her tracks every time. Her sister loved him. The loser. The jerk that used her income as a Medical Examiner so he could be the big man around town and at the casino tables in Central City. The ignorant jerk who abused her.

Ellen went back into the dining room to gather the last of the dishes. On her way out the door, she flashed Jamie a warning look. *Let it go.*

"Thanks for the loan." Jax mouth screwed up for a second before it relaxed. "We really need it to pay bills, and I'll get my car back on Monday."

"We? You promised you wouldn't let Phil know you had any money," Jamie said.

"I didn't, but I *am* married to him so they are *our* bills. Not just his, not just mine—ours. You do remember that particular concept, don't you?"

"That's not fair." Jamie's hand went to her mid-section, as if covering the area between her belly button and her left breast would shield her from further pain related to those years. Cover the scar, cover the past. The six-inch slice in her body, and the resulting scar, reminded her of more than the horror of her marriage to the charming Andrew Stanton; it reminded her of her strength, her decision not only to survive, but to thrive. But she'd never quite gotten over the failure and her poor decision related to a man.

"I'm sorry," Jax said. "It was pure meanness of me to say anything to you about your marriage. And I am grateful to you. When you bought me out of my share of the house after Daddy left you saved me. Not just Phil, who I know you couldn't care less about, but me. And you've saved me more times than I want to count since then."

"Seven."

"What?" Jax asked.

"I've bailed you out seven times. This makes eight."

Ellen walked in. "Look who's being snarky now." She placed the last of the serving pieces in the sink, folded her arms and watched the two sisters.

"I'd just like to know when Phil Sussman intends to become the husband my sister deserves. She works hard and he gambles it away." Jamie set the bucket for her compost pile by the back door. On top she set the plastic bag full of scraps that normally would have gone down the garbage disposal.

"Speaking of work," Jax stretched a damp dishcloth over the drying rack under the kitchen sink. "Jerry Coble called me today. Said you'd turned down a request to help on a search and rescue operation. Some missing camper from Idaho. What gives?"

"Did they find him?" Jamie had hated having to say no to Jerry. Socks ranked as one of the best S&R dogs in the region, and he lived to work.

"Not last I heard but that doesn't answer my question." Jax folded her arms.

Jamie's phone rang. The sheriff needed her and Gretchen tomorrow for a major search involving the FBI.

Saturday. How lucky can I get?

CHAPTER ELEVEN

Nick showed up at the site Saturday morning before anyone else. Sleep had not come easily to him the night before, but his focus was sharp. Adrenaline pulsed through his body. He paced just outside the driver's side of his SUV, unwilling to compromise even the slightest bit of ground until the searchers and their dogs arrived.

He looked out at the mountain meadow, peaceful and serene in the pre-dawn light. Birds called to one another and rabbits hopped through the long grasses, occasionally pausing to nibble breakfast. A deep, blue-gray sky shifted to a palette of oranges and pinks as the night slipped away. Three deer strode into the area near him, content to feed on the leaves of bushes near the trees, their ears perked, alert for danger.

If this location was the right place, what looked like the perfect site for a romantic picnic also held buried secrets and evidence of unspeakable atrocities. He'd already devoted most of his free time to the case as the bureau backed away over the years, but now, since Leopold Bonzer's death, the bureau would be even less concerned about acquiring closure for their files, never mind the closure for the families of Bonzer's victims. He needed to wrap this up. Unless something else surfaced, that photograph in the serial killer's cell was the last best hope he had of bringing closure to the families of thirteen victims.

The deer startled back into the trees when three cruisers and a red SUV pulled up behind his vehicle. Nick walked over to the lead car and waited while two men got out.

"Sheriff Coble, good to see you again. Seems like only yesterday."

"Good morning, Agent. I've got three deputies with me this morning and one Human Remains Detection handler with her dog." The sheriff tossed an empty cup of coffee into the front of the car and pulled out his sunglasses.

"Just one dog?"

"It's a small area, Agent Grant." Coble pulled a toothpick from his pocket and popped it in his mouth. "Jamie Taylor and her dogs have the highest confirmed hits of anyone in the Rocky Mountain region. If we need another HRD handler I'll call Rodney Casings in Glenwood Springs. His dogs are good but Rodney leaves a little to be desired."

Arnold had messengered a US Geographical map of the field to Nick last night, and he spread it out on the hood of his SUV. It was roughly the size of four football fields and Nick had already marked off search areas.

The meadow was between Aspen Falls and Snowmass Village, just outside of Aspen. The locals had always called that general area Rocky Point. Apparently some of the older townspeople called it Kegger Point, but everyone knew the general vicinity in question regardless of the name.

Sheriff Coble and his deputies gathered around. Whoever had arrived in the red SUV remained inside the vehicle. Nick figured the occupant was the dog handler. *Just as well.* "We'll begin with the area closest to the road and proceed to the tree line. You've all got your GPS units and markers?" Nick didn't have any spares and he intended to search right along with the deputies.

The men nodded.

"Good. We'll go first; the dog can follow."

Jerry Coble pulled Nick aside. "You realize Jamie and Gretchen have the best chance of finding anything, don't you? It's been decades."

Nick wanted to ask how this Gretchen person fit in to the search, but figured he'd find out soon enough.

Tension wrapped itself around Nick's throat. He pushed the words out. "You're probably right, but I'm not going to risk losing evidence because a dog or its handler didn't know what they were seeing."

"Rodney, maybe, but Jamie? She makes some of my best deputies look like rookies."

"Let's start off my way, Sheriff. We can move things around if we need to."

Sheriff Coble cocked his head. "You don't much like dogs, do you?

"Not much."

"On that note, let me introduce you."

Nick followed Jerry Coble's gaze and saw a tall, confident, striking woman walking behind one of the one of the most wretched canines he'd ever seen in his life. All that fur made him crazy. *And those teeth!*

"Jamie Taylor, meet Agent Nicholas Grant with the FBI. We're here at his request." He nodded toward the ground, a smile spreading on his weathered face. "And this fine specimen of a golden is Gretchen. Her sense of smell is the keenest I've ever seen, darn near three million times better than yours or mine. If she thought it important, she could probably tell you what I ate for breakfast last Tuesday, and a good strong sniff at the bottom of my boots would get her talkin' about my fishing trip on the Poudre River last May."

"Don't be silly, Sheriff." Jamie's smile lit up the morning like no sunlight could. "Gretchen doesn't talk to strangers." She reached down and rubbed the canine's neck.

Gretchen looked up to Jamie's face, some sort of silent signal passing between them. It reminded Nick of the look law enforcement partners often exchange before entering an interview room. The good-cop, bad-cop thing.

Then the dog turned her gaze on him.

CHAPTER TWELVE

Jamie could tell the FBI agent didn't like women in the law enforcement field. Or maybe the attitude that bounced off him like sharp knives stemmed from his dislike of dogs. And here she stood, a woman, ready to get to work with a golden retriever as her partner.

Regardless, she planned minimal contact with him. Agent Nicholas Grant, attractive in a lanky kind of way, sat on a shelf like something she'd only be too happy to add to her cart. Jamie would nip any attraction in the bud. She'd had early insight into his character, and she knew where he stood from the beginning. It simplified things. She wouldn't make another bad choice, at least not with this man.

Surprisingly, the arrogant agent understood that Gretchen would work better with a lane search pattern. They could set up a grid search if and when they found anything. Jamie preferred to work in ten-foot lanes even though Gretchen tested out at picking scents up from a thirty-foot swath, and neither was necessarily conducive to a grid search. The retriever's long silken ears were perfect funnels to enhance and direct molecules to her nose. Jamie often felt like she could take a nap and not be missed. If Gretchen could document her own discoveries and communicate them in a different way, Jamie wouldn't be necessary.

Sheriff Coble told one of the deputies to get the bundles of wooden stakes from his car. Untreated, unstained and unpainted, the two-foot stakes would be placed in the ground at relatively close intervals. The deputies would get a sense of how easily the stakes entered the soil, and they allowed the ground to breath, making the scent of any decomposition easier for Gretchen to find. If the soil felt a bit loose and mushy the deputy would mark the stake for a closer scent from Gretchen, or even closer inspection for a possible grid search. Jamie would use her own soil probe with a t-bar on the top to push in and pull out of the ground frequently.

Gretchen wanted to get to work, but Jamie made her sit and wait for the men to get ahead of them as per Agent Grant's instructions. *Fine with me. At least I won't have to put up with his biases, and Gretchen and I can focus on the job.* And to his credit the stakes used as probes should have about a thirty-minute lead on an HRD dog. Gretchen didn't need that long but Jamie waited, happy to have a few minutes to think about the job they were about to begin. She poured some coffee and took out a cranberry muffin from her pack, watching the men to see if they marked any of the stakes to indicate softer soil.

In these hurry-up and wait situations, in addition to considering the task at hand, Jamie always thought of her mom as both a reminder of why she did this job and a prayer for guidance.

They had found her mom, Star Taylor, in a meadow just like this one a little more than ten years ago, two months after Jamie turned twenty-five. She had felt so helpless then, the daughter of a victim. She vowed never to feel that way again.

After his early retirement from the private

international security firm he worked for, Bryce Taylor had relocated his family and settled into life in the Colorado high country. It was everything Jamie had ever dreamed of. Nature and space and down-to-earth people.

But one of her dad's old cases had come back to ruin their idyllic life. Star Taylor, wife, mom and friend, left to go grocery shopping one day and never came home. For nine days she was missing from their lives. For those nine days they were drilled and questioned and put under a microscope. For those nine days she tried to prepare herself for the worst but couldn't let herself actually believe the worst could happen.

Then the bad guy, ready to inflict the final blow, led Bryce Taylor on a long hunt that culminated in the literal unearthing of his wife. She'd been tortured and buried alive within hours of being kidnapped. They'd held out hope for over a week when they should have been grieving.

Afterward, the bastard had disappeared. The case was still open, but cold. Only her dad's dogged tracking of the killer gave the family any hope the murder of Star Taylor would ever be solved.

Before she had arrived on the scene this morning, Jamie had received enough information about this case to know who they were looking for. These family's lives hadn't been stopped for nine days. They'd been stopped more than ten years.

The sheriff gestured and Jamie waved back an acknowledgement. Agent Grant kept his back turned toward her.

She brought some water out of her pack for Gretchen, more to moisten her dog's nasal passages than to quench any thirst. She checked her GPS, not that it was necessary today with the smaller area and the manpower involved, but she prided herself on being thorough. Her records were impeccable, and in more than one trial over the years had proved pivotal.

"Come on girl, let's get busy." She gave Gretchen a gentle tug on the leash and they were off.

Less than fifteen minutes later Gretchen gave her first alert. She dropped to the ground and lay statue-still. Jamie flagged the stake with a yellow strip of cloth. After patting Gretchen on the head and mumbling some words of appreciation she looked around at the immediate terrain. Flat. Little chance that ground water, or other elements, may have carried the scent away from the burial location. But the trees nearby were large and might be factors. She made a note in her log and sketched the site, eyeballing the approximate length of the longest branches of the nearest tree and writing the estimate in her log.

In the middle of her training Jamie had forgotten to take into account the drip line theory and had almost failed her first field test. It is possible for scent to be carried almost two times the length of the longest tree branch from the actual source. She'd failed to take that into consideration and her instructor had presented her with a handwritten bill for the cost of excavating the wrong site. She never neglected to pay attention to nearby trees again.

Urging Gretchen in a direction that led them outside of the lane, Jamie headed toward the trees to sink her probe. Some handlers preferred to wait until the lanes were cleared, then go back and check for source issues. She didn't like to risk other finds, or overzealous law enforcement, to get in the way of systematically confirming or clearing as many alerts as possible.

"Hey! Dog person! What do you think you're doing?"

CHAPTER THIRTEEN

Nick stormed across the field the way they'd come, careful not to disturb any of the stakes. *What the hell does she think she's doing? She and her death-dog are way out of the search parameters.* It ticked him off that he had to spend valuable time and resources training this obviously incompetent female and her flesh-eating, canine partner.

His pace across the rocky meadow wrenched his aching back and he touched the bottle of oxy in his pocket without slowing. The pain didn't match the anxiety. He needed this meadow to turn out to be the dumpsite for Bonzer's victims. That necessity overshadowed every other event in his life up until this point. This search would define his career, and his future, more than anything else in his history with the bureau. And he needed to deal with a ditzy volunteer with a hairy carnivore that couldn't be trusted off a leash.

"What are you doing? This is a lane search pattern, not a 'Gee, that looks interesting over there' pattern. Don't you know anything?" He pulled up, suddenly aware of her space. He clearly, without hesitation, had invaded it, but he didn't really care.

The woman stared at him and didn't say a word. He could swear the dog snarled at him before turning its attention to its female handler and sitting on its haunches.

Both the woman and the dog were looking at something over his shoulder.

He waited a beat before turning around to see for himself whatever they were focused on. When he did he saw the handler's flag on a stake. "You found something? What did you find? Why didn't you signal me?"

"Do you generally go by Your Honor or Sire?"

A static-filled tension line connected her words to his head and pierced his brain. He touched the bottle in his pocket again. He snapped the tension line back in her direction. "I don't have time for this. Do you even have the slightest idea what you're doing?" He could give as good as he got. She might be irritated with him but she'd just have to get over it.

"Agent Grant, I don't know how you treat other professionals you come into contact with, but I have to assume I'm not the exception. You need to get a good dose of manners from someone, and that doesn't happen to be my job."

Her eyes burned as if he'd ignited some incendiary device within her. It also caused her face to redden. He rather liked the effect and that fact surprised him.

"Pay attention, Agent. I'm only going to tell you this once. Gretchen alerted at the flagged stake." The woman jabbed her finger in the air over his shoulder. "But there are other geographical elements to consider and I'm responsible for bringing them into the picture. That's what I'm doing... or rather, that's what I *would* be doing if I didn't have to stop to explain my job to *you*. Now if you don't mind, I'll do that job. And honestly? I will only be able to do it to the best of my ability if you get out of the way." She showed him her back and went to work with her probe, sinking it deep into the earth before pulling it back out. After each pull she scribbled something in her

51

notebook.

Score one for the dog woman.

"I... I thought HRD dogs needed at least thirty minutes for scent to develop from a punch," he said in what he considered a thoughtful, peace-making, pleasant tone.

"Not Gretchen. Five minutes tops. Excuse us, Agent, while we do our jobs."

His charm didn't result in its usual payoff so Nick retraced his earlier march. He reflected on the core strength, determination and intelligence he'd just witnessed. Jamie Taylor's assets extended beyond her good looks.

He had some questions for Sheriff Jerry Coble. Like for example, did this Gretchen dog actually live with the flammable Jamie Taylor, or could it be possible that it might be kenneled elsewhere?

Nick caught up to the nearest deputy.

"Get back to that flag and work with the dog handler to determine the approximate perimeter of the gravesite, then set up for a grid search. Don't touch anything other than set stakes. If Ms. Taylor confirms the alert I'll get the ME out to the site."

"She found something? I knew she would." The deputy's smile was quickly replaced by the blank mask all law enforcement professionals practiced.

"What makes you so confident she'd find something?" Nick appraised the man standing in front of him. He was a good decade younger than Jamie but that didn't mean anything. Any man would be proud to be seen with her.

"You're kidding, right?" The man didn't try to hide his smile this time.

Nick stared at him in silence.

"Sorry. You must be new around here. If you want someone dead found, Jamie and Gretchen are your best bet. If you want someone alive found, you call Jamie and get her out with Socrates. And, if you just want someone to feel better, it's Jamie and McKenzie."

"Jamie and... are these all *dogs*?"

"Yep. She's our very own Dog Whisperer."

"Are they... are they all *her* dogs?" Nick felt his intrigue for the woman beginning to bow under the pressure of the reality of the four-legged creatures he loathed.

"Who else's would they be?"

"Head on back to help the Dog Whisperer then, would you? Signal me when you know something. I don't think Ms. Taylor is very eager to communicate with me again."

"Jamie Taylor is a professional, Agent. She might not like you very much, but when it comes to getting answers for the families who are waiting, even if she hates your guts, she's your man."

The yellow strip of cloth flagging the stake had been replaced by a red one.

"There's your answer. She's confirming the alert," the deputy said. "We've got ourselves a gravesite."

53

CHAPTER FOURTEEN

While Nick waited for the ME to arrive he watched Jamie work the mountain meadow. In only a few minutes she had tied another red flag tied around a stake. She stopped frequently to give her dog some water. The animal took only a little. It looked to him like she talked to it, even put her face down close to it once. *Did she just kiss a dog?*

He thought about his earlier interest in the tall, slim woman with the fiery eyes and quick wit. *Three dogs? Not gonna happen.*

The deputy carefully strung a grid over the suspected grave. Nick couldn't have done a better job himself. A few hours ago he had considered any unfounded biases against the local LE non-existent and his perceptions of their limitations accurate. He'd been wrong on both counts.

Nick pointed up the lane grid a little farther toward another marked stake. "When you're done there she's got another one ready to go."

He pulled out his cell phone and punched in a number.

"I think we've found it. Get our forensic anthropologist up here from the Denver office. And email me the contact numbers of all the family members." He watched as Jamie put a yellow flag around a stake and move out of the lane to check the geography. He couldn't help but admire her tenacity and perfectionism.

"Damn straight I'm calling them. I'll tell them it's still tentative but I don't think it's false hope. They might need to adjust their schedules if they want to be here. It's my decision and I've made it. Just get me the numbers."

One number he didn't need.

"Mrs. Archer, I have some news."

When Susan Archer ran out of tears she told Nick she needed to hang up to book a flight and pack a bag. She would check with Liam's doctor but only to confirm whether or not they needed to take additional precautions. No way would Liam Archer sit at home and wait, bad heart or not.

Nick tucked his cell phone away and watched a white van pull up next to his SUV. The driver turned off the engine, not caring that the vehicle was in the middle of the rutted road. A woman got out and seemed to be looking for someone. He walked over and introduced himself.

"I'm ASAC Nicolas Grant. You are?"

"I'm Dr. Jacqueline Taylor, the medical examiner." She extended her hand to shake his. "I understand we have some burial sites that probably contain human remains. Is that correct?"

"The first one is right over there." Nick gestured toward the grid-marked spot and waited while the ME grabbed her bag and a backboard from the back of the van.

Nick took the backboard from her and tucked it under his arm.

She smiled. "Lead the way."

"Taylor, huh? Is that a common name in the area?"

"Common enough."

"I guess you must know the dog handler then?"

"Uh-huh. That I do."

Nick decided to let it go. After all, he wasn't interested.

When they were next to the staked and strung area, Dr. Taylor set her bag down and pulled out a large white plastic sheet to spread over the backboard, which Nick had laid flat on the ground next to her. She drew on latex gloves and set a camera and notepad within reach. Then she laid out a common garden trowel, a hand whiskbroom, a toothbrush and several bamboo picks. Nick continued to feel better about the competency levels of the law enforcement personnel in this small mountain town by the minute.

"I called my assistant on my way here." She glanced around at the red flags blooming like poppies in the meadow. "By the looks of things we'll need all the help we can get."

"I've requested the FBI's forensic anthropologist from Denver too," Nick said.

"Good. You might also call Griggs at UC Boulder. Their forensics program is one of the best in the country. A grad student or two might not hurt." She placed a pad on the ground near the 1-1 grid square and reached for the trowel.

"It's not worth the possibility of my site getting trampled, Doctor, but thanks for the suggestion." Now that he found himself working with a professional that didn't involve dogs, he felt a little magnanimous.

"It's your show." Jacqueline Taylor went to work.

The sun was high overhead when the ME finished with the first gravesite. Before moving any of the contents she'd carefully photographed everything as she unearthed it. The white plastic sheet covered with lightweight netting had been cataloged and photographed as well. Two deputies came and removed the backboard to the van. They would grab a second backboard for her, and then transport the remains of the next grave.

Dr. Taylor moved to the next flagged site.

Nick talked on the cell phone with his superiors for what seemed like hours. For a case that had collected a considerable amount of dust, this one suddenly found itself getting a lot of attention in both Virginia and Washington. Nick could picture the bureaucrats juggling for position. Someone would be able to pad their resume with his hard work. He couldn't care less. He just wanted to wrap the case up, and he could count on the people who knew of his contributions and commitment to make due note.

In truth, he'd grown weary of thinking about Bonzer, and the weight of the families and their expectations had been bearing down on him for years. He would feel like a free man when he closed this one. He could finally move forward with his life.

During another phone call, right in the middle of some dweeb grilling him for details, Jacqueline Taylor stood up and put her hands on her hips. She looked around and spotted him, then waved her arms.

"Gotta go." He ended the call and strode toward the doctor.

As he approached, she said, "I thought these grave sites were all at least ten years old."

His intestines clenched. "That's right. Bonzer was sentenced ten years ago."

"This one hasn't been here ten years, Agent. I'd say no more than six months."

CHAPTER FIFTEEN

Over the next few hours Gretchen alerted for seven more gravesites. Jamie straightened up and stretched her back. *Time for Gretchen to take a break, and I could use one myself.* She wiped a thin trickle of sweat from her hairline where an insistent throbbing had set up shop. The additional secrets that lay hidden beneath tranquil beauty for years would have to wait a few minutes longer. A gentle breeze ruffled the Aspen leaves and swept the tops of the grasses and wild flowers. She called Coble and let him know they were taking ten minutes to rest, then led Gretchen out of the lane and into pools of shade and cool air. She reached into her pack and pulled out a water bottle with a drinking bowl snapped onto it. She poured some water for Gretchen then took a drink for herself.

The retriever never wanted to leave the job at hand, but Jamie could tell her dog felt a little overwhelmed at the moment. She hadn't hit on this many scents since her training days.

"Come on, girl, let's go see what Jax is up to."

At the mention of Jacqueline's name, Gretchen perked up and took a fresh look at her surroundings. Jamie didn't need to lead her this time. To keep from contaminating the site, the two headed for the far side of the staked-out grave where Jax was bent to her work.

More official vehicles were parked on the narrow road that was little more than a pair of tire ruts. Tiny dust devils spun the loosened dirt then fell apart. The magnitude of the discovery hit Jamie for the first time. A lot of people were legitimately interested in the events in this meadow because their jobs demanded it. She just hoped they could keep the press away as long as possible.

Apparently the king of the FBI, Agent Grant, shared the same concern. She watched as he pointed down the road toward a deputy carrying yellow crime-scene tape. The three deputies who had been there early in the morning were joined by four others. They took three county vehicles with them as they pulled out to expand the previously established perimeter. A good move by the man with issues.

Jamie found a knee-high boulder to sit on. "How's it going, Dr. Taylor?" Gretchen badly wanted some attention from Jax, but she remained a professional and sat down at Jamie's feet. Only eager eyes and a swishing tail gave away her excitement.

"Hmm?" Jacqueline barely acknowledged their presence. She removed a small amount of dirt with the trowel, sifted it, then set to work with the hand-held whisk broom, her body rolled into a tight ball with only her right arm and neck extended.

Jamie cupped her hands around her mouth. "Ground control to Dr. Jax."

Her sister's head moved in her direction, but when Jax's gaze met hers, they didn't focus for the first second. "Oh, hi."

"Oh, hi? That's what you have to say? *Oh, hi?*" Jamie smiled.

"James," Jax only called her James when she was deadly serious. "We have really stepped into it here."

"What do you mean? We knew if we were lucky, we'd

be unearthing the bodies of a lot of people whom much of the world abandoned a long time ago." Jamie squeezed out an uneasy feeling and reached out to touch Gretchen's head.

Jax sat back and rolled her shoulders. "That's just it. We have new ones mingling with the old ones."

"Oh my God... that explains why a couple of her hits were so quick. Gretchen alerted really fast on some." Jamie folded her arms as if she were cold and her eyes scanned the meadow. "How many do you suppose there are?" A cloud passed over the sun and she shivered. Jamie looked at her dog, then back to her sister.

"If the old bodies and the new bodies were all victims of one killer, then Leopold Bonzer can't be our guy. If the old bodies were Bonzer's victims—" Jax shuddered and looked back at the gravesite.

Jamie finished the sentence. "Then we have two killers."

"Either way we have a killer walking around Aspen Falls."

Jamie and Jax stared at each other as they flashed back to their personal connection with murder. The memory of those nightmare days was never far away. Witnessing the quiet determination on their father's face, the two young women had watched in silence ten years ago as their last remaining parent had packed two duffel bags and handed them the keys to the house.

His firm voice had touched them with the gentleness of a father to a child. "My attorney has taken care of all of the paperwork. Everything is yours. I'll be in touch." Then he leaned in close and drew them both in a hug. "I love you, but I've got to do this. I hope you'll both understand one day."

Jamie had followed him around the country for three months until he ambushed her in a bar and told her to go home. He wanted his daughter to be safe. He wanted his other daughter to stop seeing the guy in her life. He sent her home with both edicts.

Ten years ate up a lot of long days. And in a blink it spit them out. Jamie rose and touched her sister on the shoulder, breaking their thread with the past, at least for now. She urged Gretchen back to her lane and Jax went back to work.

CHAPTER SIXTEEN

Jax noted with satisfaction that so far every skull had remained intact. Even two skulls with obvious trauma had retained all their teeth, and in place. That piece of luck would go a long way toward identification.

The forensic anthropologist from Denver would be here soon to begin work on the older corpses and she would be happy to relinquish the responsibility for that part of the process. Jax excelled at her job, but her expertise had its limits. While the anthropologist played with the old bones she could focus on the new ones. Her lab contained everything he would need to work, including the space to spread out.

In the meantime Jax would begin with x-rays on the victims who had died more recently. She doubted they'd find any sign of bullets or stab wounds. But fractures and other medical procedure evidence might help in the identification process if necessary. The trace evidence scrutiny on both the clothing and the bodies might provide some clues as well, but as long as they'd been in the ground, she didn't hold out a lot of hope they'd find very much. The process was time-consuming, but each possible cause of death they could eliminate would bring them one step closer to finding the truth.

Her cell phone rang with Phil's ringtone. She'd

learned the hard way what could happen if she didn't answer his calls right away. It usually involved the loss of substantial amounts of money.

"Hi, Phil. I'm kind of busy right now. What's up?" She fought to keep her tone light.

"'I'm kind of busy right now.' Is that any way to greet your husband?"

His own tone sounded petulant, not a good sign. A lot of noise was belting in the background. *More than likely he's in a bar—also not a good sign.* "I'm sorry. It's just been kind of crazy today." She waited for a response but soon realized she was talking to air. He was engaged in a conversation with someone else, his hand muffling the phone. She counted to ten and tried again. "How's your day going?"

Nothing.

While she waited for her husband to finish whatever conversation had taken precedence, she watched Jamie flag another stake. *We're going to be here a very long time.*

Finally her husband's voice boomed into the telephone. "Jackie Baby, you there?"

"I'm here." She hated when he called her Jackie Baby, but he never listened when she asked him not to do something. His continued use of that endearment told her two things. First, it reinforced the fact that he didn't really care about her wishes. And second, whatever he said next would not be anything she wanted to hear.

"Good. Listen, Babe, I need you to transfer some money into my business account by Monday morning. Just giving you a heads-up."

Jax's stomach twisted. *Transfer some money? What money?* They didn't even have enough to meet their current bills. Of course that was nothing Phil wanted to hear. Nothing he could deal with. "Why? What

63

happened?" *Maybe I can juggle something... again.*

"You know. The usual. Mel is holding back my commission check for some reason." Phil rushed the words as if sheer speed of delivery would make her not question him further.

The truth was she didn't need to question him any further. Resolve gave way to routine. Phil undoubtedly had found himself into the car dealership for some cash because he'd requested another advance. It was the fourth time this year.

"How much do we need to cover?" Jax closed her eyes and held her breath.

"Two grand ought to do it."

"*Two thousand dollars?* Where in the world do you think I can come up with two thousand dollars by Monday morning?" She loved her husband, but remembering why was becoming harder and harder. "Phil, tell me exactly how much we need to cover and what it's for."

Silence on the line. She fought a strange combination of tears and anger. A picture came into her mind. The end of the rope she held onto hung precariously over a cliff with hungry alligators snapping in the swampland beneath her. And her hands were sweaty. And she had a job to do.

Finally Phil said, "Look, if we don't have the money to transfer, you're going to have to ask your sister for help. Things will be bad for me—for us—if enough money isn't in that account."

Phil didn't have any answers to her questions, and what if he did? What difference would it make? They were stuck in perpetuity, dancing the same steps on the same dance floor. The orchestra had stopped and gone home years ago, but Jax still kept moving her feet.

Anger bruised his next words. "Did you hear what I said?"

"I'll make a call."

"That's my Jackie Baby."

Chapter Seventeen

He sensed rather than saw the activity in the area—his area—and continued driving along the road. He would go to the high bluff where he'd first learned about the safety buried secrets could provide, where he'd first watched a man dig into the earth and deliver a body into the ground, almost like getting rid of trash. He'd watched for thirty minutes while his fellow truant had slept off the combination of booze and weed they'd shared.

He savored the details of that quiet afternoon's education, and he'd returned often to the remote location. Three of those times he'd discovered what he thought were additional fresh graves. The other times he'd stretched out on the ground over a spot he knew contained a burial site, and tried to make a connection to the victim or the killer. He didn't care which.

Not until a little over ten years ago, when Leopold Bonzer finally admitted to killing fourteen people and burying thirteen of them, did he know for sure the identity of the man with the shovel he'd seen that afternoon. Bonzer went to prison and he went to college. While getting the pedigree his birth parents failed to provide him, he pondered how he could turn what he knew to his advantage. About a year ago he'd decided to take over ownership of the burial ground. It belonged to him now and these people were intruders.

He drove up the mountain, each switchback taking him closer to the spot that overlooked the meadow below. He'd have to hike a bit, but no one would know of his presence. He could observe, figure out what they were doing there, make some decisions.

He pulled his SUV off the road into a small clearing and turned off the ignition. The car's computer system hummed for a minute, then fell silent. The sound of a droning bee came through his open window. He followed the sound until he spotted a large bumblebee popping on and off some wildflowers about ten feet away. It was too big to actually land. The creature, adapted to its cumbersome shape and weight, overcame its reality. Flexibility was one of the great keys to the universe.

He looked at the two rolled-up tarps stacked crisscross in the back end of his vehicle and sighed. Two at a time didn't do it for him. Ten or fifteen wouldn't either. It was time to move ahead to the final stages of his ultimate plan. Tens of thousands of men, women and children. His formula pushed closer to perfection. Flexibility.

Flies buzzed and swarmed near the rock that had once served him as a lookout post. A gnarled piñon fought for survival on the slope, its roots binding the large rocks in a death-grip. The fragile, sparse branches were unable to provide shade, and the abandoned carcass of someone's pet lay in a mangled mess in the sun at the base of the pine. What wasn't dark and sticky with blood displayed shiny and white—bones picked clean. It was hard to tell what kind of an animal it had been, but the collar sticking out of a mound of fur confirmed that whatever form it once held, it had proved easy prey, like the two he found himself hauling around today and the others he'd already practiced on.

Hungry Ghosts—they were all around him. Even he was one. He hungered for—craved—to feel something, anything. Sorrow or love or remorse or guilt or compassion—they were feelings he could fake, but they were also feelings he'd never experienced.

When he'd learned about Hungry Ghosts while studying Buddhism, he'd felt a kinship with something for the first time in his life. Tormented by unfulfilled desires, demanding impossible satisfaction from any available source, hungry ghosts sought to fill a void—a terrible emptiness—within themselves. They had been depicted through the centuries with enormous empty stomachs, tiny, ineffective mouths, and necks so narrow they couldn't swallow should they ever be able to get something into those mouths. He could understand their obsession, their hunger.

He'd spent the next five years of his life traveling in and out of Asia in an attempt to find more elements with which he could identify, something that might not only explain his emotional vacuity but give him a direction to take to void it. Years later, he'd thought, *Yeah, right... void vacuity.* When he returned home he knew he needed something bigger than some silly, archaic religion to fulfill his personal craving.

He began to give form to a god of his own design, one who loved him even though he couldn't love. His god would support him in his quest to experience the same emotions everyone else around him enjoyed and would understand that until he could feel, killing played the role of a means to an end.

At an early age he'd learned how to force a tear by imagining a pierce to his eye. A cough or a strangled gag, for a man, worked as well as a total breakdown for a woman. Gazing off into the distance gave people the impression he had connected with an emotional memory. He'd fine-tuned his repertoire over time.

People, especially women, loved him. He was wealthy, successful, powerful and emotive. No one, not one person he'd ever met, would describe him as degage or without emotion or detached. In some circles people considered him too involved and over the top. He could fake passion as well as guilt. He smiled at the thought, but a close look would show it was a disconnected smile born of decades of practice.

Flat on his stomach, he used his elbows to prop himself up and he gazed down onto the meadow. It lay close enough he didn't need field glasses, which of course he wouldn't have used anyway. Too much of a chance they would reflect sunlight and give away his presence. The last time he'd had business in his private cemetery the entire place had been awash in moonlight. The silver illumination and the vision it had afforded made him feel powerful, even unstoppable. He had moved like a ghost among ghosts, better and stronger than flesh and blood.

Even so, the sense that someone was lurking in the shadows watching him had been intense, if fleeting. If there had been a witness it might already be too late. He would know soon enough. He'd have to engage in conversation with the enemy.

Uniformed cops were moving around the meadow like human counterparts to the flies buzzing around the animal carcass lying near where he was lying. Several small posts were marked with red flags. He shifted. *They found it, but how much of it?*

He narrowed his eyes and focused on the far edge of the meadow. Empty. No posts, no flags, no uniforms. He might yet have a place for the current inhabitants of his SUV, but otherwise the usefulness of this burial ground had drawn to an abrupt close. He began to formulate a plan to mislead the stupid people who thought they were on his trail and buy himself some time. He didn't need much.

He worked his way back down the slight slope to his vehicle, then stood and brushed the bits of dirt off his pant legs and elbows. *It might even prove stimulating to bury a couple of corpses under their noses later tonight. Could I get away with it? Will I feel anything?*

CHAPTER EIGHTEEN

Gretchen's tail began to droop. At some point the golden would begin to make errors and both of them would get frustrated. Jamie turned around and looked behind her at all they'd accomplished. She saw what looked to her like a sea of red. *Time to call it a day.*

When the forensic anthropologist had arrived from Denver almost an hour ago, Jax had brought him up to speed and left for her lab to begin her own workups. With potentially two separate perpetrators and multiple victims, they would have the muscle of the crime labs of both the FBI and the Colorado Bureau of Investigation. The CBI lab could not compete with the scope and strength of Quantico, but it boasted current equipment and was much closer.

Looking at her sister's face before she left, Jamie saw a level of excitement over the scientific work ahead. But another emotion lurked like a shadow. Concern was etched in the corners of Jax's mouth. Jamie knew that troubled look. She made a mental note to phone her sister later.

"C'mon, Gretch. We're done here for the day." She called the sheriff to let him know they were leaving.

"You two did good here today, Jamie. We'll see you

71

first thing in the morning."

Before she took her own shower, Jamie sat out on the deck grooming Gretchen. Socks and McKenzie were happy to chase one another around the yard, their own way to celebrate the together-again status of their little family. When Jamie finished grooming her, Gretchen shot off the deck to join her more raucous counterparts.

Jamie walked into the laundry room and stripped down to her underwear. A day's worth of dirt and grime had found its way into her clothes and she didn't want to track the dirt all over her house. Plus, taking off her dirty clothes here would save a trip with them later.

The harsh fluorescents in the small room made the scar on her mid-section jump out in an angry purple hue. Her impulse was to cover it even with nobody around to see, but she'd also begun to discover that in an odd way, she kind of liked that scar. It represented a very bad part of her life that she had survived, and she was stronger for it. She dropped her hand back to her side.

She out turned the lights and moved through the kitchen. With her first step on the stairs leading up to her room, the three dogs blazed by in a race to get to the top. Putting in the doggie door ranked as one of the smartest things she'd done in years. They still liked it better when she opened the door for them, but when they couldn't wait, the outdoors—or the indoors—was accessible. In her bedroom the three found their favorite nap spots and settled in while she turned the shower on to warm the water.

The hot water cascading over her helped heal the sorrow of the day. She imagined all of her fear and sadness flowing down the drain, leaving behind only the success and closure she and Gretchen helped to achieve. While she was shampooing, the phone rang. *Forgot to check my messages when I got home. Later.*

Revived and clear-headed, Jamie wrapped a towel around herself and went to the kitchen to put on the kettle for some tea. Too tired to tackle another home repair job but too wired for an early night, she dialed into her voice mail. Four messages. She put her phone on speaker and opened the fridge to inspect her dinner possibilities.

Her boss reminded her about the staff meeting set for Monday morning. He must have gotten wind of the S&R job she'd undertaken—on her own time—and wanted to make sure she remembered her commitment. The second one was a message from a local non-profit looking for donations. She laughed. Between home repairs and subsidizing her brother-in-law's bad habits to support her sister, the amount of money available for donations totaled pretty much zilch.

The third message made her heart stop. "Hi, Jamison. I feel kind of awkward here but I just wanted to touch base. I'll be back in Colorado for a conference in a couple of days and I'd like to get together if you can spare the time. There are a few things I'd like to talk about. If not I understand... more than you know." He left a number.

Andrew Stanton—the man she'd once believed was her soul mate. The man who had convinced her friends and family of the same thing. The same man who turned on her, isolated her, abused her, and finally left her with something she would carry with her forever. That six-inch purplish scar between her belly button and her left breast.

Last summer while Ciara was getting her belly button pierced to engage a male eye or two, Jamie stocked up on one-piece swimsuits.

She closed the refrigerator door.

CHAPTER NINETEEN

The fourth message helped. "Hey, girlfriend." *Speaking of the uber-pierced.* Ciara's voice penetrated the ice that had enveloped Jamie the moment she'd heard her ex's voice on her voice mail. "We're meeting up at E-lev 2 at about seven o'clock. My shoot is over and I'm buying at least one round." Ciara sounded ready to party, and E-lev 2, the Aspen Falls offshoot of Aspen's Elevation, was the current hot spot in town. It was more rustic than its Aspen counterpart, and the girlfriends had fallen in love with the overstuffed chairs and fireplaces in the intimate space.

An evening with her friends sounded like exactly what Jamie needed. Clean clothes, a fresh face, a clip for her wet hair and Jamie was headed to town. She phoned Jax on the drive down her little mountain. No answer. She left a message. "Hey, you okay? You looked a little ragged when you left the site today. We're meeting at E-lev 2 for some girl time. Hope you can make it. Call me." She clicked off.

She would tell her sister about Andrew contacting her face to face. Jax took his abuse of Jamie as a personal betrayal since Jax's matchmaking efforts had set them up in the first place. Jamie shook her head. Andrew Stanton had fooled everyone.

The busy gathering places of downtown Aspen Falls

forced her to park two blocks away from the restaurant. Her phone rang as she walked toward the bistro. *Jax.*

"You on your way?"

"I can't. Looks like this will be an all-nighter."

"Thought it might be. Can you take a dinner break?"

"Gonna try. I might hook up with you guys about eight."

"Try hard. We need to talk."

Inside, Jamie looked around and spotted Ellen and Ciara at a corner table. It looked like Ellen had a date. *Good for her.* Ciara spotted her and waved. Ellen and the man looked her way. *A nice enough looking guy in a geeky kind of way.* Ellen looked happy and energized. Sitting next to this man, right at this moment, she looked like that dynamic teacher Jamie had once witnessed in action, the one who had completely astonished her with energy and brilliance, like a perfectly cut diamond. The shy, retiring schoolmarm had left the building.

As Jamie approached the table, the man stood. *Manners, too... well, well.*

"Jamie, meet Arnold Abner. Arnold, this is my good friend, Jamie Taylor."

He did a double take at Jamie's name.

She nodded before he could comment. "I know. I know. I get it all the time. My blessing and my curse." She reached to shake his hand, then nodded at the waiter who appeared at her side. She ordered a wasabi Caesar salad with grilled chicken, water and a zin. Ciara had barely touched her plate but so what else was new? Ellen and Arnold had wine glasses in front of them that were almost empty.

Ellen smiled, suddenly shy again. "Arnold and I can't stay, Jamie, but I wanted the two of you to meet." The couple pushed back their chairs and stood.

"I hope I haven't made you late for anything."

Arnold looked at her and smiled. "It's okay. We have dinner reservations at The Roaring Fork but I think they'll probably hold our table for a few minutes."

Everyone said goodbye and Jamie watched the couple leave, Arnold's hand protectively at Ellen's back. Jamie turned to Ciara. "Who, what, when and how?"

"They met at the drugstore yesterday morning, can you believe it? They totally hit it off. If I wasn't so happy for her I'd be jealous. I love it when a guy is head over heels with me, and Agent Abner doesn't know which end is up." Ciara winked.

"Agent?" *Oh please don't let there be a connection.*

"Yeah. He's with the FBI. He didn't tell us much more than that. Probably have to shoot us. Isn't that sexy?" Ciara picked a piece of lettuce out of her plate and bit off an end. "The FBI part, not the shooting part." She giggled.

"How did she meet someone with the FBI at the drugstore?" *Things were getting ugly.*

"I think he's up here on that same deal you and Jax are working on. The Bonzer thingie?"

Oh crud. One of her best friends had hooked up with someone who was obviously hooked up with the king of the FBI. *I'll have to watch my mouth.*

Ciara nudged her in the ribs.

"Look at what just walked in. Honey, I love you, but this girl has *got* to see what he might have behind that brilliant smile. And those six-pack abs." Ciara stood, adjusted her clinging top and made her way through the crowd.

"Fine. Get me here and then abandon me. What are friends for?"

Jamie finished her salad—superb as always—and debated what to do next. She wasn't ready to go home, but the idea of sitting by herself at a four-top didn't feel right either. People were lined up three deep at the bar waiting for a table, and she knew what it was like to work for tips. She grabbed her purse and headed for the bar, spotting an empty seat at the far end.

Drink ordered, she noodled with the bar food and glanced toward Ciara. The girl glowed in her element. Toothsome and Muscled, the specimen who had drawn her attention, stood at her side, and two other adoring men were paying their respects as well. They looked like expectant puppies waiting for a treat.

"May I?" A man wearing an obviously expensive suit and designer casual shirt pointed to the empty stool next to her.

She did a quick scan at the rest of the full bar and nodded. "Of course."

The bartender brought Jamie her drink and the stranger laid a bill on the counter. "Please. Allow me."

"I'd rather you didn't." Jamie pushed the cash away and replaced it with her own.

Rather than put up the expected fuss, he surprised her when he smile and nodded, then pocketed his money.

Well that's a nice surprise... a little respect for my position. She gave him a closer look. He was maybe ten years older than she, no more. Medium build, in good shape. *Great shape, actually.* He was her height or a little taller with sandy hair and gray-blue eyes. *Smells pretty good... altogether not a bad option, especially since both of my friends are gone for the evening.* The fact that she also needed to erase the memory of Andrew Stanton's phone call, at least temporarily, played no small role in her appraisal.

Only his hands made her stumble. They were manicured. She would try not to hold that against him.

He looked at her and smiled. *Good teeth, too.*

He extended his hand. "I'm sorry. My name is Teague Blanton."

Firm grip. That works. She smiled back at him. "Jamie Taylor."

"A pleasure, Ms. Taylor."

Ten minutes of small talk turned into two hours of more personal give and take. Teague made her laugh and feel important. She gave him her number. He said he had some business at the bank next Wednesday and asked whether he could buy her lunch.

Ciara joined them and a warmth spread over Jamie when Teague didn't seem to fall under the model's spell. Polite and charming, his gaze was riveted to Jamie's. It made her want to giggle.

When he left, citing paperwork, Ciara fell onto his vacated barstool, grabbed Jamie's hand and demanded to know every detail.

This time Jamie gave in. She giggled.

CHAPTER TWENTY

Nick sat alone in his study while one of his favorite CDs played. The peaceful native flute of David Maracle sweetened the air, but it didn't quite reach his soul as it usually managed to do. He needed to make phone calls to all of the families, but before he could face the pain and relief, and the inevitable pain *of* relief that this kind of finality would kick into place, a few minutes of quiet would enable him to build up his own internal reserves.

People always think closure is the goal, that it's a good thing—and in the end, when it's been accomplished, it often is—but completing one more agenda item when it concerns the death of a loved one just separates them from the family that much more. The process leading up to closure is usually much more traumatic than people realize.

A soft, steady glow from lamps balanced the light dancing from the fireplace. His sandwich remained uneaten, but the drink he'd been working on was down to ice. Again. An oxy bottle lay empty on its side, three pills having spilled onto the table. He had one more bottle in his bedroom. He made a mental note to get the prescription refilled on Monday.

Nick organized the calls, beginning with families who

lived on the east coast. No sense waking people up, even though they were unlikely to sleep at all tonight after he spoke with them. His promise to each of them had been to let them know what was happening as soon as anything *did* happen. Today's results required him to keep that promise. He'd pass on his update and advise them that he expected to have word very soon with respect to positive identifications. The victims' dental records were on their way to the local ME's office by courier. He wouldn't mention anything about the newer gravesites. It wouldn't mean anything, and it could add to their pain. He picked up the phone and made his first call.

He kept the conversations short and on task even through the tears and meltdowns that burned through the connection. Several times he held the phone away from his ear to lessen the intensity and preserve his eardrums. During each conversation he worked hard to remain professionally connected but emotionally detached.

He tried to keep his previous performance evaluations in mind. As an FBI agent he should never engage in emotional exercise related in any way to an investigation. To do so could compromise his effectiveness.

His gut twisted more with each phone call. After he finished talking with the last relative, the hidden, uncontrolled part of him clamored for release. Only moments ago he'd been tight, restrained, in charge, but now he came fully to once again imagine the horrifying last moments of the lives of each victim. His heart fell open, and the unbelievable torment of the people they left behind, people who only wanted to bring their loved ones home, ripped into it. For the last decade he had connected with the victims and those who mourned them. He had processed information, evidence and pain. And today, finally, he'd gotten the job done.

Two-dimensional faces, hundreds of them, floated

around him. Some were smiling and happy, with no idea what horror their future held. Others were bloody, with matted hair and vacant stares. They'd already met their fate. The images gathered and spun into tornados of incredible strength, the torque magnificent in its fury. In seconds, faces began to fly out, spinning through space, slicing through Nick's soul.

Finally thirteen faces were circling his head, thirteen people murdered and thrown into dirt, not to respect them but to protect their murderer. He knew each of them personally, though he hadn't known them at all.

He fell onto his back, exhausted, waiting for his heart to slow down, for regular breaths, for the curtain to open that would clarify his thoughts and set them in order. He had to slip emotion back into the bottle.

His cell phone rang. He took a deep breath and tried to sit up. Pain arced through his back, digging low and deep. Nick rolled onto his stomach and reached for the phone. "Grant."

"Good work, ASAC."

"Thank you, Sir."

"I received a call from Sheriff Jerry Coble in Aspen Falls this afternoon. It's a good thing they want our help on this one. Since you handled Bonzer and were there when they found the new bodies, I told him you'd be our man on site. Plus, he likes you. You're in charge of whatever else is being dug up out there." Don Adams, the SAC for the Denver office, never wasted time.

Nick didn't respond. More faces. More families. More.

"Is that an affirmative, Agent?"

"Yes, Sir. I'm on it."

Chapter Twenty-One

He stood motionless in the deep shadows. The dense trees around him scented the air with the smell of pine and sap. People moved over his meadow with seeming impunity, tossing soil and making discoveries he wasn't ready for them to make. One uniformed cop, bored with his duty, paced and stopped, paced and stopped. He'd made the trek to the patrol car twice already to get more coffee or something to snack on. An official—a medical examiner, he assumed, presumably attached to the FBI's Denver office—was working each of the sites, a groveling technician or assistant at his beck and call.

White-hot Klieg lights drenched the work area. Meanwhile, the far end of the meadow—his end of the meadow—flowed with dark shadows, lit solely by the waning moon. *Demolition and threat there. Peace here.* He pulled in a lungful of air. Clean. Fresh. Invigorating. A sure sign that his plans for the evening would hold and he could leave them with a couple of new discoveries. Keep them busy for a while longer.

He grabbed a shovel from the back of the SUV, pushing aside the bottom portion of one of the two rolled up tarps to get to it. He noticed the rigor had left and the limbs were once again pliable. *Sweet.*

The soil of the high mountain meadow lifted heavy, its dense, dark loam fragrant with decay, death giving way to new life.

He pierced the soil and turned it up, piece by piece, the dirt, the rocks, the worms. All of it turned with his will. The ease of the progress validated his plan. The lack of pain in his body left him assured he possessed the strength to carry it out.

Three hours later, when he'd dug enough, he laid the shovel down with the gentleness of a lover. His quest would give him what he craved and the Hungry Ghost in him would finally be appeased. The sudden rapid beating of his heart told him affirmation was near.

Soon.

On the ground, he pulled up a handful of the moist earth and held it to his nose. The loam held the intimate aroma of confidentiality, the pervading scent of timelessness. He spread his fingers to allow it to break free and fall in clumps around his knees. He felt in its cool texture the beginnings of emotion, the quest for meaning that drove him.

These two were the last. If his secret burial ground had remained secret, he probably would have made a couple more tests. But they would have confirmed what he already knew.

He was ready.

Chapter Twenty-Two

Nick observed the pretty, but tired, medical examiner as she sat behind her messy desk. It wasn't the worst he'd ever seen, but it wasn't the precise, managed desk he presumed a woman of science would maintain. He leaned forward, then consciously pulled his body back to settle into the chair. "Can you be more specific?" No good would come of trying to intimidate someone on his own team.

Jacqueline Taylor exhaled and shifted forward in her own seat behind the desk. "Agent, it is what it is until I tell you different. You're the one who's pushing for answers. If you have to push, you also have to accept that the answers might change down the road."

At nine o'clock in the morning the clouds were already building outside the offices of the medical examiner, threatening to obscure even Cobalt Mountain from view. Nick worried about what the changing weather might mean to the progress being made at the burial site. "My apologies, Dr. Taylor. I understand we're discussing preliminary findings here, but can you be a little more specific as to what we're dealing with?" Nick considered the ME and the dog handler and their relationship to one another. He could definitely see the connection. Smart, dynamic and stubborn—a dangerous combination.

"It's my opinion—preliminarily—that we have two

84

separate entities responsible for the deaths of the individuals we've examined—preliminarily—from the Rocky Point Meadow site."

"Why do you believe that's the case?" Nick pulled out his notebook.

"Aside from the gap between the groupings of the killings, which is a good ten years, there is the obvious differentiation in the method of the killings." Dr. Taylor pulled two files open and offered them to Nick.

"That difference being?"

"The older victims all sustained visible trauma of some kind. For example, they were struck over the head or their feet were mangled as if they'd been caught in a trap. Two of them experienced blows to the ribs sufficient to cause major breaks before they died."

"And the more recent victims?"

"We're still waiting to hear but there are no clear indications of physical assault. I suspect—again, preliminarily—we're looking at something they ingested."

"Like poison?"

Jacqueline nodded. "Maybe. Or maybe some kind of toxin they absorbed cutaneously, or maybe something incorporated through their lungs or even injected."

"Did you see any signs of injection?"

"Not on the bodies we've seen. The degradation has precluded us from doing visuals that would be of much value, but we haven't yet prepared all of the tissues for toxicology. They'll tell us a lot."

Nick hated when uncertainty obscured his direction.

"So what you're saying—preliminarily—is that we have a killer out there right now who is killing people by some means that doesn't leave noticeable trauma."

"That's about it."

"Any idea why?"

"That's your job, Agent."

CHAPTER TWENTY-THREE

After Agent Grant left, Jax remained at her desk. Exhaustion pulled her deep into the chair. While her on-call, part-time assistant cleaned up the autopsy room in preparation for any new cases—and there *would* be new cases—Jax tried to complete her reports. She hoped to get some sleep before the next round.

Suddenly Alicia, one of the admin clerks on Sunday duty, was standing in her doorway, coffee pot raised high. "Coffee, Doc?" She was new, energetic, and annoying.

Jax smiled and shook her head. "Not now, thanks. Maybe not again in this lifetime."

Alicia walked in, her tight leather skirt working its way up her thighs.

"You used to be married to Phil Sussman, right? The guy who was the All-Star quarterback for the Wildcats?" She seemed a little eager, a little loud.

Jax looked closer. *Well hell... new and energetic with a leather mini-skirt does not automatically equate to youth. The woman has crow's feet.* She wanted to gather facts. This was not the time to entertain the "used to be married to" portion of the woman's question. "Did you attend Aspen Falls?"

Beneath the thick makeup a blush worked its way up Alicia's neck and cheeks to her hairline.

"For about a semester." Her confident bluster receded almost to a whisper. The woman had figured out that this conversation would not include a girlfriend chat.

"Move away?" Jax forced the words out. *Best to appear pleasant.*

"You could say that. I moved into the maternity ward at Memorial."

Ah. Jax remembered the girls in high school everyone expected to get pregnant. Leather mini-skirts fit right into that image. She quickly went from wondering how this woman could possibly have passed the background check to work here to considering how many kids by different fathers she had birthed to the baby Jax wanted but didn't have.

"Don't think I was a slut or nothin'. It just took that one time. And I just had the one kid." Alicia tugged down her skirt and tugged up her chin. "Who I raised."

Forced to examine her own judgmental thoughts, Jax swallowed and her scrutiny turned inward. "Being a single parent is one of the toughest jobs on the planet. I admire you."

"Yeah, well... my folks helped." The woman fiddled with a thread sticking out of the hem of her tight sweater. "He's the guy who goes to the casinos, right? Parties big? Phil? Your ex? In Central City and Blackhawk?"

A brick, ice-cold on the outside and newly forged with intense heat on the inside, dropped into Jax's stomach. She could taste the clay. Raw and gritty, it coated her mouth and threatened to choke off the air to her lungs. *Damn him.* Pride, a temporary savior, poured in and wrapped itself around the sharp cornered chunk of dirt in her gut. Her husband's actions made her add this sin to her repertoire of cover-ups. It became one more item on a growing list.

"Sure, every once in awhile. He likes to blow off

steam." She bit her lips before she spit out the lie. "We both go from time to time. Why do you ask?"

Jax watched as Alicia filled in the white board in her mind. The coffee pot tilted precariously and the clerk stepped back into the hallway, her free hand pulling uselessly on the hem of the tiny leather statement that almost covered her upper legs.

"Yeah. Well, I thought so. Heard you guys liked to head over there every now and then. Maybe one of these days—"

"Yeah. Maybe one of these days."

This wasn't the first time Jax had been confronted with this side of her husband's character. Just because she kept it a secret didn't mean no one else knew. In addition to the list of creditors she had to juggle, she'd become adept at keeping a list of women she needed to avoid.

She had to dig down deep to remember why she loved him.

CHAPTER TWENTY-FOUR

Sunday morning broke with exquisite perfection. With promise of a brilliant blue later, the pre-dawn sky folded smoky purple and silver hues together, a hint of rose peeking out of the stillness between the trees. Jamie opened the door to the deck of her bedroom to breathe crisp air filled with the tingling scent of pine mixed with overnight dew. From this side of her house she could see clouds building beyond the mountains. That blue sky would be interrupted before it got started.

Dressed in heavy socks, her favorite blue jeans, a tee, a turtleneck and an over-sized cable-knit sweater, she sat on a deck chair and pulled on her boots. *Probably be down to my t-shirt by mid-afternoon unless it snows. In Colorado you never know.* Back inside she pulled her hair back and wrapped a scrunchie around it before applying some light makeup. Then she was ready for some caffeine. Lots of it.

Glowing light from the small lamp she kept turned on in the kitchen pooled around its base and cast a kind of spotlight on the phone. She punched the button on her coffee maker for French roast, glad she'd taken the time to prepare it the night before, and tried to ignore the lit object. The phone and the message from Andrew Stanton it still held mocked her. *There are a few things I'd like to talk about. If not I understand... more than you know.* Like she's supposed to trust him all of a sudden?

While the coffee brewed she flipped on the overhead lights and filled the dogs' bowls. She would have time for a cup on her deck, and then she and Gretchen would hit the road for another day of duty. She could hardly wait. Focusing on work she loved would be a good thing.

Two of the dogs came bounding through the doggie door.

"Perfect timing, you guys. Where's McKenzie?" Jamie walked out on the deck, expecting a streak of white to come flying up the steps.

About to call out, she saw something out of place and instinctively raced down the stairs. She tore through the back yard. The side of the small storage shed that held her lawn equipment and backup propane was gaping open. Broken boards were scattered over a four-foot area. Whoever had broken in also had pulled up floorboards and weakened the remaining ones to such a degree that the twelve-pound dog had fallen through and gotten stuck.

Jamie fell to her knees and reached out to pull him to her. She finally exhaled when he raised his head at her touch. He was alive, but not by much, and he seemed to be caught on something under the flooring. She reached underneath him and jerked her hand back. Blood coated her fingers. Back again under the shattered plank she scrabbled by touch and found a bent nail curled in such a way that McKenzie's leg was trapped. She looked around for something to give her leverage. *Nothing. Why don't I keep tools out here?*

McKenzie laid his head back down, expelling a wheezy whimper with the movement. He watched her, his brown eyes calm and warm.

Jamie lifted her sweater and unbuckled her belt. She

90

snapped it out of the loops on her jeans so hard that the last one pulled loose. With both hands she felt to hook the buckle behind the nail, protecting as much of McKenzie's leg as she could with a finger.

She pulled. Nothing.

She moved the buckle a little closer to the edge of the nail and pulled again. The nail creaked against the wood. She pulled harder and the nail, still attached to the wood, moved enough so she could extricate McKenzie and pull him to her chest. She raced back to the kitchen to grab her keys. *How long has he been out there?*

Jamie tried to think back. McKenzie had curled against her side while she was reading the newest Hallinan novel before turning out the lights. She'd gone to sleep with the little guy on her bed, but at some point she had become aware he'd hopped down. No big deal. His dog bed was on the floor next to her bed. *Damn doggie door.*

She called Scott Ortiz at home and asked the vet to meet them as she sped to the clinic with all three dogs piled into her SUV. McKenzie lay on the passenger seat beside her, swaddled in an afghan her mother had crocheted before she died. *Mom would understand the blood.*

CHAPTER TWENTY-FIVE

Only a few minutes later than planned, Jamie slowed down to acknowledge the uniformed officer at the perimeter of the search site. She pushed the button to roll down her window and the fresh air puffed into her face.

McKenzie was going to be fine. A few stitches and some strong antibiotics. The vet also had agreed to keep Socrates with him for the day. Socks wouldn't like it much, but Jamie needed to know everyone was safe while she and Gretchen were working. The destruction of her shed seemed purposefully violent, as if it were intended as some kind of message.

"Morning, Joe."

"Jamie." The tall, once good-looking cop sported a gut that expanded a little over his belt. His hairline did the opposite under his hat. Joe made a point of searching for her name on the list clipped to the board in his hand.

She wanted to tell him to get over himself. He had carried a grudge against her ever since high school. As bad as Jamie's choices about men had been since, turning down Joe Hoffman for a date ranked high in her Good Decisions column.

"C'mon, Joe. We've got to get to work."

"You're clear." He checked his watch and made a notation. "You'll need to park right behind me and walk in."

"You're joking, right?" It was a good half-mile hike up steep terrain to get to where they'd been working yesterday, and Jamie needed coffee.

"Sorry. Orders. We're full-up with trucks to transport evidence."

Jamie saw the smirk before Officer Hoffman regained his aloofness. *Sorry my ass.* She watched as he leaned over and scooped up his Starbucks cup.

"Is there any coffee up there?"

"There was. Probably none left though."

She took her foot off the brakes and pulled forward. Burning a bit of tire on some loose gravel would feel good, but it wouldn't mean much at the end of the day. Tucked into a parking spot that would have to do, she rounded up her gear and loaded it onto her shoulders and waist. Gretchen leapt out and explored for a few seconds before coming to heel, waiting for her leash so she could get to work.

Jamie and Gretchen moved off toward the site. As she walked she thought about her dad's message. Why hadn't he contacted them again? Was he still in the area, or had the trail taken him in a different direction? No way could she second-guess Bryce Taylor. What she could do was concentrate on her job.

If there were any more graves to be found, Jamie wanted to find them today. Tomorrow morning she'd be back at the bank and useless to the families who were waiting for word.

She also wanted to find a few minutes to speak with Sheriff Coble about the vandalism at her home that had left McKenzie injured. She couldn't put her finger on a rational reason, but she felt something pointed and sinister about the breaking up of her shed. As far as she could tell nothing had been taken, but the maliciousness of the destruction didn't feel like the result of teenage delinquents, and it left her feeling alone without much of a safety wall between her and whomever had ripped the solid planks out of her storage building while she slept.

She made a mental note to stick with the facts when she talked to Jerry unless he asked her opinion, and the two questions he would want answers to—who and why—weren't ones she could help with. She closed her eyes and put the vandalism to the back of her mind.

The morning gleamed with exquisite beauty. If not for the job they had to do, Jamie would have let Gretchen off the leash to capitalize on the moment, which would allow Jamie herself to arc to the sunshine and strike off on a path that had nothing to do with a grid search. Instead, she kept Gretch on a tight lead, close to her side until they got to the work zone. Once they arrived at the lane, she'd let the leather leash ride out a few more feet, a signal to Gretchen they were down to business.

A few hundred yards remained for them to trek when Jamie pulled Gretchen up short. There was an unexpected movement ahead. She dropped her backpack and rummaged for her binoculars. She adjusted the focus and watched, a tremor running through her as Agent Grant filled the viewfinder.

She watched as he pulled something from his coat pocket, a bottle of some kind, and based on the amber color, a prescription. He worked the lid off and tipped it into his hand. Whether one pill or twelve, Jamie had no way of knowing, and wouldn't have thought twice about it until she saw him look around. Then he put his hand to his mouth and swallowed. With a shrug he slipped the bottle back into his jacket. Agent Grant had something hiding in his closet.

CHAPTER TWENTY-SIX

By two o'clock the entire meadow was jacketed with stakes, red flags limp in the calm, warm mountain air. The threatening clouds had come and gone hours ago. Together, Jamie and Gretchen had found seventeen gravesites in two days. She pulled off the jacket attached to her duty belt and chucked it into the back seat of her SUV, followed by the belt itself and Gretchen's empty water bowl.

She walked around to the back and picked up the probe she'd leaned against the bumper to clean off and stow for the next time she needed it. She bundled the stakes they hadn't used and put the yellow and red flags back into their separate storage containers, along with the leather gloves she hated but was sometimes forced to wear.

At this point she didn't know which graves were old and which were fresh. That was for someone else to discover. If she wasn't so tired, she'd stop by to see Jax and get the latest progress on the identifications, but exhaustion convinced her a phone call later would work just as well.

Sheriff Coble had agreed to send a deputy out to her house tomorrow after she got home from work to take a report on the vandalism. The department was stretched thin today and she didn't expect them to find anything anyway. Still, she didn't know what the repairs might cost. If they were more than her deductible her insurance company would want a report.

Her cell vibrated and she pulled it out. Didn't recognize the number. An out of state area code. *Andrew?* Her hand trembled as she held the phone, waiting to see whether the caller would leave a message. At least then she could control her response. The message light came on. She skimmed for a voice message or a text.

PRETTY SURE I WANT DINNER 2NITE. DINNER 4 2? - TEAGUE

She caught a deep breath and laughed, the tension draining from her body. It wasn't Andrew. It was Teague. Flattered he hadn't waited for their lunch next week, she texted back *DINNER 4 2 + 3 DOGS OK W/U? MY PLACE. 7?* She hit send and waited.

The answer came back in a few seconds: *6 OK? HAVE FLITE AT 10 ASPEN ARPRT.*

After texting back that six o'clock would work, Jamie felt energy seep back into her bones. She'd been wanting to try a new paella recipe, but abandoned that idea until she knew a little more about Teague's culinary tastes. Instead, she would pick up the ingredients for a sure-fire hit: rosemary pork loin with baked apple, fresh beans and Tuscan breadcrumbs. It would be perfect for a fall evening.

She watched as Nicholas Grant wound his way down the dirt road toward her. She lifted a hand to say goodbye. He was talking on his phone. She didn't expect a wave from him, but some acknowledgement would have been nice. She didn't get any. *What a jerk.*

She opened the door for Gretchen to jump in, then

finished securing her equipment so it wouldn't bounce around too much on the rutted road. Behind the wheel, Jamie finished her report on her laptop, including a detailed map marking each site. She'd email it to the sheriff when she got home.

She called the vet's office to see whether McKenzie was cleared for release. No doubt Socrates would be ready to go. The Search and Rescue dog had probably tested every fiber of the vet's patience. Confinement for long periods of time was not Socks's long suit.

"McKenzie can go home, but he'll need to be on some antibiotics for a while. That cut was pretty bad. I want to see him back here in ten days unless you spot signs of an infection earlier."

She thanked Scott for opening up on a Sunday, and arranged to pick up McKenzie and Socks after she grabbed a few groceries for tonight. Some wine and fresh candles too.

Singing along with the radio, Jamie drove toward town. Gretchen lounged on her special blanket, opening one eye on occasion as if to make sure her person hadn't rocked out of control. Jamie smiled through the words as she belted out her off-key tune. She loved her dog's sarcastic sense of humor.

The male clerk behind the counter nodded approval at her purchases. "Cooking up another one of your magic dinners?"

"From your lips." Jamie pushed some loose hair behind her ear and smiled.

"One of these days you're going to take pity on me, my meager salary and decided lack of culinary skills, and bestow an invitation."

Colorado ski towns had an amazing amount of well-educated people who chose to do menial jobs just to be close to the slopes. Most were young, but some, like Jackson, were in their forties, hanging on to their dreams by a bent ski pole. At least towns like Telluride and Aspen Falls were more year-round communities where there was enough of an economic base that residents could find employment twelve months of the year and didn't need to go home when wildflowers replaced snow.

"Jackson, I promise. One of these days."

Jamie pulled into the garage, all three dogs energized at being on their home turf. McKenzie sported a plastic bucket on his head so he wouldn't mess with his stitches. Jamie shook her head. *He'll probably bump into things. He'll get the hang of it in a day or two.*

With instructions to wait, Jamie went to the rear of her house to erect some kind of barrier between her rambunctious brood and the ruined shed, which could still pose a danger. When she rounded the corner she couldn't believe her eyes. New lumber had been erected replacing the exterior walls that had been torn down. The new sides were painted to match her house, something she'd intended to do next summer.

At the entrance to the shed Jamie saw a padlock, a key taped to its side. She opened the door and checked out the interior. Two-by-fours were snugged together tighter than ever, forming a solid floor for the structure.

She knew exactly who to hold responsible for the repair work. "Thanks, Dad," Jamie said, then returned to the garage to release the three previously confined units of energy. Whatever evidence the vandals may have left was gone, but Jamie didn't think it would have mattered anyway.

Three acrobats of fur bailed out of the vehicle and shot into the back yard, McKenzie almost breaking his neck with his head apparatus. Jamie smiled. Within ten minutes they'd be clacking their nails on the hardwood floor in her kitchen, optimists looking for a snack before dinner.

Most of the ingredients for the impressive feast she'd planned for Teague were inside the two canvass bags she was lugging into the house. She had plenty of time before her guest arrived. She anticipated a long, cleansing shower. Her new teal top with the metallic accents would be perfect with black dress slacks. Suddenly life was fizzing and bubbling again.

Jamie plopped the bags on the kitchen counter and sat down to begin peeling off her clothes. Boots removed, she pulled off her socks and began a pile. Everything else soon followed and Jamie shivered in the cool air. She dumped the clothes in the hamper and went into the kitchen to find some rawhide bones for her crew. A large one each for Gretchen and Socrates, and a smaller one for McKenzie. She whistled and in seconds they were sitting at her feet, their tails whipping up their own weather systems and their faces turned expectantly toward her.

"Eat slowly." She handed the treats out. *Yeah, right.* Slow to any one of them meant looking up once to make sure the others weren't getting more than their fair share.

Jamie padded up the stairs and a few minutes later was reveling in the warm water raining over her head. Life was good, and the evening ahead made up only a small part of it. She took some extra time and put some of her favorite body cleanser onto her loofah.

After her shower, she blew her hair dry and for once loved the way it layered and fell in soft feathers around her face. Some fresh makeup, her planned outfit with just the right jewelry, a spritz of Bijan and voilà, she was ready. She slipped on her black satin slippers and made her way down to the kitchen, stopping briefly in the family room and put on a Chris Botti CD to listen to while she began the initial preparations for dinner.

She pulled the pork loin out of its wrapping and rubbed the surface of the meat with olive oil, then sprinkled on a little salt and pepper. She liked to let the meat sit for a few minutes before cooking. She opened the refrigerator and found the perfect leftover French bread with which to make the Tuscan topping. She started to hum along with the CD, the herbs gathered around her on the counter.

She froze at a noise in the family room. She hadn't seen anything out of place when she turned on the music, but then, she really hadn't looked. *One of the dogs? A log shifting in the fireplace? No, more like someone putting a glass down on a table. Not a slide but a deliberate placement, a noise meant for me to hear.*

Jamie thought about the destruction of her storage shed and McKenzie's injury. *Did they come back? What do they want?*

She slipped a knife from the storage block and moved to the wall that separated the kitchen from the family room. She strained to hear any sounds over the pounding of her heart.

Someone cleared his throat.

Jamie edged to the doorway and looked into the softly lit room. A man was sitting casually in one of the chairs by the fireplace, completely at ease.

Andrew.

CHAPTER TWENTY-SEVEN

"Hello, Jamie." Smooth. Calm. Regal. A royal holding court.

Memories of his abuse crowded her mind and she shook her head. "Andrew, what are you doing here? How did you get in?" She gripped the knife, hard.

"First of all, as usual, you misunderstand my intent." He used to always tell her she had failed to realize his intent. Then again, it was hard to miss the intent behind his fist, or behind his constant, demoralizing comments. He had treated her like someone with sub-par intelligence for so long that near the end she had almost believed him.

"I understand that you broke into my home; I understand that you are now sitting in my family room, drinking my wine and generally assaulting my life." Jamie willed her heart to slow.

"Well, as usual, you're missing a lot of salient points."

"By salient point, do you mean not calling the police? Because if that's the salient point you think I'm missing, I'm about to correct it."

"I did not break into your home. The key was where you have always left it, beneath the third rock from the door." Andrew sat back in the chair and placed his feet up on the table. "To tell you the truth, I'm surprised you haven't figured out another hiding place."

101

Jamie felt her face grow hot. She had locked her house this morning only because of the vandalism last night. She had never been a reason to lock the doors. McKenzie stood next to her, a low growl in his throat. *Did Andrew wreck my shed?* It didn't sound like something he would do, but over the years he'd twisted her up in so many knots she wouldn't put it past him.

Jamie spat a question at him: "How long have you been in Aspen Falls? Were you here last night?"

"Were you dreaming about me again? Missing our intimate moments?"

She closed her eyes against the horrible memories flooding her mind: the ropes, the duct tape, the box cutter, her shame. She didn't trust herself to speak. McKenzie's growl grew louder. To protect him, she plucked him off the ground.

"I'm sitting in your family room, that's true," Andrew said. "And let me say you've done a wonderful job bringing sophistication and casualness together in an ambiance that paints an intriguing picture of Jamie Stanton."

"Taylor. Not Stanton." She hated the way her words came out in a whisper. She set Mckenzie down.

"Ah, Jamie," Andrew said. "You'll always be Stanton to me, but I digress."

Andrew inspected her, his gaze traveling up and down her body. "Do you remember our home? The one in Limon? You've come a long way in your decorating skills. Our place always looked like hell."

"Limon is where you took me to separate me from my family," Jamie said. "Where you could do whatever you wanted to me and I'd have nowhere to run." Jamie began to tremble as old fear and new anger bubbled to the surface.

He picked up the wine glass and tilted it to his nose. "I

am also drinking your wine," he said, disregarding her as he'd always done. "But it occurs to me that you became proficient in wine under my tutelage. So perhaps this is a wine we have shared?"

Jamie clenched her jaw and rolled the knife handle in her hand.

"And, dear Jamie, with regard to assaulting you? That is precisely why I'm here."

She gripped the handle, hoping that the manufacturer's promise of balance would apply to self-defense moves. She waited for him to continue.

He cleared his throat and moved to get up. "Do you mind if I get some more? This is really extraordinary wine. I'm quite impressed."

Jamie looked over at the open bottle. If he wanted more he could get it himself.

Andrew got up and poured himself more wine, then turned to face her. "You've matured a bit since we were together. In a good way, of course." He looked at her with admiration, and maybe a little of something else. "Did I have anything to do with it?"

Jamie continued to stare. He didn't deserve to know anything about any changes. They were hers, not his. The pain that had led her to those changes was hers, not his. He gave her the gift of that pain, but she had applied it and grown from it.

He settled back in the chair. The refreshed wine glass in one hand, he fingered one of the afghans her mother had made with his other hand.

Something twisted in her heart to see him touch the familiar pattern, the yarn that once had slid through her mother's fingers. He was touching love that had nothing to do with him, love he could never understand.

"Your mom left some beautiful things behind when she died." He looked at her. "Including you."

"I'm calling the police," Jamie said and moved back into the kitchen.

In the time it takes a bully to recognize a bigger threat, Andrew appeared at her side.

"I'm sorry, Jamie. I handled this all wrong."

Andrew? Saying he's sorry? Jamie froze, her hand reaching toward the phone. In all of the years she'd known Andrew Stanton, he'd never uttered anything close to a sincere apology, or even a fake one. She spun around to look at the man she'd once loved.

He was still almost unbearably handsome, and even the lines around his eyes looked distinguished. A few more flecks of gray were apparent in his curly hair, but it remained thick and luxurious, somewhere between tousled and perfect.

"You still manage to bring out the worst in me," Andrew said.

Jamie had always been drawn to Andrew's hands, and her gaze tugged away from his face to search for the hands she used to love to watch, to feel on her body, to kiss.

But those beautiful hands also had inflicted pain, with intent and with great force. Those beautiful hands had taken a box cutter to her one night after he'd raped her. She pulled the knife in her hands up in front of her at the same time she saw the wedding ring on his finger.

Andrew followed her gaze. "I wondered how long it would take you to notice." He took the knife from her grip and slipped it back into the wooden storage block.

Chapter Twenty-Eight

The words came out of Andrew's mouth like butter that morphed to acid as they knifed and burned into her heart. "My wife is everything you could never be, Jamie." It was a familiar talent her ex-husband had perfected long ago.

She backed against a countertop, hating the fact he held this much power over her after all this time. Her hands shook and her legs began to tremble. She crossed her arms and held tight.

"Amanda is delicate. Fragile. She appreciates everything I do for her, Jamie. She knows how to handle herself in social situations and knows who the head of our household is. Unlike you."

Anger finally pushed her paralyzing fear aside. "Why are you here? Tell me now, Andrew, or I will call the police."

"We both know they couldn't possibly get here in time to make any kind of a difference." He moved to her kitchen desk and began thumbing through things at random. Bills, correspondence, ads she'd pulled for home improvements, recipes she wanted to try. "I came in person because this is the one way I know I can make you comprehend the importance of the circumstances in which I find myself. I'm sure you'll think of it as my need to control, but really, I just need to assure myself that you understand completely." He shoved the neat stacks haphazardly around the desk.

"Actually, Amanda has one other very important asset: her father. He's quite wealthy, and my wife is his only child. Amanda is a bit spoiled, Jamie, but she's also well trained. She's such a relief compared to you. And, well... the money has a way of holding my attention, if you know what I mean." Andrew laughed, then turned to face her.

"My father-in-law wants me to hold political office. So do I. I'm intrigued with the notion of power and influence. I think I'll handle it extremely well. And given enough time in politics, should I grow weary of marriage, there might be some attractive alternatives. Time will tell." His voice dropped off and he went back to poking around in the detritus of her life that just this morning had seemed so important. "I'm here, Jamie, because there will be someone contacting you as part of a check on my background. My father-in-law and his friends are not going to want to pour millions of dollars into my campaign without proper vetting. I need you to be very clear on what your answers will be."

"He's checking you out now? Why didn't he check you out before you married his daughter?"

"Oh, he did, believe me, but he didn't go very deep. I know all the right people, I make an extremely good living, and I don't have a record."

Yeah. Thanks to paying off all the right people in a small town.

"This is the big time, with big stakes involved. There's no doubt in my mind that someone will find you and want to know about our marriage and our divorce. I need to know whether I can rely on you."

"Or what? What will you do to me, Andrew, if I tell the

106

truth?"

He slipped his hand into a pocket and in one smooth movement pulled out a switchblade and popped it open. "Jamie, Jamie, Jamie. I was afraid that might be your position. You see? You never could learn—"

Suddenly three ferocious canines were barking and drooling, hackles up, ready to attack. Andrew backed away but whipped the knife back and forth in front of him.

"Heel! Heel!" Jamie felt panic rising. Andrew wouldn't hurt her, not as long as she had a weapon nearby—he didn't like pain—but she didn't want any of her dogs injured.

The air grew thick, infused with a combination of deep, sharp barks, all of which signified intent and focus on the threat. Jamie yelled again, but she'd lost command.

Just as Andrew grabbed her and slammed her face-first against the wall with enough force that her nose popped, as if through a tunnel Jamie heard the sound of splintering. *Someone kicking-in the door.* Blood poured down her chin as Andrew held her firmly against the wall. She opened her mouth to breathe.

The ferocious vocals from Gretchen, Socrates and McKenzie quelled to menacing snarls as they made contact. Gretchen and Socrates each claimed an arm, and McKenzie, even with the plastic bucket on his head, sank his teeth into one of Andrew's ankles.

His breath hot on Jamie's neck, Andrew hissed, "Call them off! *Now!*"

Blood splattered the wall as Jamie yelled, "Heel!" Andrew pressed her against the wall again. Gretchen was the first to drop back. Socrates and McKenzie, when they realized they had one fewer dog in the hunt with them, also backed away.

A harsh voice came from the doorway. "Drop the

knife! Drop it now or I'll shoot!"

Andrew both jerked his head to look at the doorway. A man dressed in steel-gray slacks, a cashmere sweater and a leather jacket was standing among the debris. His pistol was pointed directly at Andrew. In his other hand were some flowers.

Teague had arrived for their dinner.

Chapter Twenty-Nine

Thirty minutes later, Jamie's house contained enough people to be Party Central, but without the music. It definitely was not the evening Jamie had envisioned. Andrew had been placed under arrest, but she knew he'd post bail at the first opportunity. Teague had taken a low profile after talking to the sheriff. She didn't blame him for trying to sit out all of this chaos.

Would he ever call again? She wasn't sure that she would call if she were in his shoes.

She thought about the gun. A lot of people possessed guns for self-protection, especially if they travelled for business. At the end of the day Jamie experienced no distress in the fact that Teague carried, just relief that he did and that he had been ready to use it.

Ciara and her two gorgeous standard poodles, Bella and Sophia, arrived first. The model, on her way to Aspen when Jamie called her, had just passed the turnoff to Jamie's house. Sheriff Coble arrived next with two deputies, followed by Ellen and her new beau and yellow lab, Sam. Jax and Phil came in right after Ellen, though Phil begged off for an important meeting. He took Jax's car with him and left his wife behind. A couple of neighbors who lived in homes closer to town also dropped by. They had witnessed the procession of speeding vehicles, and had come to make sure Jamie hadn't been killed by an axe murderer.

The sheriff made a phone call and someone was on his way to secure the front entryway of her house. She'd call her insurance agent the next morning. She suspected they would not be happy to hear from her again so soon even though they hadn't had to pay for the shed.

Jamie explained to Teague that the man who had attacked her was her ex-husband.

She knew that had Teague not been there, she would have let Andrew leave. Jamie hated the cowardice her ex continued to inspire in her and vowed to change.

Jamie gave her statement to Jerry Coble, who said his deputies would be back at first light to check out the damage to her house. She wouldn't need to stick around in the morning for them to complete the report. They'd call her at the bank if they had any questions.

In the meantime, the sheriff would make sure a deputy drove by her home at regular intervals for the rest of the evening. Someone would call her when Andrew posted bail.

When the uniforms left, an almost palpable cleansing breath came from everyone still in the house. Ellen thought to put Jamie's food in the fridge. There would be no pork loin tonight. She'd stashed a couple of pizzas in the freezer for emergencies, and figured if tonight didn't count, nothing would. She turned the oven on and pulled them out to place on her pizza pans.

Ciara came up behind her. "Is your new friend staying the night?"

Jamie shook her head, too tired to pretend to be offended at her friend's question. "He has a ten o'clock flight out of Aspen."

"Then Bella, Sophia and I will stay with you. No way you're going to be way out here all by yourself."

"I have my crew." Even as she mentioned her three protectors, Jamie knew she'd appreciate some two-legged company for the evening.

"Well, your crew is now expanded by three."

"Thanks, Ciara."

Ellen joined them. "Make that five. Hank and I are bedding down here too." She bent down to scratch behind Hank's ear.

"What about, um... Agent...."

"Arnold. Arnold Abner. I know, his name confuses me, too." Ellen smiled. "He's headed back to Denver tonight anyway, so Hank and I are all yours. And we're not taking no for an answer. Besides, Hank misses the company of your crew."

"You know I love you guys, and I'm not gonna turn you down. We'll have one of our sleepovers. A pajama party."

Ciara looked at her and winked. "Ellen might need to borrow some PJs, but I don't use them."

Ellen said, "We know. We know."

Ciara smiled and batted her impossibly long eyelashes.

Teague walked into the kitchen.

"Um, do you mind?" Jamie's vision remained fixed on her personal hero as she asked her friends to give them some privacy.

Alone, Teague took both her hands. "I can cancel my flight if you need me to."

"You've done enough. Nothing more is going to happen tonight, and Ellen and Ciara will be here to keep me company." She took a step closer to him. "I'm sorry about our dinner plans."

Teague took her face in his hands and kissed her. "No one is more sorry than I, Jamie, but we'll make up for it on next week, I promise."

With that, Teague Blanton moved up a notch on Jamie's emotional ladder. He made her feel safe, treasured.

Less than an hour later, Jamie, together with her sister, two girlfriends and six dogs, were sitting in front of a blazing fire, the only sign of drama the boarded-up entry into her home, which thankfully they couldn't see.

Soon all of their eyelids began drooping as the adrenaline gave way to exhaustion. Jamie struggled to remain vigilant. *These women are here to support me.* She didn't believe Andrew would return, but apparently he remained as unpredictable as ever. She wouldn't be able to live with herself if one of them was hurt because of her. She went to the kitchen and put some heat under the kettle that always sat on her stove. She'd become fond of an afternoon fix of tea, hot chocolate, or Starbucks instant coffee, so she kept the kettle on hand. She readied a teabag in a cup and moved to look out through the French doors leading to her deck. The full moon lit the area with luminous silver light.

Was Andrew responsible for the vandalism of my shed? She shook her head, unable to think of any rational reason for him to threaten her in that way even though McKenzie's response left little doubt. Destruction of her property was not likely to entice her to give him a favorable review should she get a call regarding his background. *Where would he run? Is he standing out there now, watching me? Ready to get to me when he knows I'm alone?*

The landscape off her deck was familiar. She knew exactly where every rock was, where the Indian paintbrush would bloom and where the columbine flourished every summer. She knew where the deer were likely to graze and where they took refuge from the heat. She had carved out a piece of the Rocky Mountains and she knew it intimately. It had remained untouched by the cruelty of the outside world until now.

A movement caught her eye, a shifting of shadow, then stealth. She studied the shape. *A bear? No. A man.*

She turned off all the lights, even the ones she generally left on so she wouldn't step on a rawhide bone in the middle of the night. The interior plunged to black stains, elongated by the moonlight. Jamie stood in one of those stains and focused her gaze on the man who had moved from a standing position to a crouch. *Something familiar about the way he holds his shoulders... the way he moves his head. Dad.*

Bryce Taylor was standing outside, separate and alone, watching the house he'd raised his own family in. The number of people, the police, all would serve as a deterrent to him coming closer. He wouldn't want to risk running into anyone in an official capacity. They might have questions he didn't want to answer. During ten years on the heels of a killer, Bryce Taylor had done one or two things law enforcement might frown upon.

Jamie hugged herself and watched in silence. She had a few questions of her own.

CHAPTER THIRTY

Nick parked his SUV in front of the house. The boarded-up entry gave testimony to the events he'd been told about as he'd appreciated his first cup of coffee for the morning. Jamie Taylor had not enjoyed a relaxed evening at home. He took a sip from his travel mug and looked around. The dog handler owned some acreage here, though he couldn't tell how much. At any rate, the land appeared well tended around the house—even looked like there might have been a summer vegetable garden around back.

Nick appreciated the exterior. A lot of natural Colorado stone, wood beams and grand, vaulted windows. Whoever built this home had put a lot of pride in the construction. It didn't just blend in with the surroundings, it became a symbiotic focal point. Respectful, integral and dynamic.

Nick rolled his shoulders, dislodging the hovering sentimentality. *What am I doing here? Okay, yeah... need to make sure my case isn't involved with what happened here last night.*

At least that's what he told himself. Actually, Jamie Taylor had gotten to him. It was that simple and that complicated. The woman exuded strength and intelligence, a certain attitude toward and engagement with life, and on top of all that, her looks could knock every other woman in contention to the mat. What wasn't to like about that?

And she'd been wounded. Her wounds gave her the attitude she carried around like a shield. Her wounds softened her edges and made him want to dig for both answers and understanding, and protect her from questions at the same time.

Then again, throw in his own trust issues, the hours he spent on the road, the pills he seemed to need more and more of, and the fact that he was more or less set in his ways, and a new relationship didn't stand much of a chance. *Hell, any relationship doesn't stand much of a chance. Besides, she loves dogs, and at least three of the beasts live with her.*

About two weeks after his seventh birthday, his dad had taken him to visit Grandpap and Grandma and his Uncle Gage. Gage was his dad's younger brother by about twelve years, and he was about to go away to boot camp where, if Nick's mom and dad were right, he'd learn to be more responsible and make better choices.

In Nick's seven-year-old eyes, Gage Grant ranked pretty close to a rock star. He was a little on the wild side, but his soulful brown eyes could plead for forgiveness regardless of what he'd done.

Uncle Gage and a buddy were going to a high school football game in a neighboring town, then out for pizza after. The adults made a lot of fuss about the older boys taking Nicky along with them, and in the end, the two teens had relented, probably because Nicky's dad agreed to spring for the pizza.

Only they never did go for the pizza or even make it to the football game. Instead, Gage and Aaron took Nick way down some country roads where they promised him he'd have the time of his life. He'd see some action and maybe even make a dollar or two. They were going to someplace off the map, secret, unless you knew the right people. They were going to do a bit of gambling.

On dog fights.

Men were walking around, checking out the caged dogs. Sometimes they banged on the wire to get a reaction. The snarling sounded horrible and foam dripped from the dogs' mouths, but the men seemed to like it. They made notes on little pads of paper while they smoked their cigarettes or cigars. Nick watched as money changed hands and the men made more notes. Sometimes no money changed hands, but stuff still got written on those little notepads.

Nicky liked dogs, but he'd never seen dogs like these before, snarling and baring their teeth. He became scared and wished he could go back to his grandma and grandpap's house to see his dad. The next thing he knew, he'd lost Uncle Gage. He frantically looked around, but he didn't see anyone he knew. The snarling and mean laughter and cigar smoke started to choke him.

Panicked, he ran, leaving the noise behind. Uncle Gage would find him soon and everything would be okay.

A short while later, a cooling breeze lifted the stinging sweat from Nick's body as he walked along the back of the site near the trucks with cages in their beds. Bees buzzed around the wildflowers that lined the rutted drive that marked the edge of the fight grounds. Thirsty, he spotted a well with a spigot just inside a fence. It didn't look like the other fences, the ones that enclosed the bad dogs, and the gate didn't have a lock, just a latch.

Nicky lifted the piece of metal and quietly pushed open the gate, starting to feel grown up again. The house that sat back behind the well looked empty. His thirst pulled him to the spigot. He pumped it once, twice.

Halfway through his third pump something snarled behind him, and he turned to see white fangs coming right at his face. Before he could scream the dog pulled him to the ground.

Nick squeezed the memory away, turned the engine off and opened his door. He'd just check on Jamie, maybe confirm that she really did keep three dogs on her property, then head into town to see what progress had been made on the identifications. He put one foot on the ground, but wild barking and flying fur made him jerk his leg back inside his SUV and slam the door. Six huge, salivating dogs were ready to take him down. One, a wild, banshee-type canine with some kind of plastic thing on its head was flinging itself around the marauding pack. The plastic cone seemed to enhance its crazed behavior. The other dogs were big and muscular, but that little one behaved like an unpredictable dart with a fiendish homing device.

He started the engine and did a three-point turn to get away from the madness as quickly as he could. *Pharmacy should be open by the time I get there.*

CHAPTER THIRTY-ONE

The Hungry Ghosts twisted themselves around his body. They were with him all the time now. Mostly he'd made peace with them, but their presence still made his skin tingle and heat to just below a burn. Alcohol, pills, sex—nothing dispersed them. Not even killing.

He lifted the heavy Persian rug and pulled it across the slate floor to a space near the entrance. When he dropped it, a deep *thwack* popped the air. He thought it looked better in its normal spot between the two leather sofas, but no one would think too much about it if they were to walk in.

He stepped behind his dark wood and leather desk at the far end of the room, slid open a panel and depressed a button. A four-by-six section of the floor beneath where the rug had lain a moment ago dropped a few inches and slid open. Circular stairs provided access to what lay below.

At the bottom of the stairway, he pushed another button and what was now the ceiling slid closed. The sound of the latch slipping into place released a sense of excitement and freedom in him unlike any he experienced anywhere else.

Seven cameras allowed him to see not only the exterior of his house, but the main level as well. He would never be taken by surprise.

A closet held protective clothing, including a self-contained breathing apparatus he wouldn't need today. Instead he slipped on a lab coat and a pair of latex gloves. Safety goggles lay on the counter. Everything gleamed. He'd installed a commercial grade positive air system to expel any harmful contaminants through specialized filters. Dust was almost nonexistent in this space. The purity of the room relaxed him. There was nothing complicated, no pretense. He didn't have to process information other than what he discovered scientifically, and that particular methodology always came easy to him.

The tank, the focal point of the room, stood behind glass doors that were vacuum-sealed, keeping it sterile and separate.

He entered a code and the three-quarter inch glass doors parted. His weight on the special flooring caused the doors to close behind him. He settled the safety goggles firmly on his face, snapped the latex gloves free of any wrinkles and picked up one of several sterilized eye droppers and a slide. With his wrist, he depressed another button and a section of the top covering the tank slid open.

Holding his breath, he inserted the eyedropper to very near its end and withdrew a small bit of fluid, which he distributed to the slide. He placed the dropper in a sterilizing solution and slipped a cover on top of the prepared piece of glass.

Once he stepped back into the main part of the lab and the isolation doors sealed, he placed the slide under a microscope and removed the latex gloves. As he looked through the lens, he knew he had crossed the finish line. He'd artificially created *Karenia brevis*. Saxitoxin. Red Tide. The term Red Tide was being replaced by HAB, which stood for "harmful algal bloom," but he preferred the picture the older description painted. So biblical.

When he first created his lab, he had left himself wide open to possibilities. He researched everything from medieval weapons of torture to psychological dismemberment, and although that concept intrigued him, the length of time it took to achieve results proved dismal. Biological threat agents held promise, so he focused on finding the right one. Saxitoxin quickly rose to the top of the list.

In nature, when the *Karenia brevis* algae is present in high concentrations, huge death rates occur among fish. When first discovered, tests proved the toxin from the super concentrated algae paralyzed the central nervous system of the fish and made it impossible for them to breathe. Paralytic Shellfish Poisoning in humans can happen when an unsuspecting victim ingests a shellfish that has been contaminated by the algae. Unless some kind of artificial respiration is available, it's pretty much lights out.

Several things kept Saxitoxin at the top of his list: only 0.2 milligrams would prove fatal for the average weight human, and much less was required for children; it could be administered through food, water, or air, with air being the preferable method; there was significant potential for misdiagnosis, meaning there was less threat to him; and no vaccines, antidotes or other effective treatments existed to counter the effects, other than an artificial respirator.

Over the last several months, he'd perfected a controlled environment in which he could create the perfect storm for his algae and then distill it to a concentrated powder for airborne use. Powder was easier to transport, it maintained its potency longer, and he could better manage its delivery.

The first few test subjects had died with less than

satisfactory results. Either he'd needed far more Saxitoxin, resulting in a potential mess and more risk to himself, or they'd died too quickly for him to even begin to tap into some emotion, and of course that was the point of the entire exercise.

He looked through the microscope, satisfied at the change his last minor tweak had effected in the algae. He would make one more trial run to make sure he had the right balance. Then, if all went well, he'd begin to distill Red Tide in the larger quantities his plan required.

Years of research and plans and work had culminated in the little drop of water under this lens. He thought he felt a little ripple of pleasure, but it disappeared before he could tell for sure.

Chapter Thirty-Two

Corinne Rawlings rolled up her sleeping bag and strapped it to her backpack. The remnants of a frosty Rocky Mountain morning clung to her fingers and nose. She shivered, so cold she thought she might never be warm again. *Good thing Brian and I are heading home this afternoon.*

They'd been lucky with the weather for their vacation, which they'd been forced to postpone twice because of their work schedules. Now it was time to get back to Boston and the grind. They would return to Colorado to celebrate New Year's and get some quality skiing in. No outdoor camping at that time of year—just plenty of flying powder and roaring fires, hot drinks and hotter sex. At least, that's what their tradition dictated. Corinne grinned, partly from memory and partly from anticipation.

"Hey, Bri, I'm thinking I'd like a green chili burger for lunch. Think we have time to get to the Augustine Grill in Castle Rock before we need to head to DIA?"

"I don't see why not. We have a late flight." Brian tamped out the remnants from their fire. "Assuming, of course, we aren't hunted down by a deranged, plague-ridden mountain lion between here and the trailhead."

Corrine strangled a laugh. "Thanks, my love. That's just what I needed from you before we hike out of here."

Last night they'd heard some odd sounds around their campsite. Stealthy, not like foraging raccoons, with which they'd had plenty of experience in Boston. Whatever it was, this creature had acted different from any wildlife Corrine had ever been exposed to. It seemed out of place somehow, as if it were lying in wait.

Corrine had come up with two alternatives: either it was a sick, rabid animal or a crafty vampire. Brian had not let up since she'd told him of her conclusion.

"Either that or Bela Lugosi is hiding behind an aspen waiting to pounce."

Corrine laughed outright. "He'd have to be pretty skinny." She shook last night's sounds out of her head. Her thoughts could run amok, and she didn't want what happened in her head to follow her all day. And besides, the Colorado morning promised a beautiful day with no scary axe-murderers anywhere on the trail.

But it was cold. The sooner they got moving, the sooner she'd warm up and she could begin discarding some of the layers she was wearing. At least the Rocky Mountain cold didn't come close to the damp cold of the Bay State, and the sunshine here provided hope for warmth.

Corinne shivered again, not entirely from the cold this time, then smiled. Everyone knows vampires can't do sunlight.

Brian made a last check to confirm the fire truly was out of commission, took a quick look around their campsite to make sure they weren't leaving more of a footprint than necessary, and they were off. Brian whistled a special down-up-down tune, and Shelby, their seven-year-old beagle, bounded between them to begin the three-mile hike back to their rental car.

Shelby went with them everywhere, and she enjoyed the status of an internationally travelled dog. They had started her on airplanes as a puppy, and because they took several trips a year, Shelby took it all in stride. Neither Corrine nor Brian could imagine a vacation without their dog.

Since this trip had been delayed, the vacationing kids were back in school and they'd had the entire area to themselves for the last four days. They had enjoyed not having to share their space with anyone, but Corrine looked forward to getting back to their friends and their active social life. But she loved the smell of a mountain morning. There was a purity about the natural scents in rested air, before the sun brought out all of the manmade bits. They'd be home in Boston soon enough and she'd have to work hard to remember this moment.

They hiked uphill about a hundred yards before the steady drop down to the trailhead. No other hikers were in sight, and they allowed Shelby to run off-leash, enjoying her last few minutes of freedom. The beagle didn't always stay on the trail, especially if an interesting scent beckoned, but she didn't wander too far. Corrine never worried.

Brian led the way, stopping at the difficult spots to make sure Corrine could navigate them with her backpack and bedroll. Every once in a while, Shelby offered a bark of unabashed pleasure.

The trail leveled off and the couple stopped to catch their breath. Gear dropped to the ground almost as fast as their butts dropped to the sun-warmed rocks. Brian stripped off his jacket and sweater to stuff them in his backpack, but Corrine chose to keep her jacket a little closer, and tied it around her waist.

"You are beautiful when your face is just a little dirty." Brian leaned over and kissed her.

"If you mention anything about my earthy aroma, you're going to have a hard time walking the rest of the way to our car."

The faint sound of bees caught their attention, but they couldn't quite tell where it originated. Brian stood and pivoted, his hands outstretched in a radar pose, as if he could pick up the direction by some sort of skin sensors, a quizzical look on his face. Corrine stayed on the rock, ready to gather up her gear in case they needed to make a quick run. A swarm of bees did not happen to be part of the Rocky Mountain experience she wanted to take with her.

Brian said, "Would you look at that...."

She looked in the direction he was facing and blinked. A plane, like the ones those hobbyists fly in competitions, only larger, was flying down the trail in their direction. She looked around for the guy with the controls, but she couldn't see anyone.

The couple held hands and watched as the model plane came closer, the sound of its electronic engine acting as a swinging pendulum, lulling them.

Cold returned to Corrine, this time running fingers up her spine and around the back of her neck. She squeezed Brian's hand at the same time he squeezed hers. Her mouth went dry. The fear of last night punched her stomach, fresh and large. Brian turned to look at her and she expected to see her panic reflected in his face, but he was smiling like a kid at the fair.

"No. Brian. There's something wrong. We need to ru—"

The plane flew directly overhead. A popping sound reached them as it banked upward, sunlight glinting off its wings. A gentle mist fell over them before settling to the ground.

She stood. "Brian, we—"

Corrine would never forget the look in his eyes as Brian grabbed her and pulled her behind him as he raced down the trail. The kid at the fair had disappeared, replaced by a man determined to protect the woman he loved. From what, neither of them knew.

She felt like dust had gotten in her eyes, in her lungs. But there hadn't been any dust or dirt in the air. It was getting hard to breathe.

Brian tripped and struggled to stand, but he didn't let go of her hand. He regained his balance and they jumped and lurched along the trail. They didn't talk or scream. They saved their breath to propel themselves onward.

Her legs and arms began to tingle, almost burn. Then she was on the ground next to Brian, trying to reach for his hand before she realized they were still holding hands. He pulled her toward him in an embrace. Her face wet with tears. Hers and Brian's.

Loud, steady buzzing made her look up. The plane seemed to hover over them, and she thought she saw a camera lens mounted on the belly. *How strange.*

Corrine's chest tightened as she and Brian looked into each other's eyes.

The air had been sucked out of the universe by a toy.

Chapter Thirty-Three

"Yes, this is Nicholas Grant." Nick pulled off his Sorrell boots, phone clamped to his ear by his shoulder. At five grand a pair, they weren't the most expensive western boots on the planet, but they were expensive enough to be comfortable except when he wanted his slippers. And he really, really wanted his slippers.

"Yes, I used to be married to Sandra Bellamy." *What's going on here?* "Who did you say is calling?" Nick sat back in the chair, his stocking feet forgotten. *What new trick is Sandra pulling?* "Look, my schedule is full. Sandra and I were divorced eight years ago. Just because she's retained some new lawyers doesn't alter the fact that we both finished that chapter in our lives with, I'm sure you're aware, a binding agreement."

That time represented some of the worst months of his life. Whirlwind romances could affect men as much as women, and his and Sandra's courtship definitely fell into the whirlwind category. At first it was magical. Sandra had come across warm and compassionate. Her beauty stunned him every time he looked at her, and Nick felt it reached inside as well as outside. But not long after the exchange of their vows, her façade began to slip.

Sandra's definition of a partnership involved a spending partner and an earning partner. She could spend with the best of them. During their dating days, she told him his deep bank accounts didn't matter. He believed her. He believed his character and charm and sense of humor and honor would rise above his net worth. He had been naïve.

When she found out he could, and would, put the brakes on her shopping sprees, Nick became a piece of lead in her life that grew heavier by the minute. She tried manipulating him sexually until she figured out he thought of sex as an intimate connection, as making love. When she tried to turn it into a bargaining chip, he moved to the sidelines until he could figure out a way to end the game.

"Our divorce settlement can't be breached. What? Yes, I know the premise presupposed a childless marriage." Had there been a child, Nick would have fought for sole custody, and he'd have won. He'd held out hope until the final day, but by the end of their union, Sandra had managed to demonstrate complete disregard for anything bordering on commitment. And since there had been no child, end of story.

Nick leaned forward, his head in his free hand. "Sandra is dead?" They'd been divorced eight years, but he remembered the way she had looked the last time he'd seen her. "How did she die? And exactly why are you calling to tell me?"

The man on the other end of the line said something about cancer, Nick's legal rights, Colorado Child Protective Services, and his daughter.

CHAPTER THIRTY-FOUR

Nick didn't sleep well. Wild attack dogs came after him in his dreams, then left him to go after the defenseless baby he tripped over in a mountain meadow full of gravesites. The nightmare jerked him awake a little after two in the morning. He threw the covers off and walked to his library. A few chapters of a new novel would be just the thing to calm his mind and settle his nerves. He needed rest to be able to focus on the new case he'd been thrust into. And to try to figure out what he should do about the latest development that threatened to completely alter his life. *Latest development? Threaten?*

He supposedly had a daughter. He would have some tests done to confirm the biological link, but in his heart he already knew. She was almost eight years old, living in Alexandria, Virginia, the town he'd lived in with Sandra. A little girl, with a personality and a past and a name: Kylie.

He tried the name out. "Kylie. Kylie Grant."

"What do you know about me, Kylie? What have you been told?" Nick pulled a book off of a shelf without even looking at it. "What the hell am I going to do with you?"

After receiving the phone call, he'd contacted his personal attorney to verify the information. Even given the hour, Paul had called back in forty-five minutes. The caller was legit, not some scam artist who knew a few facts, including the important one that Nicholas Grant possessed a few hundred million dollars. It wasn't someone hoping to make a score.

Nick called United and booked a seven-thirty a.m. flight to O'Hare since there were no direct flights from Aspen to DC. From there, he'd fly to Reagan International and meet with the attorneys handling Sandra's estate that afternoon.

He also called his SAC in Denver and told him he needed forty-eight hours, but would stay in contact. He didn't mention he might be bringing a daughter home with him.

A text message to Felicity and Jerome to alert them that they needed to plan on the possibility of a new member of the household brought an immediate call from Felicity. Before the woman could start to plan a wedding ceremony, he informed her the subject was an eight-year-old girl, that nothing was certain, and that he had no intention of going into any details with her at this hour.

Before settling into a chair to read—or pretend to read—Nick walked over to the wet bar and filled a glass with water. A full prescription bottle of oxy sat on the inlaid countertop. He shook out a few of the pills and started to throw them into his open mouth. As they were about to leave his palm, he made a fist and opened his hand. Five pills. He reached for the bottle and scooped three of the little green pills stamped with *80* back inside the amber chamber. He would cut back, beginning now.

Chapter Thirty-Five

Jamie looked for a sign confirming that her dad might still be around Aspen Falls as she drove to work that morning. Not surprisingly, she didn't see a thing. When he didn't want people to know of his presence, they didn't. A security expert who had worked all over the world, Bryce Taylor didn't make mistakes. He had wanted Jamie to see him in the darkness the other night, to let her know he was close, to protect her if necessary. And maybe to let her know he was close to finding her mom's murderer.

The thought, yet again, of her mom's death made Jamie draw into herself. For anyone, especially someone she loved, to have been buried alive just to prove a point made her furious. She understood her dad's motive. Her mom's death and the manner of it also had been a major factor in her doing what she did.

At the same time, her dad's focus, his commitment and passion—his obsession—meant she'd lost both parents ten years ago, not just one.

As she was about to enter that wallowing stage that she hated, her phone rang. She appreciated the diversion.

"It's Ellen. I think I'm in love."

Jamie smiled.

Ellen raced ahead, almost tripping over her own words. "Is it too soon for me to be in love? Should I slow this down? I don't want to slow this down. Don't you just *love* him?"

FBI Agent Arnold Abner and Ellen had been as tight as fresh paint on a wall since the morning they'd met at the drugstore. Ellen had sprung open like some rare flower. *If Arnold Abner made that happen, then yeah, I love the guy.*

Ellen's emotional rush continued for a bit, and the call ended with a promise they'd all get together soon.

Jamie pulled herself back to the task at hand. The Corbett loan, which was almost ready to be underwritten, was on her desk. She had to make sure all of the necessary information had been obtained to facilitate approval. Most of her applicants these days had a dicey thing or two in either their credit or employment history or both to deal with. She made sure any issues were addressed and answered in a way that would be satisfactory to the loan committee. She had grown comfortable living in that strange position where she had to advocate for the borrower while preserving the lending integrity of the bank.

At the bank, after reviewing the Corbett file and writing her own cover letter explaining the pros and cons—heavy on the pros—promoting loan approval, Jamie looked at her own list of potential economic disasters. All were related to her home.

Her insurance company had shown themselves to be an upstanding partner in the repairs she needed to make to the entry wrecked by the hero of the hour, Teague Blanton. She couldn't help but feel her claim might have been received in a more positive light by the insurance company because of her referrals to them over the years through the bank. Still, she was tremendously relieved to know the expenses would be covered, at least partially.

Too bad she couldn't expect to have help meeting all

of the other expenses required to simply maintain her home, let alone bring it up to its full potential. *One thing at a time.*

The mist of her thoughts parted, and Gabe Ahrens, her boss, appeared in one of the chairs in front of her desk. His appearance both startled her and left her a little alarmed. Gabe usually summoned. He didn't appear.

"How's everything going, Jamie? Are you happy?"

What in the world? She looked at him, totally uncomfortable with the dynamics. "Everything is fine, Gabe. You?"

"I'm thinking ahead, Jamie... thinking ahead. I'm wondering whether you might be part of how I envision my future."

She stared at him, unable to find any words or grasp the gist of the conversation. She was a little afraid to try.

"I want to send you to a special training course, Jamie. One that will give you the skills you need to become my second in command here at the bank. I need a successor if I want to move up, and I think you're that person."

"Gabe, I—"

"No need to thank me, Jamie. Of course, you understand it will require more of your time. You'll need to not only prove your dedication, but show your willingness to pay your dues. One day, you'll be able to run this branch on your own."

"I'm not sure about this, Gabe." Then she looked at her boss's earnest face and relented. "I mean, I'm not sure I'm ready for this."

Gabe smiled the smile of someone who had just bestowed a magnificent gift on an undeserving—or maybe unsuspecting—subject. "Don't worry about anything. I think you're ready. The future is yours, Jamie. You just need to decide you're ready to meet it."

He pushed the front legs of his chair off the ground. "And just so you know where your bread is buttered, you know that twenty-thousand dollar line of credit we shelved a few months ago? The one you wanted to use to make some repairs and improvements to your home?"

Of course she remembered it. She'd felt about as tall and as welcome as a stink bug when she'd been told the bank didn't see extending her credit an appropriate use of their funds at that time.

"Well, it's been approved. You can access those funds as necessary. And you'll find the interest and repayment terms are better than the going rate. Oh, and of course there will be a substantial raise in pay as well."

Jamie felt the strands of a spider's web wrapping around her. "Thank you. I appreciate it." She couldn't look him in the eye, and that bugged her. She forced her gaze to meet his.

"Just see that you don't let the bank down." Gabe settled his chair back on the floor and leaned toward her desk. "Or me." He rose and walked a few steps away before he turned. "I'm counting on you, Jamie."

Jamie knew she should be flattered. The bank wanted to promote her. If she chose, she could make this career her life. One day, she could manage this branch and then potentially move on to bigger and better things. But rather than a rosy future spread out before her, Jamie saw a trap. They were dangling just enough money to keep her interested. But the money would be good. She could make repairs to her house, buy a new car, take some really great vacations. She could donate as much money as she wanted to Search and Rescue.

On the other hand, she'd have to completely give up her work with her dogs. All of them. No more searching for missing hikers or providing closure to families of loved ones who had died. Even McKenzie's visits to hospitals and hospices and homebound people would have to stop. That part of her life would be over. She would have to be happy fixing the house, cooking for people she loved, and working at the bank. *Two out of three's not bad, right?*

She shook her head. *I'll thank Gabe and the board for this opportunity, but no way can I give up—*

Her phone rang. "Jamie Taylor."

Jax sounded tired. Defeated. "Hey, it's me."

"You okay?"

"I'm fine... no, that's a lie."

"Tell me."

"I need to talk to you about a loan. Business."

"Okay. That's what banks are for. What do you need?" Phil and Jackie's house was mortgaged to the hilt. Jamie had laid her job on the line for them to get the third mortgage last year. And although real estate in the area had held its own even through the tough times, they didn't have much equity left to play with. *She must need a short-term signature loan. I can probably authorize as much as a thousand.*

"Due to some unforeseen expenses, Phil and I... we thought eight hundred would be enough to get us through the next thirty days, but we've just discovered we need fifteen to meet our obligations."

"Fifteen hundred?" She could probably stretch it that far, even if she had to add a couple hundred from her savings account.

Jax sighed. "No. Fifteen thousand."

Chapter Thirty-Six

Jax had just asked her sister for a loan of fifteen thousand dollars through the bank. She closed her eyes. *Fifteen thousand. Fifteen lousy little thousand.* It wouldn't even come close to what they needed. *It'll just buy us some time... maybe.* But she couldn't come that clean with her sister. Not yet.

To Jamie's credit, she didn't choke when she heard the amount. "I'll see what I can pull together and get back to you."

Jax poured another cup of coffee. She'd worked in the lab until three o'clock this morning and had been about to go back to work when Phil mentioned that things were "a little worse" than he'd said before. *A little worse? Y'think?* Then he'd promptly left for the car lot, mumbling something about an early meeting.

The phone rang. *Jamie, so fast?*

She answered.

An electronically modified voice wormed into her ear. "Don't hang up. You want to hear this." She readied her finger to disconnect.

"Dr. Taylor, are you listening?"

Jax moved her finger off the button. "Who is this?"

"I need you to do something for which you will be paid handsomely."

"Who are you? Why are you calling me?"

"Dr. Taylor, I will not now, or ever, answer any of your questions." The flat, metallic voice clawed into her brain. "I am, however, prepared to pay you two hundred thousand dollars to delay the toxicology tests on the newer corpses in your lab."

Jax sucked in a breath. Her mind filled with possibilities. The killer, or someone working for the killer, knew of their find, and believed the toxicology report would show cause of death. But the tissue samples, even on the most current bodies, were decomposed enough that they might not have answers. *Are there more bodies? Could the killer be a medical professional? How did he get my name and number this fast?*

"Two hundred thousand dollars, Doctor, in cash. We never meet. All you have to do is delay requesting the tests for a few days, or delay reviewing the reports. I'm not asking you to falsify the data in any way. You will be paid well for a few days of not doing one little thing."

Two hundred thousand dollars. I could pay off the goons who are after Phil and put some money back in my retirement account. No. What am I thinking? "Why are you calling me?" Another question, and she already knew the answer. She controlled the lab and she needed money. Apparently there were even fewer secrets in the small town than she'd thought.

"I'll be watching, Dr. Taylor. I'll know your decision. And Dr. Taylor? You would be wise to decide in the affirmative and take the financial advantage. To decline would not be healthy."

The call ended abruptly and Jax began to tremble, which soon gave way to hot tears of anger. Phil's behavior had placed them—placed her—in this horrible position. If not for his actions, she would not have been targeted as someone who could be tempted. *Why in the world do I stay with a man who only uses me?*

She walked down the hallway toward the master suite and paused in the doorway of a smaller room next to it. Soft light from the windows created a peaceful setting for the rocker, crib and layette arranged with love and care and dreams.

CHAPTER THIRTY-SEVEN

Nick watched wipers push the rain away on the limo's windshield. They hadn't moved more than a block in the last five minutes. He looked at the stalled traffic on either side of the vehicle, then at this watch. He lowered the privacy window. "Look, do you know a different route? One where we can actually make some progress?"

"The whole area is like this, Sir. D.C. is shorthand for gridlock."

Nick punched the button to close the window, then found the control for the air and turned the temperature down. Sweat was pouring from his body.

He thought about the last several years—the cases he'd worked, the vacations he'd taken, the women he'd been with—and all that time, he'd had a daughter. Had she known she had a father out there somewhere? Did she wonder why he didn't call or visit or even send her a birthday card? *What the hell could Sandra have been thinking to do this to her own daughter?*

Nick's knee began to bounce and he clamped a hand down on it. After an intense moment, the bouncing slowed and stopped. Things were getting to him.

He reached in his pocket and pulled out his amber friend. He had taken a drastic cut in the amount of oxy support he gave himself, but maybe his timing could be better. *No, dammit. No time like the present.* He shook just two more little green pills, rather than his normal five, into his hand. Instead of washing them down with water, he reached for the Macallan bottle and poured a generous amount into a crystal tumbler. *Maybe a different kind of amber will help calm my nerves.*

Nick opened his briefcase and pulled a folder out of it. He had no hope of getting to the attorney's office in time for his appointment. He let them know about the traffic situation, and asked them to please hold his appointment if possible. They assured him his appointment took priority.

His memories spun back to the days when he'd been heady with the opportunity to make his own mark in the Bureau, and in life. All he wanted was to work in the field, to make a difference. Too many people, including his wife, wanted him to move up to the more prestigious administrative positions. Nick had been offered several, and he'd declined each time. Eventually, the offers stopped.

Sandra had liked his bank account, but it chafed her that Nick didn't move in the Country Club set. When it became clear she would rather party than settle-in with him for an evening at home, he let her go, at first, just to the parties. Later, after she had a string of wild affairs with losers having fun on his dime with his wife, he made it more permanent. Sandra's lifestyle and moral ambiguity notwithstanding, she had never wanted kids. *So why did she keep Kylie? And why did she keep her a secret from me?*

He didn't have to wait long to get the answers.

CHAPTER THIRTY-EIGHT

"We understand, Agent Grant, that you want to confirm for yourself that Kylie Bellamy is your biological daughter. However, for the sake of expediency, let us presume for the remainder of our meeting that she is."

Nick had divested himself of his jacket. His tie hung loose around his neck. He couldn't stop sweating. "Fine. Let's just get on with it, shall we?" Nick dug his fingers into the back of his neck to try to ease the tension. He watched as an assistant filled his water glass for the third time.

Edward Lockwood, partner in Mills, Lockwood and Sterling, laid his Mont Blanc pen on the desk. "Are you not feeling well, Agent? Perhaps we should reschedule."

"I don't have time to reschedule. I'm working on a case and I need to get back to Colorado." He swallowed, forced his body to relax and his eyes to meet Lockwood's. "Just tell me what you have to tell me."

The attorney consulted his file and cleared his throat. "Very well." He handed Nick some documents. "At the time of the dissolution of your marriage, Sandra was involved with another man. An extremely wealthy man, even by your standards. Ms. Bellamy, as evidenced by the affidavit you're holding, was pregnant, and determined her wisest course of action was to present her pregnancy to her lover, assert that the child belonged to him, and remarry. That is what she did."

"And why did she believe the child was mine?"

"To put it delicately, our client asserted that you were the only man she didn't take precautions with when intimate."

Nick struggled to control his voice. "And her reason for stating so now? For the affidavit? For all of this?"

"When Ms. Bellamy's late husband died, he left everything to his wife with a provision it would all to pass to Kylie upon Sandra's death. Ms. Bellamy learned of her inoperable...." Lockwood consulted his file. "Her diagnosis of inoperable glioblastoma occurred a little more than a year ago, and shortly after that time she requested we make arrangements for her estate, and Kylie. She said that you, better than anyone, knew what it meant to live an authentic life even with a great deal of money at your disposal."

Nick's look of incredulity must have struck a chord because Lockwood paused for a long moment.

He continued. "Agent Grant, I understand how your history with Ms. Bellamy—Sandra—could leave you disillusioned about her motives, but people do change, especially when faced with the end of their life. Sandra loved Kylie in her own way. She wanted the little girl to be cared for, and for all of her questions to be answered."

"Questions?"

"Your daughter—assuming she is your daughter—is a very observant child. She has been asking questions about her paternity. Her mother didn't feel equipped to answer them."

Nick doubled over in pain and fought the need to vomit. The room spun.

Lockwood issued a directive to someone to call nine-one-one. Nick thought, *This is not what I had in mind when I woke up this morning.*

Three hours later, IV in place and clothes neatly hung, Nick looked around his private room. *Not bad for a hospital.* He had no intention of staying, even if he was sick. *Maybe especially if I'm sick.* He kicked one leg out of bed.

"Whoa there, Buddy." A nurse the size of a linebacker marched up to his bedside. "You're not ready to go anywhere yet."

"That's where you're wrong. I need to—"

Another voice, a baritone with authority, joined the conversation. "No, you need to listen to me. You can self-destruct if you want, but you won't do it with my blessing." The man's face reflected a combination of compassion and determination. His lab coat and his demeanor identified him as a doctor. He impaled Nick with a glare from fierce, coal-black eyes.

Nick pulled his leg back under the bedding.

"Today is going to be the worst day in your life. Shit happens." The doctor pulled a chair from a corner of the room, planted it at Nick's bedside, and sat with the gracefulness of an athlete. "Now, do I have your attention?"

Nick answered with a squint.

"Good. I appreciate an appreciative audience."

"Who the hell do you think you are?"

"I'm the man who's going to save your sorry ass."

"Excuse me?"

"You have a drug addiction. That's not a good thing in anyone. It's especially not a good thing in an FBI agent."

"I'm handling it."

"Yeah, I know. That's why you're here. You were trying to kick by yourself. Not smart."

Nick sucked in some hospital air. It didn't help his

mood. "What is the 'shit' that's happened?"

"Well, Kemo Sabe, you had the decidedly mixed luck of coming apart at the seams in an attorney's office. An attorney who, as a reminder, does not represent you."

Nick didn't like what he was hearing. The lousy mood he had been in a few minutes ago took a nosedive.

"Edward Lockwood recognized the signs of withdrawal, having had two former associates at his law firm go through them. As such he was obligated to notify Virginia Child Protective Services and, well, combine that with the completely bizarre timing of a raid by the DEA on a doctor's office in New York who had your prescription information sitting on his desk along with an FBI contact number and you can see how people got curious."

The FBI. Terrific.

"Your employer is sending a representative here now, I imagine to inform you that you'll be taking an unrequested leave. So you see, Son, you might as well lie back and relax. You're not going anywhere for the time being."

Chapter Thirty-Nine

Jamie put the final touches on a loan request that really didn't need any. The borrower could have bought the assets of the bank twice over, but considered this a way to give back to the local community. Jamie smiled. Margaret Pomeroy was building a home for her aging parents on some land she owned along Sopris Creek near Snowmass. In addition to the jobs her construction business created, the money her late husband had left her supplemented any number of local non-profit agencies. Margaret Pomeroy didn't need to hunt for ways to give back to the community, but she did it anyway, and with grace.

She hit Send on her computer and the loan application made its way to the underwriter. Mrs. Pomeroy did not have to substantiate her income, assets, or debt for the rubber stamp loan approval waiting at the other end. Still, Jamie had made sure the submission could stand up to a third-party audit.

Earlier, Jamie had filled out the necessary paperwork to take out a loan against her 401(k) for fifteen thousand dollars. The money should be transferred into her account tomorrow and she'd be able to help her sister. She'd also have to tell Jax this couldn't happen again. Phil Sussman might ruin his financial future and he might ruin Jax's financial future, but no way would she let him ruin hers. She had to be solvent to provide some sort of long-term security for both herself and Jax should the need arise, and right now it looked like the need would surely arise.

Her extension rang and she answered it while clearing her desk.

"Hey, Jamie."

"Teague. Are you back in town?"

"No such luck. I just wanted to hear your voice."

Jamie's face heated up, and other places on her body responded as well. She remained silent.

"It's going to be a few more days before I can get back to Aspen Falls. Will you wait for me?"

"Probably."

Laughter filled her ear and made her almost giddy. "If I have to fight someone off, I will, you know. I'm pretty sure I've proven myself."

"You have. I suppose I can always make room for a knight in shining armor."

"Not *a* knight, Jamie. *Your* knight."

"If you say so."

"I do. Save Thursday night for me? I have to be in Denver for some meetings over the weekend, but I don't want to wait to see you again."

Jamie hadn't felt this good about a man—or herself—for as long as she could remember. It tickled her with a strange, wonderful, and altogether foreign feeling. She liked it.

"Call me Wednesday and we'll work out the details."

"I'll do that. I have to run. Hope you'll think about me between now and Thursday. If you think about me only a fraction of how many times I'll think about you, Jamie Taylor, thoughts of me will fill your days."

Jamie kept her hand on the phone several seconds after the call ended, somehow extending the connection.

She hadn't felt so special, so treasured, in a very long time. Teague had dropped into her life at a point when she had pretty much decided it would be her and her dogs for the rest of her days. That future wouldn't have been a bad thing, but the possibility of real love sounded so much better.

Her desk readied for the next day, she checked her calendar to see what she'd scheduled for the first thing in the morning. A loan committee meeting at eight followed by a meeting with a young man interested in a small business loan for an art gallery. Jamie shook her head. Unless he possessed something special and a lot of staying power, it would be a tough sell. Art galleries were a nickel a dozen between Aspen and Aspen Falls.

She shrugged on her coat, drew the strap of her purse over her shoulder, and said goodbye to the staff. They'd be there until the six o'clock closing time.

A cold gray sky oozed between the mountains that framed Aspen Falls. It wouldn't be unheard of for Aspen Falls to get snow this early. Jamie thought about the windows she needed to re-calk and the firewood she needed to order. She walked toward her SUV, mentally calculating both timing and expense.

Her key chain pulled up in front of her like a compass, she pushed the button to unlock the doors. That's when she looked up and saw him leaning against the driver's side.

Andrew pushed himself off the vehicle and braced his feet. "Hello, Jamison." He smiled and placed his hands in his pockets.

Jamie stopped. "I can't believe you're still here. After the other night, I thought you'd hightail it back to your new wife, new digs and new life."

"I'm sorry about all of that, I really am. Things just got out of control." He cocked his head to one side. "You know, that seems to happen to me a lot where you're concerned. You're a bad influence on my manners, Jamie Stanton... oh, excuse me... Jamie Taylor."

"What do you want now?"

"All I'm looking for is for a little help from you. If someone should call you about my character, you just need to tell him what an upstanding guy I am. That's all."

Jamie squared herself and moved within striking distance of the man who had bruised her heart and sliced her body. "You'd better pray no one calls. The best you can hope for is that I'll tell them we haven't been together in years, that people change and life goes on. The only reason I won't tell them what a bastard you really are is that I suspect your new wife is a good person, and maybe you treat her a whole lot different then you ever treated me.

"So here's the deal, Andrew. You leave now, never to show up in my life again, and I'll be ambiguous. I won't lie, but I won't volunteer the fact that you're an ass. However, if you're still here in five minutes, I'll let them know exactly what I think of you. Your best bet is to leave now. As long as their questions are generalities, I'll respond in the same manner."

"And if they ask you something specific?"

Jamie shook her head. "You'd better hope they don't."

"You know what I can do to you."

"I'm not the same wide-eyed little girl you controlled all those years ago. You'd best be thinking about what I can do to *you*."

Andrew popped out a laugh. "Are you *threatening* me?" The broken laugh turned into a snicker. He finally pointed a finger at her and walked toward the back of the vehicle. "You'd better do as I've asked. If you don't, you'll have a lot more to deal with than a little bit of vandalism to a shed, and I'll enjoy myself a lot more."

"Bring it on." Jamie felt good saying the words, even if she did urge them out just above a whisper.

CHAPTER FORTY

Jax sat in her car, watching the lunchtime crowd as they sat on benches and at tables scattered around the square. They seemed to be living their lives in some weird parallel universe. They looked fresh and optimistic as they turned their faces to the sun. A few actually were talking on their cell phones, and others were texting, but they all seemed relaxed and happy. In her current state of mind, they all looked to her like unsuspecting victims.

Ever since she'd received the call yesterday afternoon, she had lived in a tense sort of alien atmosphere, her effectiveness diminished. Fear and anger and hope and resentment burrowed under her skin and dug in. She needed to flush them out and think. She tried to understand what had led her to this point, and who might be behind the offer of the money. Two hundred thousand dollars would represent a lot of breathing space for her and Phil. It wouldn't make everything better, but it would lighten the load. What did two hundred thousand dollars represent to the man behind the offer? *Someone knows my financial situation, someone who has a lot of money and wants me to delay the toxicology tests. But why only delay? Why not outright falsification?*

Delays happen all the time due to human error and technology breakdowns. But could she live with herself if she knowingly caused one? *Why am I even considering this?* Jax reached for her ceramic mug filled with coffee from The Coffee Pod, situated her purse straps over her shoulder and shoved herself out of her car. Her office and lab had been state of the art eight years ago, but budget constraints had not allowed them to upgrade to current technology.

Still, it was better than the basement storage closet the county had converted when she'd first begun her career. Jax would never forget the old and second-hand equipment she was expected to use to provide fast and accurate information. Seven years out of date rated far better than twenty.

The forensic anthropologist from Denver was still working in part of her lab. The man was as quiet as the remains he worked on, and Jax easily forgot he had set up shop in a third of her space. He would probably be wrapping up the intense physical work in the next few days. The bodies were intact, and they had a select pool of possible victims to work with.

Jax and her assistant had managed to do three autopsies. The autopsies had taken longer than usual because of the state of decomp, and her assistant had balked at the continued detail Jax insisted on. She wouldn't let up on the examination or cut corners. If anything, she made sure they were more meticulous.

Thirteen of the bodies had been interred for over a decade, and four of them had been placed in the cold earth within the last six months. It made her lab a very busy place. They would be ready to send out the tissue samples to determine any toxins late this afternoon. The CBI in Denver would make the toxicity tests a priority, and they would have the results back in less than a week, rather than the month the tests usually took.

Jax realized she'd answered part of her questions.

There would be no delaying anything from her office, for any reason. Now, she needed to talk to someone and brainstorm the possibilities. *Jamie.* With a little bit of shame, Jax realized she hadn't even considered talking to Jamie about this until she herself had decided to do the right thing. Jamie's passion for justice might be part of what had rubbed off, ultimately, on Jax. Whatever the reason, she'd give Jamie a call after she finished up the last autopsy, seen the tissue samples safely off, and schedule some time so they could talk.

The afternoon passed in that kind of amazing time warp in which a person is so intent on a project they forget all about the clock. When she and her assistant finished the last autopsy, it was after five. They carefully and respectfully placed the remains back in the refrigeration unit.

"You go ahead and hit the road," Jax said. "I'll finish cleaning up here, and then I'll get the paperwork ready. The CBI courier from Aspen won't be here for another hour."

"Thanks, Doc." The young college student backed to the door as if afraid Jax might change her mind.

"Doc?"

"Yes, Oliver?"

"I'm proud of the work we did here. I'm glad you made us—me—do it right."

Jax smiled. "Get out of here."

Jax washed down the autopsy table. The negative pressure vents that surrounded it always reminded her of giant cheese graters, and she took special care to make sure they were cleaned thoroughly. The vents designed to suck in anything that might be released into the air while they were doing an autopsy, and having four bodies in various states of decomposition on the table in the last couple of days, she wanted to make certain it was well cleansed.

Finally, she walked out of the lab, divided her autopsy apparel into the biohazard trash, the hamper for laundering, and the bin for sterilizing, and moved toward her office to begin the paperwork. *And call Jamie.* Exhaustion settled over her shoulders in a good way. The precision with which she met the needs of her profession affirmed her. Jax wondered if she'd get a follow-up call from her not-to-be benefactor. She shook a little at the idea. *What if he goes from a carrot to a threat?*

Her private line rang.

"Dr. Taylor." She squeezed out her name.

"It's me." *Jamie.* "They called Gretchen and me back out to the site after I got off work. We've got two more, and Jerry wants you out at the site tonight."

"On my way." Jax hung up and called the courier to reschedule the pickup for the next afternoon. They weren't very happy, but it wasn't like they were coming from Denver. They'd pick up the samples tomorrow and get them on a plane to Denver with very little skin off anyone's nose.

Jax grabbed her bag and wondered whether someone would be watching her exit the building.

CHAPTER FORTY-ONE

Jamie hunched next to Gretchen, one arm around her dog, and watched Jax at work. She was proud of her sister and knew this had to be every bit as hard on Jax as it was on her. So many people had been murdered and then buried here. She imagined the soil a dark red with their spilled blood, their unfulfilled lives driving it deep. She heard the crack of the shovel against the earth as it split open a seam to hide the evidence of their abrupt deaths. The Earth Mother must have wept.

Jamie believed everyone's story had an ending. Even those who believe their stories continue long after their time on this earth ceases, have an ending on this side of heaven. There should be dignity in that ending, and something that marks it, even if only from a medical examiner. The End never comes for people and their families, when there isn't proof. Men, women, and children who were simply lost never get that final good-bye.

Jamie shivered. *Why did the killer choose this particular meadow? Does he have a connection to Leopold Bonzer? And where is Agent Grant? Why isn't he here making my job more difficult?*

Jamie's phone rang.

"Taylor."

"Jamie, I need you over here. I'm about half a klick due north of where you are."

"Sheriff?"

"Now."

She stood, stretched her legs, and looked north. Other than an old logging road and a steep climb to get to it, Jamie could see nothing. She wondered why the sheriff needed her. Whatever the reason, it couldn't be good. She tugged on the lead. "C'mon, Gretch. Let's take a little walk." She looked at her sister. "Jax, Jerry Coble just asked me to meet him up the hill. You okay?"

"As long as they leave these lights on. And tell Jerry these two haven't been dead more than two or three days."

"What's going on, Jax?"

"Damned if I know. I'm not even sure I want to know."

Near the top of the hill, Jamie looked back. She could see the entire meadow. Moonlight shimmered like a fine mist through the high clouds, giving shape and life to the Cimmerian darkness beyond the illuminated work area.

There was a bark and a low growl above her and to the right, and then everything went quiet. She took a step.

"Jamie, that better be you comin' up behind me."

"Yes, Jerry. It's me." She made her way carefully up the rest of the incline, Gretchen tight at her side. With slow, measured steps, she slipped up alongside the sheriff and waited for him to say something more.

He pointed. About ten feet away was what at first looked like some large, broken logs leaning against the trunk of pine tree. She tried to see whether there was something else, something significant, in that direction, but her gaze kept returning to the pile of logs.

Then one of the logs moved and let out a mournful howl.

Jamie blinked. "Is that a beagle?"

"Right now it's acting more like a wolf hybrid. Won't

let me anywhere near it... or the two people it's lying next to."

"Oh, dear God!"

"Right. So between you and God, do you think you could manage to get Wolfgang out of my way so I'm not forced to commit dogicide in the line of duty?" He was trying to lighten the mood for her benefit.

"I think we can handle this."

With a soft, smooth glide, purposeful but not threatening, Jamie moved out from behind the sheriff and knelt about eight feet away from him. She needed to distance herself from any perceived threat. Gretchen stayed put, but remained ready for action if she received a signal from Jamie. "Hey, sweet thing. You've got quite the responsibility tonight, don't you? I know you're in the role of protector and everything is different than it was not long ago, isn't it? We're here to help you, if you'll let us." Jamie moved a little closer.

The beagle growled, but only for a second and the sound trailed off into the rhythms of the night.

"You don't have to be alone, you know." Jamie signaled and Gretchen loped to her side. The other dog shifted and bared its teeth.

Before Jamie could stop her, Gretchen rose and moved toward the pine tree and the beagle intent on standing guard.

About five feet from the other dog, Gretchen slowed, her movements minute, as if she were seeking permission to approach. Then, as if blocking out movements for a game to come later, she walked forward, stretching out her front legs, her hindquarters in the air. She made a mewling noise and lowered her back end to the ground. Then she crawled like a soldier moving toward a dangerous target.

CHAPTER FORTY-TWO

Jamie caught her breath. To call out could unleash a primitive response from the beagle, and she wouldn't risk Gretchen's life. Instead, she readied herself to jump into the fray if necessary. For now—for this moment—she would trust Gretchen's instincts.

Within the next few seconds Gretchen came alongside the other dog, offering a mixture of understanding, condolences and protection of her own. The beagle backed away.

Jamie stood, intent on keeping her posture and movements non-threatening, and edged closer. The beagle looked in her direction and she froze. Some sort of non-verbal communication pulsed between the two animals, and the beagle went prone on the ground in front of Gretchen.

"Good girl. Thank you, Gretchen." Jamie waited for a signal from her dog. She got it when Gretchen leaned over and licked the ears of the dog at her feet.

Jamie moved slowly into the almost-visible ring that surrounded the tree, two dogs and the two unmoving forms at its center. She knelt well before she reached touching distance, then inched forward on her knees. She kept her tone soft and controlled. "I'm here to help. I'm not going to do you or your people any harm." She reached her hand out, palm up, and let the beagle focus on her scent. A mournful cry formed in the beagle's throat and sorrow filled the hillside.

Jamie felt for a pulse on each body, but they were cold.

"Sheriff, we're good here, but you need to call Jax and get her up this hill."

"You're sure, Jamie?" He'd already pulled out his cell.

Jamie sat on the ground, one dog on either side of her. She gave both of them some of the treats she always carried in her pack. A little extra went to the beagle under Gretchen's watchful and approving eye.

Jerry Coble, arms folded, watched Jax examine the man and woman as best she could, given the circumstances. The sheriff had already brought a portable Klieg light up to the new site.

Jax photographed the bodies from multiple angles and asked Jamie to diagram the scene for her. Tomorrow, in the daylight, the LEOs would do a thorough search of the surrounding area.

When Jax retrieved the wallets she handed them to Sheriff Coble. He opened them and read aloud. "Brian Rawlings. He'd be... thirty-six. Boston, Mass." He shuffled the ID and opened the other wallet. "Corrine Rawlings. Thirty-four. Same address." His voice rang low and mellow on the mountainside, respectful and sad.

Jamie watched as Jax continued her preliminary examination. She'd helped Jax study for hours before her exams. Her sister would carefully disrobe each victim enough to get their body temperatures rectally. She would determine livor mortis—where the blood has settled—and rigor mortis.

Jamie reached over to the beagle's collar and checked for a tag. "Well, hello Shelby." At the sound of her name the beagle's ears twitched. "What happened to you?" She scratched behind Shelby's ears and the dog moved closer, pressing tight against her thigh.

Time passed. Jax worked. Coble paced. Jamie thought about the families who were about to receive the worst possible news. Families who at this very minute were experiencing the last of what they would forever consider "before the call." Everything else would be "after the call."

"I've done what I can here, Jerry. I'd say they've been dead between eight and thirty-six hours. Most probably about twenty-four. I can't see any signs of external trauma, which ties them into the others. It looks like they asphyxiated."

"On what, if there wasn't any external injury?"

"I don't know. Someone could have smothered them, but then there should be obvious signs of defensive wounds unless they were drugged in some way first. I want to get them back to my lab so I can do a closer examination."

"I've called for transport. They should be here in about twenty minutes. You two go on home. I'll wait."

Jamie stood up. "I hope you didn't call Animal Control."

"Nope. Knew better."

Jax packed her bag and Jamie brought out her spare lead. She thought Shelby would probably follow without a problem, but she might have some angst over leaving the two people she loved.

Back where Rocky Point butted up against the dirt road, Jamie opened the back door to the SUV and Gretchen bounded in, then turned to make sure Shelby followed. The beagle struggled a little bit with the high jump, but she hit the floor first and popped up on the back seat like she'd been there before.

Jax watched, then said, "James, I need to talk to you

159

about something."

Great. Just great. Jamie already had felt the pressure for more money. She was going to have to put a stop to this at some point. But when? Tonight felt all wrong. "Can it wait until tomorrow?"

"No. It can't. Well, *I* can't. Look, I know it's late and we're both tired, but this is important."

Jamie sighed. "Did you have dinner?"

"You're kidding, right?"

"Let's go to my house. I can get the dogs settled in, and I'm sure there's something to eat."

"Thanks, Jamie."

"You bring the wine."

Chapter Forty-Three

Nick did his best to settle into the seat of his chartered plane. They'd received clearance from the tower for takeoff and the jet took only seconds to pick up enough speed to be airborne. Regardless of everything that had happened, he was headed home.

Home. Funny how Colorado had become the place of his heart so easily. He'd grown up on the east coast. He'd gone to school, made a living, joined the FBI and gotten married all on the east coast. Less than a year ago he'd moved to the Rocky Mountains, but that part of the country had laid claim to both his present and his future. *Such as it is.*

He was going home, a father without his child and a law enforcement officer without authority. He was a recovering addict with a boatload of pills that held the potential to become his new drug of choice.

In a few short days, he'd gone from thinking he'd never solve the case he'd been working on for a decade to actually getting closure for families to finding out he had a family of his own to losing everything. And mixed up in all of it was a tall, skinny woman with a man's name and a bunch of dogs. And he couldn't get her out of his head.

The co-pilot ducked out of the cockpit and nodded in

Nick's direction, then moved toward him in the spacious cabin.

"We're clear, Sir. If you want to use any electronics, feel free. The attendant is preparing your dinner. Is there anything you'd like while you wait? A drink perhaps, or something more?" Her smile held a hint of promise.

Nick was used to women coming on to him. He figured his looks were just a little above average, but his wealth wasn't. It was easy to guess the attraction. The flags these women waved, the desperation or greed that drove them, made him tired, bored and cynical.

"Thanks, I'm fine." *Except that right at this moment, you made me want a fistful of my oxy. You are a psychic vampire, ready to suck away every forward step I've taken.*

She turned to walk back to the cockpit.

"Wait." He flashed her the smile he knew could knock women over, bankrolled or not.

She had already turned back and posed, smoke almost pouring around her body. "My name is Glade."

"Fine, Glade. I'd like a glass of zin. And a shrimp cocktail. And a copy of today's Denver Post, which I was told you'd be sure to have on hand."

The co-pilot visibly stiffened. Her tone lost all the smoke and sizzle she'd previously displayed. "I'll let your attendant know."

Glade, the co-pilot who thought she'd hit the jackpot, marched back toward the front of the plane, pausing to bark some orders to the young girl assigned to serve Nick's meal. To Glade's credit, as audible as the bark was, she'd turned the volume to seethe.

Just because he was on medical leave from the bureau didn't mean he no longer had something to contribute. He punched a number into his cell phone. "Arnold, it's me." Nick hoped Agent Abner wouldn't ask him too many

162

questions. *With any luck, he hasn't heard of my status.*

"Hey, Nick. What's up? Anything to get me a prolonged stay in Aspen Falls?"

"You fall in love or something, Agent?" Nick grinned at the sudden silence. He pictured the younger man's face and bit the insides of his cheeks to stop from laughing. "Good for you," he said. "A lot of good looking women in the mountains of Colorado."

"I only know of one, and that's all I can handle."

"I've got ya, Buddy. One is sometimes more than enough. Listen, I need Sheriff Coble's direct line or his cell." Nick held his breath.

"Yeah, hang on. I've got it here somewhere."

After Nick got the number, he gathered his thoughts. This would take a little more finessing. Arnold Abner thought Nick was pretty impressive, but Jerry Coble was his own man and was not easily impressed. And Nick needed to be back in the middle of this investigation.

A few minutes later, Nick had secured a face-to-face with Coble for the next morning. He'd plead his case and make the sheriff an offer he couldn't refuse.

He kicked his seat back for a nap.

An hour later his eyelids flew open. They should be getting close to Aspen by now. Nick set up in his seat and focused his hearing. Something was wrong. He'd flown enough of these jets as both passenger and pilot that a change in pitch was instantly noticeable. He ran through the possibilities in a few seconds, and he knew. One of the engines had cut out.

He stood and moved to the cockpit, then hesitated. The sudden silence in the cabin meant only one thing— they no longer had even one working engine.

Inside the cockpit the pilot and co-pilot had hauled back as hard as they could on the sticks, working to keep the nose up.

"What can I do?" Nick asked

"Pray," the pilot said.

CHAPTER FORTY-FOUR

Nick lay still, his eyes closed. The smell of aviation fuel permeated the air, mixed with popping sounds. He was covered in electrical wires and other debris. When he moved his arm to clear his eyes and nose, pain shot through his back. *Damn.* Someone was shoving something off his legs.

"Are you all right, Agent Grant?"

The pilot. Nick spat dried leaves from between his lips. "I've jacked into an old back injury, but otherwise I think I'm fine." He cleared dirt from his face. "The co-pilot and flight attendant?"

"They're both out, but I don't see any signs of trauma. The emergency beacon is set, so we shouldn't be too long." The man stood up and rummaged through what was left of part of the overhead compartment. He pulled out a first aid kit and several blankets.

"I don't think we'll have to stay here overnight. We've landed in some kind of pasture. But just in case, here's a blanket."

"I'm fine. Put them on the others. They might be going into shock."

Nick reached into his pocket. *Empty.* He took one long blink and swallowed. *It's a new day, Gunga Din, and bound to get interesting.* He sat up. Winced.

"You know my name, what's yours?"

"I'm Steve Robbins. The co-pilot is Glade Lewis, and the attendant is Veronica Beale." They shook hands.

"We were only about thirty minutes out of Aspen when we went down. If the rancher doesn't get here first, we should get some air support or ground rescue within an hour or so."

Nick nodded. "Do all of you live around here?"

"Glade and Veronica both live in Glenwood Springs. I'm in Snowmass. You?"

"Closer to Aspen Falls."

Nick was reminded constantly that people with money weren't that big of a deal in the Aspen area. It was one of the reasons he'd moved here. He wouldn't be surprised to learn that Veronica, the flight attendant, had more money than Nick and Steve put together, and just loved her job.

Nick could relate. He loved being in the field, making a difference. If he wanted, he could do nothing but jet between continents, going from party to party or spa to spa. When he first hurt his back, he'd thought about it, but only for a short while. Those lives were empty. It wasn't just the adrenaline, but the impact of his job and the mental focus it required.

A Ford F-150 pulled up, its headlights piercing the fading light. A rancher stepped out of the cab, boots and Stetson complimenting his Levi 501s and the plaid shirt under his Levi jean jacket. "Anyone hurt?"

Nick said, "Mostly minor injuries. The co-pilot and attendant might have more serious things going on. The pilot seems okay, and I just have a back injury that's kicking up some steam. We were lucky."

The rancher took in the scene and nodded. "Could say that."

The air was split by the revving motors of vehicles approaching over rough terrain. *Someone knows a siren*

166

going full-blast would have no positive impact in a rancher's field in the Colorado mountains. He was grateful that the daughter he had never met would not become an orphan today but he could use some pain relief.

CHAPTER FORTY-FIVE

Jamie stared at Jax. "So you're saying that someone obviously connected to the killings offered you two hundred thousand dollars to mess with the toxicology results?" Jamie pulled her legs off the couch where she'd been stretched out, and got to her feet. Pacing helped her think. *Whatever we've gotten involved in, it's big.*

"Not *mess* with them, per se. Delay them."

Jamie gave her sister a stern look. "You're kidding, right? Like it matters?"

Jax's gaze slid to the grandfather clock in the corner. She had been tempted, and it bothered her.

Jamie thought, *Time to lighten up. We have more important things to think about than whether Jax can be bought.* She picked up a copy of the *Aspen Falls Gazette* and checked out the front page for the third time that day. The headline read *Bonzer Bodies Un-Buried*, but so far the sheriff's department and FBI had been able to keep the story about the newer victims from hitting the papers. It would be national news soon enough.

She barely glanced at the story below the fold. Another terrorist had been arrested in Denver. Jamie's ribs thrummed with anticipation. They were on to something. She knew it. "What do toxicology tests screen for, exactly?"

"Standard tox tests check for all kinds of drugs and alcohol. They're grouped under broad headings and tested. If a positive comes up, more tests are run to determine the precise drug. Those things can pretty much be determined in a few hours."

"What about the FBI lab? Are you sending some tissue samples to them?"

Jax nodded. "We are. They'll also screen for some poisons, and a few other things."

Jamie stopped pacing. "So unless you see something in the autopsy that triggers a test for something that's not on the list, it's possible the real cause of death will never be known."

"Sure. At some point you run out of tissue. We screen for typical substances, but unless there's a suspicion of something else, something specific, that's all we can do."

"Why would someone want to delay results that would be more or less typical?"

"I don't—"

"Would it be atypical for a lot of unconnected dead people to have the same drug or whatever in their system?"

"Of course, but I don't see what difference that would make," Jax said.

"So assuming we're not concerned about alcohol poisoning, it must be a drug or a poison someone is trying to keep from being discovered. But why?"

Jax shook her head. "I have no idea."

"Think," Jamie said as much to herself as to her sister. "Maybe whatever it is ties directly to the killer. If we can figure out the why, maybe that'll go a long way toward helping figure out the who." She resumed pacing back and forth in front of the fireplace. "A supplier?"

"Jamie, I've thought and thought about this. I can't come up with anything. A supplier is possible, but it's one

169

element that would point to only one source." Jax tugged one of their mom's afghans up to her neck. "This is Aspen Falls, neighbor of Aspen. Drugs are flown into that airport from LA and New York and Asia on a regular basis all packed and secure, not to mention the stuff coming up from Mexico. One thing pointing to one supplier doesn't make sense statistically."

"Okay," Jamie conceded. "Why else would someone not want the results released?"

"Something new?" Jax ventured from under the afghan.

"What, like a new drug? A new drug that's killing people?" Jamie went into the kitchen and came back a minute later with two glasses of wine. She handed one to Jax. "Why would they offer you money? If I was trying to distribute a new drug and it kept killing people, I'd just back off. Let things cool down. Come up with another formula."

The sisters sipped their wine in silence.

A cold chill pushed itself up through Jamie's body. "What if it isn't a drug? Who would pay big bucks to buy a little time?"

"What are you talking about?" Petulance oozed from Jax. She often got cranky when she was tired or stressed.

Jamie figured her sister was allowed, and she was about to make it worse. "What if he was making a big deal about the toxicology screen—the *standard* toxicology screen—because he knows there's nothing there. That way, regardless of what you decided to do with his bribe, he'd still be buying himself some time."

"James, I'm a scientist, not a behaviorist. I have no idea what you're talking about."

"Okay, let's be scientific." Jamie exhaled and gathered her thoughts. "Let's look at the facts we know and what we can reasonably surmise from them." She held up one hand. "Now, we're not law enforcement or attorneys. We're just two sisters talking, so surmising is allowed. Wait." Jamie went back to the kitchen and came back with the bottle of wine and some nuts. She sat down. "Okay, the bodies, which you've already established were killed in different ways by two different people were found in the same location. Why?"

"Either our current killer knew Leopold Bonzer or, more than a decade ago, he found a fresh grave or witnessed Bonzer burying someone."

"Good." Jamie was glad Jax seemed to be getting into the game.

Jax said, "But Bonzer didn't have any friends that anyone knew about, and people just don't stumble onto dumping grounds. So statistically speaking, our guy must have witnessed Bonzer burying someone more than ten years ago."

"Which means our current guy spent at least some time here back when Bonzer was doing his killing."

Jax nodded. "Probably even lived here."

Jamie popped a few nuts in her mouth. "So he's not a copycat."

"Nope. He just took advantage of someplace accessible, but remote."

Jamie said, "Okay, now I'm going to share something with you that I know something about: serial killers."

"You do?"

"One of the presenters for my continuing ed program last summer was a profiler. And not the *Criminal Minds* TV-profiler type. The real deal. There are a few statistics, and although there's no guarantee these are even close, we're just two sisters talkin', right?"

Jax nodded. "Shoot. "

"Serial killers don't contact MEs to ask them to delay a tox screen. Or offer two hundred thousand dollars as bribes. If a serial killer thought someone was on to him, he'd lie low. He'd change his MO or move to another state. If he contacted law enforcement or an ME, it would be to taunt them, to show them he's smarter than they are. So this guy, or this group, are not serial killers."

"So—two sisters having a conversation here—what the hell are you saying?"

Jamie picked up the newspaper and pointed to the article below the fold. "I'm saying one option we need to consider is terrorism." Jamie worked to push the words out, and still had a hard time believing she'd said them. They sounded so dramatic.

"A terrorist in Aspen Falls?"

"Do you have a better idea? Listen, without the bribe, we'd be looking at an equally bizarre possibility—a serial killer—but with the bribe it's a whole new basket of bones."

CHAPTER FORTY-SIX

Jamie's phone call early the next morning to Jerry Coble resulted in a meeting for eleven-thirty. That would work with her schedule at the bank. Her afternoon was clear, so if it ran long there wouldn't be a problem. She didn't need any more conflicts with her boss.

Jax had filed a report first thing that morning regarding the bribe, and she planned to be at the sit-down with the sheriff. Jamie wasn't a hundred percent confident in her supposition they were looking at a terrorist element—especially in Aspen Falls—but she thought they were at least headed in the right direction. This was a lot bigger than Leopold Bonzer.

Jamie fielded the expected telephone inquiry regarding her ex-husband. The caller sounded bored and young. Obviously they weren't very interested in doing an in-depth background check, nor had they heard about Andrew's recent arrest. The phone call lasted less than five minutes. With luck, Andrew might be out of her life for good. He'd have enough to handle with the press in California and his father-in-law should he ever get a hint about Andrew's past.

Jamie went on autopilot during the loan committee meeting. Nothing outrageous had been proposed, and she felt fortunate to work for a bank that still wanted to lend money when it made sense. The young man who wanted a loan to start a new art gallery had three things going for him: one, wealthy parents; two, an idea to rent art for a fee, either on a one-time basis to impress people, or to rotate among businesses to keep their selection fresh; and three, wealthy parents. She had a few questions about his business plan, and he promised to get her additional information within a week.

A little before eleven, Jamie called E-lev 2 to place an order for three take-out lunches of Phad Thai. Elevation in Aspen was only open for dinner, but E-lev 2 provided a nice lunch menu. While on the phone, she decided to be on the safe side and order four. One of the sheriff's deputies might be sitting in on the meeting and she didn't want to slight anyone. If there were more than four people, they could figure out how to share.

By the time she got to the sheriff's office, she was running late. The clerk at the front desk waved her through to the conference room and she shoved the door open with her shoulder, her arms laden with food, her purse and her briefcase. She nearly dropped everything when she saw who was seated at the table.

Jerry Coble said, "Thanks for lunch, Jamie. You remember Agent Grant."

She nodded. "I do."

Nicholas Grant, bruises on his face, eyed the four bags. "Ms. Taylor. I see you were expecting me."

"I prepared for the unexpected." *Be nice, Jamie.* But she hadn't liked it much when he winked at her and laughed.

Jamie sought out Jax and fixed her with a glare. Her sister should have figured out some way to warn her of what she was walking into. They'd talked about the agent's lack of appreciation for Jamie and her dogs.

Jax stared right back at her and didn't blink, and her

174

lips were curled in the slightest twinge of a smile.

Fine.

She set the bags down on the table and moved as far away from the FBI agent as she could and still be part of the conversation. Everyone pulled a lunch toward them and dug in. Jax looked pointedly at the untouched bag until Jamie tugged it toward her and fiddled with the contents.

The sheriff stabbed a forkful of noodles and shrimp and looked at both Jax and Jamie while he chewed. "Agent Grant is working with us in an unofficial capacity and reporting directly to me. I just want to make sure you both know that regardless of his status, we're lucky to have him and his insights on this case."

This just keeps getting better. Jamie couldn't even take a bite.

Jax spoke up. "Unofficial?" Jamie threw her sister a mental hug and forgave her for not giving her a heads-up call.

"For reasons that are nobody's business, Agent Grant is on leave from the Bureau. He has offered his assistance. I've talked with his superiors, and he's on this team."

Jamie remembered the morning she had watched the FBI agent dry swallowing a handful of pills through her binoculars. *Better and better.*

A little over an hour later, they'd drilled Jax up one side and down the other about the phone call she'd received. They noted and examined every nuance, every word, and every pause in the conversation. The lunch debris cleared away, they moved on to Jamie's idea that there might be a terrorist element involved.

"Two hundred thousand? C'mon." Nick Grant pushed back from the table. "If we were talking Al Qaida or anything similar, the bribe money would be significantly more."

"Unless that's what they knew you would think." Jamie shoved her chair back. She wanted to pace. She wanted to get some agreement, some direction.

She wanted to talk about drug addiction, and why someone with that kind of baggage should be trusted on the team.

Nick cocked his head and looked at her. Jamie resisted brushing her hair away from her face. "Possible," he said, "but I don't think so."

"Do you have a better idea?"

Nicholas Grant shook his head. "Not at the moment."

Jamie, vindicated for the time being, wished another idea would surface. *Anything to get some answers, even if it means letting the dog-hater win.*

Chapter Forty-Seven

He made the drive to Denver easily and checked in to the hotel. It was Saturday and the hotel lobby was full of travelers. His choice normally would have been the Ritz-Carlton Suite, but it was three thousand dollars a night and he didn't want to call attention to himself. He settled for something smaller and less conspicuous.

An escort service provided a companion for the evening. He was hungry for a great steak and personal service, and a lone diner at Elway's would stand out. The stupid girl didn't understand when, after their meal, he called a cab and sent her out into the night. Under other circumstances, he might have been up for some fun, but tomorrow was a big day. He wanted to review the details of his plan and re-run all of his calculations. He was confident the young woman would find something to do with the rest of her evening and would soon forget the boring businessman with whom she'd shared a meal at one of Denver's best restaurants.

At eleven-fifteen, he turned off the reading light and rolled onto his side. Sleep would come quickly.

Hours later, sunlight sliced into the room where he'd left the draperies open to awaken him. *A good omen.* He tossed the blankets aside, looked for the television remote, and grumbled while he worked through the hotel's programming. He rubbed his face and cursed. *Need the local weather*. Finally, he found a weekend team he recognized and turned the volume up while he went into the bathroom.

The sports guy, Sam Adams, was discussing the Bronco game and giving his score prognostication. "Denver twenty-seven, Kansas City twenty-four."

Yeah, right. Not today, buddy. Not today. This game would be his and both Denver and Kansas City would be left to pick up the pieces.

The weatherman said, "You might want to take another run at those scores, Sam. We're looking at some significant winds that could play a role in today's football game.".

Damn. He turned off the water and stepped back into the bedroom.

"The Denver area is getting an early surprise gift from our friends to the north. We don't expect to see any moisture out of this, but we will endure some strong, sustained winds beginning about one o'clock and continuing well into the evening hours. If you're going to the game, you'll want to be prepared."

Damn, damn, damn.

Between the end of the weather segment and the time it took him to walk into the living room area of the suite to make an espresso, he'd gone to Plan B. His ability to adjust was one of the things that had made him wealthy. He hadn't come this far, gone through this much, to quit because of one windy day. There would be more home games at Sports Authority Field.

178

CHAPTER FORTY-EIGHT

Jamie reached for her wine and smiled. Ciara had been entertaining them at the E-lev 2 with a story from her latest modeling job. It had been a relaxing Sunday afternoon, and every one of them needed it.

"And then, at the very last moment, when the asshole had every element in the picture just the way he wanted, with me twisted into a position usually only obtained by double-jointed humans, the electricity went out and he lost his lighting." She laughed and tipped her martini glass to the rest of the table. "Here's to mean-spirited photographers everywhere." She took a healthy swallow.

Ellen looked at Jamie. "You've been quiet. What's going on that we should know about?"

"Other than pressure at work, pressure from my ex, and pressure to make home improvements, not much, I'm afraid."

Ciara signaled to their waiter for a refill. "What about that gorgeous hunk of male you've been seeing?"

Heat rose to Jamie's face. "Teague?" She mentally pushed it down.

"Are you seeing more than one?"

For some inexplicable reason, the heat went up a notch. At any minute her face would melt away. *These are my friends. Why am I so uncomfortable?* "Of course not.

Teague is the only one I've had any kind of real date with in ages, and even that was a dinner date that ended before it began, with my home being filled with law enforcement and friends and neighbors asking all kinds of questions."

Jax looked at her, daring her to be honest. "What about Nick Grant?"

"I'll tell you all the truth," she said. "I have a certain amount of physical attraction to Agent Grant, but I'm certain he would be one of my notorious bad choices." She looked around at the amazed looks on the faces of her friends. "Oh, please. Tell me what you really think."

Ciara leaned forward. "I've been with a lot of men, Jamie, but Nicholas Grant? I met him the other day with Ellen and Abner. Nick Grant has layers. He's got layers worth taking out a shovel to get to. A little too much trouble for me, at least for the moment, but give me the right place and time? Honey, you'd have a race on your hands."

Jamie, amazed at the depth Ciara imagined Nick Grant to have, had no clue how to respond. She looked to either Ellen or Jax for some help.

Ellen smashed the end of a shrimp quesadilla between her fingers. "Arnold told me Nick Grant is one of the most respected FBI agents in the region. That's got to mean something, right?" She took a bite, avoiding all eye contact.

Jamie stared at her for a moment. "You know something. What else has Arnold told you?"

Ellen, unable even for a moment to hide something she felt, turned a blotchy red and her eyes pooled with tears. But she drew her lips inward and sat silent. The look she gave Jamie was both pleading and accusatory.

"Wait." Jax put an arm around Ellen. "Before we go any further, I have something to say that everyone here, and most especially my sister, needs to hear."

The three other women fell silent.

"For whatever reasons, neither Jamie nor myself have made the best choices when it comes to men. Just so you understand I'm being completely honest and open here, I'll start with myself." She paused for a moment and took a deep breath. "I know what all of you think of Phil, but right now, he's my best shot at happiness, which, to me, is having a child."

Jamie sat stunned and open-mouthed. She stared at her sister. *Where's this coming from?*

Ellen folded her hands, inspecting them closely as if for a flaw of some kind. Ciara took another long swallow from her fresh martini before setting the glass on the table and looking intently at Jax.

Jax smoothed one of the cloth napkins on the table. " I know what Phil has cost me in terms of money, pride and time, but if I get a baby from him, it all will have been worth it. I know my choice in a husband sucked, but I made it and I'm stuck with it. I said all that to say that being married to him has given me a kind of insight into what really makes people tick deep down where it matters, where they usually try to hide."

Jamie shifted in her chair, aching to stand up and walk out of the restaurant.

Jax looked directly at Jamie. "So here's the big sister speech. I don't know much about Teague Blanton, but there's something about his charm and absolute perfection that makes me feel oily, and not in a good way. Nicholas Grant, on the other hand, probably has some secrets." Jax looked pointedly at Ellen, then back to Jamie. "But there's something good and solid and honorable about him. If one of these two men are about to become deeply embroiled in my sister's life, I hope it will be the one who, right now, she can barely stand."

Jamie was as mad at Jax as she had ever been. "Who

the hell are you to talk about oily and honorable? Just because you've experienced the faithlessness and disrespect of your own husband doesn't make you all-seeing when it comes to other men, and especially not the men in *my* life."

Ellen reached for her hand, but Jamie pulled it away. "You all know that I made a horrible decision where Andrew was concerned, but not one of you knew beforehand. And if you did, we have some other problems. I've grown since then, and would no more stay with a man who cheated on me in every way possible than I would with one who left me with physical scars." She looked at each of them to make sure she had their attention. "Teague Blanton has treated me with nothing but respect, and a man with secrets, like Agent Grant, is one of those long shots that no sane woman should make time for. Think about this: the man doesn't like dogs, and he can barely cover up his own feelings about them. *Dogs.* Are you kidding me?"

She stood, dropped some money on the table, and looked at Jax. "I'm sorry, Honey, I really am, but Phil is never going to give you what you want. Even if you do have a baby, you'll have to deal with the baby's father and life will be always be hell."

She turned to Ellen. "And you. You know something about the handsome, yet troubled, FBI agent." Jamie's voice took on a theatrical note, but she couldn't stop. "Whom, we know, is currently on some kind of secret leave. Well, sweet Ellen, my misdirected sister and I have been informed that we will still be working with him, so if there's something we should know—something that could impact our progress on this case—you'd better get over keeping your pillow-talk secrets and spill this one."

"I can't, and I won't. Jamie, do you hear yourself? This isn't like you." Ellen looked hurt. "If Sheriff Coble is good to go with Agent Grant, what gives you the right to be all over his case?"

Jamie sat back down, the wind knocked out of her. It was a good question, and one that she didn't want to think about.

CHAPTER FORTY-NINE

"Sometimes our friendship and love gets a little intense, you know?" Jamie squeezed someone's fingers, she just wasn't sure who they belonged to. Eight hands entwined on the table top at E-lev 2. "We see each other at our best and our worst. Thank goodness whatever day we became friends I had my best game on. I made you fall in love with me and count me as a friend, and then I opened up my box of flaws. I couldn't get through this life without each one of you."

She waited for a moment, then pulled out a hand and wiped a tear. "You are all important to me in so many ways. Ciara, you make me want to live my life bigger than it is. You keep me reaching and striving to be more than I am." Jamie looked at Ellen. "And sweetheart, you make me understand what's really important. Thank you for keeping me grounded."

A moment passed.

"What about me?" Jax smiled, but Jamie could read the insecurity underneath the pulled-up mouth.

"Jacqueline Angelique Taylor, you know the exact spot on my butt that needs kicked from time to time to take a look at what's going on around me. You remind me that family is what matters, and that with love in our lives, we can overcome anything." Jamie squeezed again. "You guys keep me centered, and it's a good thing... because when I'm out of whack, I think and say some of the dangdest things. Things I'm always sorry for."

Ellen smiled. "I have an announcement to make."

Jamie looked at her friend. *No way!* It had been less than a month.

"Arnold and I are engaged. We're getting married next month, and I want all of you to be my maids," Ellen looked at Jax, "and matron of honor."

All four women jumped from the table and hugged and cried, thrilled for their friend.

The next hour was taken up with discussion and questions and plans surrounding Arnold Abner and the details of the big day.

Jamie was content, and so happy for Ellen. *Leave it to the quiet one to meet someone, fall in love, and get married in only a few weeks.* Before she was ready to stop celebrating, both Ciara and the bride-to-be had to leave. It had been a special afternoon among a long list of their special afternoons, but with Ellen's news, today ranked near the top.

After the other had left, she and Jax shared a few moment of comfortable silence.

"You really are something, you know." Jax shoved the bowl of nuts in Jamie's direction.

"Yeah?"

"For someone who doesn't always know what's going on with herself and shows it, you can be remarkably self-aware. I don't get it."

Jamie smiled. "Well, I guess I've had a lot of practice."

"Whatever."

The sisters sat awhile longer. Neither needed to make conversation. Besides, Jamie was exhausted and she needed to think.

Jax pulled up her purse and began to dig for her keys.

"I need to run by the lab."

"What for?"

"I have some notes there and I want to take a look at them, finish my reports on the last two victims."

"Did you get the samples off to the CBI?"

"They all went out this afternoon, except for the last two. They'll be couriered tomorrow morning."

"Mind if I tag along?" Jamie didn't like the idea of her sister going to her lab alone this late at night, but she wasn't about to tell her so.

"Aren't you tired?"

"Yeah, a little, but it's on my way home and I haven't been there in a while. You might have redecorated or something."

"Yeah, right. The county is so flush with funds, Ty Pennington put his genius to work on my office. And the morgue."

"So you're good if I'm there?"

"Sure. Why not?"

The bill finalized, they drove separately the few blocks to Jax's office.

The parking lot was empty, but well lit except for the far edges that bordered Aspen Falls Park and another office building. Patches of darkness spilled into the parking area like overturned bottles of ink where those two entities joined the municipal lot. Jamie and Jax both parked next to the building, under bright lights.

"Kind of eerie here at night, isn't it?" Jamie asked.

"You get used to it. I'm here a lot after hours."

Yeah. Like when your husband has decided to party-on down at Central City or Blackhawk. Jamie bit her tongue.

Jax fit her key in the lock and they walked into the lobby. It looked bigger somehow, and filled with ghosts.

They rode the elevator to Jax's floor without talking.

Jamie considered that the silence in a Medical Examiner's office was not the same as the silence in any other office known to man. There *were* ghosts here. Sadness. Grief. Regret. Guilt. Torment. And a curious element of hope.

They walked down the hall. Jamie waited while Jax unlocked the door and flipped on the light.

At first glance, everything looked normal. The county-issued waiting room chairs, in a horrible blue plaid, sat empty and alone along two walls. A coffee table held the fanned-out copies of the latest periodicals, while their older siblings were stuffed in an upright magazine holder next to a water cooler. A sad hibiscus plant clung to life in the far corner.

Jamie couldn't help thinking, *A waiting room assigned to death.*

Jax's demeanor changed. "What the hell?" She crouched lower as she went around the corner into the receptionist's area. Papers were strewn all over the floor. "Oh, no!" Jax took off for her lab at a run, Jamie right behind her.

Destruction greeted them like a rabid dog on a rusty chain. What had been an organized, professional space a few hours ago had turned into a biohazard dumping ground. It would take days, if not weeks, to replace the damaged equipment and certify the space for use again as a medical examiner's lab, assuming, of course, the county had adequate funds to put out in front of whatever insurance they had in place. In the current economy, that was highly questionable.

CHAPTER FIFTY

Jamie fought to keep her eyes open on her drive home. Exhaustion had settled over her like a lead blanket. The police report had taken forever, and even though she hadn't been much help, she wanted to be there for Jax. She rolled the window down and turned the music up.

The dogs would be hungry for food and attention, and she felt up for one of the two. All she wanted was a pillow, and about ten hours of nothingness.

On the drive up to her house, she stopped. The windows in her home weren't lit exactly, but a soft glow was coming from inside that didn't feel right. The sleepiness puddled around her feet and left something strange and spiky in its wake. She put her SUV in Park, killed the engine and opened the door. She slipped out and pushed the door closed as quietly as possible, until the interior light went out. She sprinted to the house, her steps as light as she could make them. *Please let this be nothing. Just some light I forgot to turn off before I left this morning.* It had happened before.

Another thought struck her. *Where are the dogs?* Surely by now they'd be barking in anticipation of her arrival. They could always sense things, hear things, smell things. *Why aren't they clambering toward me? Why isn't the slightest sound coming from the house? This isn't right. It just isn't right.*

She picked her way around the side of her house, stopping every few steps to listen for something that would tell her what was going on. She heard nothing. She thought about pushing the number on her cell phone, the one that connected her to the sheriff, but she didn't dare. If someone was listening, the noise would give her away in a flash.

At the back corner of her house she stopped. She searched the expanse beyond her back deck, but saw nothing.

"Damn, Jamie. I thought I taught you how to be quiet in the woods."

"Dad?"

"You'd better be glad it's me. Anyone else would've had your head, or worse, by now."

"Daddy? Is it really you?" Jamie flew up the stairs and into the arms of the man standing just outside the doors leading to her deck.

She had dreamt of feeling his arms around her again, and now, for a few moments, she was gathered in his strength. She was ten again, secure in a place where fathers protect their daughters, and the daughters believed them unconditionally. "How did you... I mean, when did you... I mean, why are you—"

"I'll explain everything, but for now, do me a favor. Go back and pull your SUV into the garage just as you normally do. Okay?"

Jamie had so many questions. Her father had resided on the fringes of her and her sister's lives for ten years. Like an off-stage whisper, he circled from time to time, but his focus had remained on the hunt for the man who had murdered his wife. They'd all lost so much.

"James, *now* please, before someone sees you doing something different from your normal routine."

Bryce reached down and pulled McKenzie into his arms.

When Jamie parked her SUV in the garage, she took a few deep breaths. She loved her dad and respected the sacrifices he'd made. All of their lives had been impacted by her mom's murder, maybe her dad's most of all.

Once back inside, she walked through her normal routine. Keys, purse, coat... all put away. She checked the dog's bowls, and as suspected, they were full. The dishes, rinsed, were stacked in the sink. Someone had a good dinner tonight.

A bottle of Blanton's sat on the counter. It hadn't come from her liquor cabinet. Next to it was a wine goblet and an open bottle of one her favorite Ravenswood zinfandels. For not being around much, Bryce Taylor knew her better than she thought.

She realized for the first time that a fire was blazing in the fireplace and a Norah Jones CD was playing in the background. A tray of her emergency appetizers from the freezer had been thawed and heated and arranged with care on the table. Two clean plates and cloth napkins sat next to them. Her dogs, which included Shelby until Brian Rawlings' parents arrived to take home this special connection to their son, lay curled together in the warmth of the flames.

"Dad?"

The toilet in the main floor powder room flushed. Jamie shook her head and grabbed the nearly empty tumbler that sat on a coaster. She walked back to the kitchen to pour herself a glass of the zin and replenish his bourbon. Seemed like maybe her father was in a talking mood. She'd listen to what he had to say, stay calm and not ask too many questions. *At least not yet.* The fatigue she had experienced less than twenty minutes ago had melted away. An undercurrent of energy made her alert and focused.

Bryce Taylor walked back to the family room. Jamie watched her dad and realized with a shock how much he had aged. He looked thinner, and the stiffness with which he moved reminded her how much time had passed since they'd last been together. Four years could take a lot out of a person. For sure it had taken a lot out of her dad. He picked up his bourbon and held it toward her for a toast. When she met her glass to his, she noticed the lines that carved deep into his face, emphasized by the shadows thrown by the firelight. A part of her wanted to go someplace and cry.

"You're having an interesting time," he said.

She remembered looking out through the back of her home and seeing her father standing sentinel; the repaired shed. Jamie nodded, but remained quiet.

"Andrew gone?" His voice flowed, soft, gentle, unchanged from when she was a little girl. At least something had remained the same.

"As far as I know."

"Don't be surprised if he turns up again. Bad pennies do."

Again, she nodded.

"And all of this other stuff—the FBI, fresh graves."

"How do you—"

"Not important." He put his drink down on the coaster, then took a few appetizers and put them on a plate. "You sure can cook. You got that from your mom. When we first got married, she didn't know the difference between baste and broil, but she learned fast. I remember... well...." He stared into the fire.

Jamie watched her father and wondered what he had gone through these last ten years. She would never know everything, regardless of how many questions she asked. Her parents had shared a love very few people experience.

191

And look where it landed Dad... alone and bent on his own form of revenge.

Bryce jerked his head to the side, as if mentally throwing off his memories, then turned to face her. "He's here, Jamie. He's back in the same place where he took your mom. I don't have a name yet, but I've got the connection, and I've tracked him right back to Aspen Falls."

CHAPTER FIFTY-ONE

He'd been telling himself no for hours. No more killing until the big moment. What would be the point?

Light from the fire flickered on the polished floor and blended softly on the leather of the chairs adjusted toward the warmth. Angles and clean lines made up the rest of the room, softened by the placement of silk rugs.

The formula was perfected. To use it again would be a waste of time and money. *Except maybe I want to kill again. Maybe I even need to before the main event. Really, what could it hurt?* And if this one was killed in a completely different manner than the others, just a random murder, there could be no connection.

He held his scotch up to the light in front of him and watched the way the gold color bent the shadows. He could control the entire design of the contents by moving his wrist a fraction of an inch. His party.

He rifled through the possibilities in his mind. If he could draw out the moment of death, maybe he'd connect with the human being just about to cease his or her existence. A little brutality might be good for his soul. He'd tried the torture route before, but you never knew about these things.

He imagined different methods he could employ. He hoped for a quickened heartbeat as he vividly pictured what he might do to a body, but nothing happened. He pushed his imagination some more, filling his head with the pain and tears and agonized screams of his victim. He searched his mind, his body, for anything that indicated a human response, but he got only the void he'd always gotten. Even in the moment, he would feel detached.

Still, it was something to do while he waited.

What if I picked someone a little nearer to my own circle, someone whose death would be devastating to people I know? Then I could observe the devastation first hand. He drew up a mental list of candidates and checked them off one by one. *No, too easy. No, not that one either. Her friends were marginal at best.* He considered two men, but rejected them because of the increased danger of exposure. He didn't want to risk not achieving the emotional ejaculation he'd been searching for his entire life. He pulled up one more name, turned her from side to side in his mind, like positioning a mannequin in a store window. He didn't know much about her, but maybe it was enough. *Yes, she's the one.* The woman was at a good point in her life, well loved, and she made a difference in the lives of other people. For her friends to learn she had died a painful death might be worth the effort.

He slid his feet into slippers and moved to the bar to pour himself another drink. He reviewed his choices of music, selected a playlist, then walked back to his chair near the fireplace to continue formulating his plans.

Less than thirty minutes later, he got up and put two more logs on the fire. The wood spit and flared, sending sparks up the chimney and shooting coals onto the planked floor at his feet. He considered it a form of private applause.

Tomorrow night would be perfect.

CHAPTER FIFTY-TWO

An unobstructed view existed between the building he was watching and the parking lot, but to sit and wait in his car would surely draw attention from someone. Better to sit at one of the nearby picnic tables.

People passed back and forth, but no one paid him any attention. Being out in the open meant he had nothing to hide.

It was a good decision not to sit in his car. She must have had a meeting, or some extra work, or something to keep her inside the building longer than usual. He flipped open the magazine he'd brought along, leaned back against the table from the bench and crossed his legs. He smiled at a few of the people who bothered to acknowledge his presence.

Finally she walked out to her car, a briefcase in one hand and a soft drink in the other. He watched as she twisted her wrist to hold the leather satchel and the drink in one hand, slipped the key in the door, then loaded up her front seat. *Such routine movements for someone who doesn't have long to live.*

Fading sunlight glinted off her hair. *She must have taken extra time with it during the day. It doesn't look droopy or frazzled. Maybe she isn't going straight home.* He casually rolled up his magazine and stood. *Might be a long night.*

He slipped into his parked car and tailed her out of the parking lot. He took his time, ready to make a turn if she acted at all suspicious. He enjoyed this part. He'd never stalked a victim before. They'd all just been handy.

But this one. She had been chosen. Not by some random god, but by him. Would he feel something? Would it make a difference that he knew her? A tingling ran up his spine and he waited for more. Nothing. Still, he hadn't actually done anything yet, so he could still hope.

The smell of French fries filled his car from a corner restaurant and he realized he hadn't eaten for hours. Afterward, he'd celebrate and indulge in a huge steak and maybe a small bowl of perfect lobster bisque.

She pulled into the parking lot for E-Lev 2. He thought about the fabulous menu and cursed her for making him wait. He couldn't go in. There was too much risk he'd be recognized. He imagined the fine food being prepared and presented to people who barely had a moment to appreciate its perfection. People who paid entirely too much attention to each other. People who were there to see and be seen. *Cretins.*

He settled in to wait. Part of the intrigue was knowing what was going to happen to her when she didn't have a clue, or at least not a clue she paid attention to.

He pulled out his iPad, found some free WiFi in the area, and logged on to his brokerage account. He placed a series of puts and calls, then took some of his earnings. He bought as much gold as he could, then put the rest in oil. Even though he had plenty of money and financial gain played no part in his ultimate goal, he thought he might as well take advantage of the situation since it was a situation he controlled.

She was leaving the bistro. He signed off and stowed his iPad. After a few blocks he relaxed. She was going home. As long as no one else joined her, his game plan was on.

He parked well away from her house and stepped out of his car. The night air carried a chill and the promise of winter. He pulled the collar of his jacket up and picked up his pace.

Soft light shone in the windows, but there was no outside light. *Good. She isn't expecting anyone.* The front steps announced his presence moments before loud barks came from the fenced back yard.

He rang the bell and stepped back so she could see him at the door when she turned on the lights. *That would be her pattern... a little cautious, on the smart side, but still a person who operated out of basic trust.* She'd open the door for him.

And she did.

He registered the look of surprise on her face. Before she could question him, he said, "I know this is an interruption of your evening, but I really need to talk to you."

She cocked her head to the side, smiled and opened the door wider. "I was just about to pour myself a glass of wine. Would you like one?"

"Thanks. That would be nice." He closed and bolted the door, then followed her deeper into the house.

Two hours later, when he'd grown bored with torturing her and could think of nothing left to do to her, he walked into the kitchen and selected a long, sharp knife. Within moments, he had slashed her throat in a strange smiley-face cut. While blood pulsed into the air, then slowed to a dribble, he cleaned up. No fingerprints, no obvious DNA, none of her blood on the clothing he'd worn under the travel-raincoat he'd stashed in a pocket and which he would dispose of before he went home.

He posed the body in what he thought was an

interesting configuration, did a thorough walk-through, turned off the lights, then left, leaving the door wide open. He wanted her found sooner rather than later.

CHAPTER FIFTY-THREE

Jamie's house once again filled with people, quiet and absorbed. They spoke in hushed sentences, as if a normal tone of voice would be disrespectful. A normal voice would call attention to the speaker and damage the equilibrium everyone was fighting to maintain.

People moved in whispers. Doors opened and closed, opened and closed. The sound of hugs was carried on each little rush of air.

Ciara's training, which incorporated graceful gestures, allowed the model to reposition from greeter to server to hugger, yet remain within the muted protocol. She acknowledged everyone who entered, shared their grief, and morphed into the next required role. She performed the necessary tasks, but her eyes were vacant. She grieved, but at the bottom of it all, she was a professional.

Jamie sat, pulled into herself in the corner of the couch, and registered everything in a vague sort of way. Reality was yesterday, not this. Today was some sort of a kick-in-the-gut, badass dream, and like many dreams, this one didn't make any sense.

Ellen? Tortured and then murdered? It was beyond any nightmare. It was the corroded, fetid underbelly of some monster in another world. It couldn't be true. She wanted to wake up.

She thought about the new love she'd seen in Ellen's eyes. They'd been lit with a kind of promise. She remembered the times she'd seen her friend in action in a classroom. Put the naturally reticent woman in front of a group of inquiring minds and she turned into a force to be reckoned with.

Fresh tears spilled onto Jamie's cheeks and she needed to blow her nose. Arnold was around here somewhere. She should probably go find him. But the minute his name floated into her mind, it floated out again, replaced by memories and loss.

Teague knelt at her feet. "Is there anything I can get you?"

She cried a little more at the thought of his concern. He had been with her when she received the news. He had made the call to Ciara, and he had talked to Ellen's parents in Iowa, her brother in Colorado Springs, and Ellen's principal, Irma Moses. *Irma's here now, somewhere.*

Glad to have Teague's support, she could do with a little less hovering. He was holding her, watching over her to make sure she made it through this horrible, life-changing event. Even when he wasn't right next to her, she could feel him watching her.

"I'm okay, thanks. Could you try to find Mrs. Moses and talk to her? Maybe set up a time when we can get together? She'll want to set up some kind of memorial for the kids. I want to be a part of that."

He squeezed her hand. "I'm on it. But if you need me back here, all you have to do is call."

Jamie almost laughed. She sank deeper into the corner of the couch. *How could anything ever have the same meaning it had before?*

She watched as Arnold Abner slouched over to sit by himself on a barstool in the kitchen. Her heart went out to the FBI agent. No one knew what to say to him. Shoulders drooped, head hung low, he clearly didn't care.

Nicholas Grant pulled up another stool and positioned it mere inches from the grieving man. He didn't touch Arnold or speak. He just sat on the stool, eyes hooded and hands clasped.

McKenzie shifted on her lap, steady and there for her, willing to soak up some of her heartache if only she'd let him. She absent-mindedly stroked his fur. Socks made the rounds looking for dropped food items of any kind. He loved people, but treats, especially unplanned treats, were something to revel in. Hank and Shelby lay together by the fireplace, looking sad and lost. *Where's Gretchen?*

Ciara came and sat with her. Usually brilliantly lit both inside and out, she sat in a kind of dullness. Jamie reached for her hand.

"Please," Ciara said. "Please give me something to do."

Jamie pulled Ciara close. The grief Jamie felt loomed bigger than anything even she and Ciara had shared. She squeezed the woman's hand. "I haven't seen Gretchen. I think she must be out back. Would you please find her and bring her to me?"

Jamie watched her friend make her way to the back door. She closed her eyes. Removed herself from the circle of people who had formed their own shape of sorrow and her own grieving body. She removed herself from thought.

Someone touched her shoulder. Teague. He moved a pillow on the sofa so he could sit close to her. "Can I get you anything?"

"No. Thank you. Ciara went to find Gretchen. I kind of need my dogs around me." A moment passed, and Jamie felt bad. "And you too, of course."

"Of course."

The door opened and closed in the rear of the house. Cool air rushed over Jamie as Ciara walked in. "Hey,

Honey, Gretchen won't come for me. She's well into some scent by your moss rock."

"That's okay. I'll go get her in a few minutes. I could use some fresh air anyway." Jamie stretched her lips in what she hoped would pass for a smile.

Nick and Arnold Abner left, neither saying a word, but Nick had given her a look that unsettled her, even in the midst of despair. She felt a strange kind of embrace from his gaze, one that infused her with the certainty of what Ellen would have wanted. *Forward steps. Don't wallow.*

Irma Moses was standing at the sink rinsing the dishes as fast as they piled up. Ciara was loading up trash bags and Teague was pulling the drawstrings taut, ready to go to the bear-proof garbage bins in the garage.

Irma folded the dishcloth and approached Jamie, who was still sitting on the sofa. "Honey, I'm heading home." Irma leaned over and hugged her. "Can I do anything else for you before I go?"

"I'm fine. Thank you for everything. I'll see you next week to make plans for the school memorial."

Ciara came into the room next and settled in as close as possible. She reached an arm around Jamie and they both pushed back into the cushions.

"I have to leave for Santa Fe tomorrow morning. If there was any way I could get out of this contract I would but—"

"Don't worry about it. I know you don't have any choice. And you'll be home in a few days. You just get home and get some rest. It's what Ellen would want."

Ciara nodded, then gave her one last hug and walked out.

Jamie had never felt so alone, even with Teague in the kitchen.

CHAPTER FIFTY-FOUR

Jax shoved her key into the lock. She didn't want to be in her lab this afternoon, but she had paperwork to do. Before she left Jamie's, they had made plans to get together later. She didn't want to go home, either. That would mean Phil, and she wasn't interested in dealing with that element at the moment.

The cleanup from the vandalism revealed that it had been more form than substance. No major damage, just a huge mess. Whoever wrecked the lab had used stuff from the employee refrigerator. All of the collected evidence remained locked up and secure; the equipment not as damaged as she'd feared.

Maybe some results had come in. She didn't expect them to tell her much, but they represented one more step in the process. Some cases, like the recent ones here in Aspen Falls, only got answers through the process of elimination. Other cases never reached a satisfactory conclusion.

Some tea would settle her and help her focus. She grabbed a mug, filled it with water and stuck it in the microwave, then pulled one of her favorite teas out of her personal stash: Mighty Leaf's Chamomile Citron. A few minutes later, she was savoring the aroma. It would be better with a proper kettle and all the traditional hoopla, but the county wouldn't give her a stovetop to work with.

In her office, she tossed her coat and purse on an unopened box of supplies sitting in the corner. As she swung her chair around, she grabbed files from her inbox and sat down heavily, a sigh escaping her lips. She checked her computer to see whether any of the tests had come in. None had. She opened the file on top and started to read, then dropped her head into her hands, her fingers pressed against her scalp.

Ellen had been murdered. That was bad enough, but she had endured torture and pure horror before dying.

An ME was coming up from Denver to do the autopsy. Jax would be in the room to assure herself the Denver ME was thorough.

She pushed her hair back from her face and focused on the file in front of her. If Jax could just get through a little paperwork, she could leave and get back with her friends. *Focus.*

Her private line screamed into the silent office. She took a moment before she answered. "Taylor."

"Dr. Taylor, it's Scott Ortiz. I've been trying to get hold of you for hours."

Why would the local vet need to talk to me?

"First, let me extend my condolences. I heard about Ellen Grimes. I know she's... well, was a friend of yours."

She nodded, then realized she needed to provide a verbal response. "Thank you."

"I know this isn't a good time, but I've discovered something you should know."

"Go ahead." *What in the world would a vet have discovered that an ME should know? Unless Phil's gone and done something stupid, like giving steroids or a cocaine derivative to racehorses.* She shook her head. *I really am tired.*

"I'm aware that several people have died recently of

unknown causes and—"

"I don't know what you're talking about, Dr. Ortiz."

"Please, it's Scott. And Aspen Falls is a small town, with a tight-knit professional community."

She took a sip of her tea.

"Don't worry, Dr. Taylor. I found out about the apparent murders from official sources and I haven't spoken about them to anyone else."

"I appreciate that. And it's Jax."

"Okay, Jax. Here's the thing." He paused as if gathering his thoughts. "People started bringing me carcasses of wild animals a few weeks ago. It's unusual to see so many dead animals with no sign of plague or trauma, so I decided to run autopsies."

"Autopsies are expensive."

"Tell me about it. My bank account might never recover. But I needed to know what was going on. Most of the animals that were brought to me were too decomposed to get good tissue samples for analysis, but the more recent ones weren't."

"And?"

"Most of the animals were emaciated, with little to no food in their stomachs—"

"That can be explained by a lot of things."

"Agreed. But some also presented with evidence of respiratory problems and others had brain lesions."

"I'm listening." She had seen a slight indication of respiratory issues in the bodies she'd examined, but nothing conclusive. Asphyxiation had played a role in the last two victim's deaths.

"I retrieved enough good tissue samples on the last three rabbits and one fox to run tests. I think I've discovered what killed them." He paused. "I know this is going to sound crazy, and you're the first person I've spoken to about this. I guess I need to get some kind of corroboration that I haven't dived off the shallow end of the pool, which at this moment sounds much more feasible than what I'm about to tell you." He took a deep breath. "I tested for toxins, and saxitoxin came up the winner."

"Saxitoxin? As in Red Tide? In Colorado?"

"Every one of the last four animals tested positive for it. There is no doubt."

"But how? And why?"

"Your guess is as good as mine, but if you think there might be a connection between the animal deaths and your current cases, we need to tell Sheriff Coble."

She sensed that he wasn't finished. "What else, Scott?"

He cleared his throat. "As a precaution against animal-borne diseases and illnesses, my policy has always been to request the location of each dead animal brought to my clinic, whether by an individual or by the county. Sometimes the individuals have to guess, but the county crews know I want the information and they're very good at making a note. The thing is, although some of the animals were in scattered locations, a significant number came from one particular area. It's not very populated, but the homes there are priced in the high end of the stratosphere... like fifteen million and up."

"Where?" Even in Aspen Falls, that price tag carried some weight. Of course, just because there seemed to be a concentration of animal deaths in one particular area, it didn't necessarily connect. The political fallout could be huge. "How many homes are we talking about in the area?"

"No more than four."

"You need to get with the sheriff on this *now*. I'll come in when you need me."

"So you don't think I'm some kind of crazy conspiracy nut?"

"You might be a conspiracy nut, Scott, but as far as this case is concerned I'm as much of a pecan as the next guy."

"I'll take it to Coble and for your information I'll fax you the list of homeowners in the area with the highest number of dead animals."

"Good. Send your autopsy results too, the ones where you confirmed saxitoxin."

"Sending them now."

Two minutes later, she was standing in front of the fax machine gathering the papers as they came out. She took the stack of information to her desk and sat down to take a quick look.

When she got to the listing of homeowners near what she now thought of as Ground Zero, she recognized the first name, a well-known Hollywood celebrity with more money than brains. Her gaze travelled down the list.

She stopped, shocked, at one that came a lot closer to home. *Interesting.*

Jax trusted that Scott would have called Sheriff Coble right after sending her the fax. She forwarded it on with a note. The personal connection of that one name unsettled her. Her paperwork could wait a little longer.

CHAPTER FIFTY-FIVE

There are different kinds of stillness.

There's the stillness after sex with someone you love, in which the intense emotional connection lingers with softened edges and amazing mental images.

There's the stillness after a party, in which a hint of sparkle and laughter remains in the air. It's the stillness of friendship and tomorrow's promise.

Then there's the stillness after people gather to mourn, in which the depth of emotion leads in another direction, to a place where everyone is alone. Grief is a place, even in the most lush surroundings, that is solitary. There is nothing but the loss. Jamie longed to go there, to touch her loss and make it familiar, to begin to understand so she could live through it. She needed to feel Ellen's love envelope her so she could find the strength to breathe again.

But Teague was right there. "I want you to come home with me for tonight."

"I'm fine, Teague. Really, this is where I want to be."

He shook his head. "Not good enough. Your friend was murdered. Who's to say you won't be next? Get a friend or a neighbor to take care of the dogs. You're coming with me."

She sighed. "Okay." She grabbed her coat and scarf.

"I'll call Irma and ask her to come and get the dogs for the night." As an afterthought, she walked to her desk and left a note for Jax. They'd planned to get together later.

Jamie made arrangements with Irma, whose home had more than enough square footage to handle the five dogs for one night. She pulled out some dog food that Irma would be sure to see when she came by to round up her guests. Jamie tugged on both her coat and scarf and went into the back to find Gretchen and get her in. Her heart buoyed at the sight of the golden.

"We're all going for sleepovers tonight, Gretch, but I'll see you tomorrow." Gretchen loped into the house ahead of Jamie.

Tail in the air, the beautiful animal went in search of her comrades after first checking to see whether there was anything interesting in her food bowl. Jamie followed close behind.

Gretchen suddenly stopped in front of her. Her tail dropped and she turned to Jamie with a confused look in her eye. Then she walked with purpose over to Teague and lay flat on the floor, her alert posture.

Of course, Teague didn't notice, but Jamie did.

Gretchen had alerted at the feet of the man Jamie had begun to think might be her life partner, her soul mate. She set aside her time for grieving. She needed to think. Even though she knew better, she tried to construct a plausible scenario that would cause Gretchen to register death, to alert as she had. *Where could Teague have been in the last few hours that would generate Gretchen's alert? Where could he have come in contact with decaying tissue?* She could think of only one answer.

The tiniest smile split Teague's face.

Jamie went into the family room and sat on the sofa, too terrified to move, still wearing her coat and scarf. She and Teague were alone. As much as she wished for other people to be around at this moment, at least the situation would not jeopardize the lives of others. If she could avoid it, she'd just as soon it would not jeopardize her own either.

Teague Blanton was at least peripherally involved in the death of one her dearest friends. An hour ago there would have been no question. Jamie would have been grateful for Teague's protective stance, and she would have been foolish. Now, every word, every gesture, became critical.

She tried to push the truth away from her mind, to reject it as too horrific to be real. *It simply can't be Teague.* But in her heart she knew.

There are different kinds of stillness, but deception wasn't really still. Deceit swirled, dipped, moved just beyond reach, threatened to erupt through the floorboards to expose her. She'd always been terrible at hiding things from others.

But Teague's deceit lay low to the floor, like fog. His deceit was subtle, sinister. Jamie shivered. *Does he know what I learned from Gretchen's alerting at his feet? Maybe he thinks Gretchen just laid down in front of him.* She listened as Teague turned on the dishwasher and closed some cupboard doors. His next move would be to come to her.

She closed her eyes and forced herself to slump deeper into the cushions. She listened as he paused in the space between the kitchen and the family room. She sidled against the padded arm of her sofa, feeling his gaze as he evaluated her, watching for any sign of awareness. She steeled herself. He would make his own decision soon. She would call the sheriff when he left.

She smelled him as he got closer to her, the heat from his skin on hers. The cushion that had been her home for the last several hours dipped with his weight. She wanted

to throw up.
Something pricked her neck.

CHAPTER FIFTY-SIX

Jax turned over the conversation with Scott Ortiz in her mind as she drove to her sister's house. There had to be a correlation between the animal deaths and the murders. *But saxitoxin?*

Red Tide, from which biotoxins are produced, including the daddy of them all, saxitoxin, is a naturally occurring algal bloom, but it's found primarily in large bodies of water like the Gulf of Mexico. *How the heck did it get to Aspen Falls?*

Assuming she and Scott were on to the *what* and test results on the recent victims confirmed it, the question became *who* and then *why? Why would some sicko use a biological weapon to kill people? Were they targeted or chosen at random? Is it something more?* She checked her rearview mirror and punched in her sister's speed-dial.

Jamie didn't answer her phone. *Dammit.* Jax prayed it was because Jamie had unplugged it for some rest, or maybe that she and Ciara had gone to get something to eat. *But we'd planned on getting together. Jamie wouldn't have gone off with Ciara without calling.* Jax double-checked her messages. Nothing from Jamie.

She pulled onto the long drive, turned off the engine and checked the sheet of addresses again. *How coincidental that this guy should live at Ground Zero. Under different circumstances, Jamie would get a kick out of it.* She opened her car door and the silence tickled her anxiety button. *Where are the dogs?* She also thought one or two mourners might have stuck around so Jamie wouldn't be alone. She walked up to her sister's front door, her footsteps sounding loud and measured in the quiet. The door was unlocked. It wasn't unusual, but it bothered Jax anyway.

"Jamie?" The silence seemed to answer her back.

Jax called her sister's name a couple more times. No response. No Jamie. No dogs.

She walked farther into the house.

The dishwasher in the kitchen indicated a clean load. Jax checked the coffee pot. It was filled with Jamie's French Roast and ready to go. She walked over to the desk and saw a note on Jamie's stationery laying attached to the granite counter. *Irma has the dogs. Gone to Teague's. Will wait for you there. Don't go to bed before we can talk.* Jamie had written down the address and basic directions.

Jax compared addresses. *The same. And Irma Moses has the dogs.* Okay. That explains their absence. *Why didn't Jamie just take the dogs with her to Teague's? Or leave them here?*

"Hello, Jax." The voice was deep, penetrating. He was so confident that he didn't need to repeat himself.

She couldn't move.

"I was disappointed, but not surprised, that you decided not to play the game with me."

Play the game? What's he talking about? Oh, shit! The two hundred thousand dollar bribe to delay the toxicology tests! Oh, God! Jax gripped both her address list and the note from Jamie as if they would keep her safe.

213

"Your husband played, and he accepted a much smaller sum to play with me. But then, your lab is still functional, isn't it? I guess one gets what one pays for."

The lab? My lab! Phil!

"You're looking for your sister. I can take you to her." His voice was clear, concise, promising.

Jax moved toward the voice, her arms raised in an instinctive self-defense posture. She felt a pinch in the back of her neck, and things shivered a bit before they went gray.

"Just relax. My plane is waiting."

Chapter Fifty-Seven

He had already moved Jamie from his home in Aspen Falls. She had required some additional medication for the transfer, but it couldn't be helped. The new location would be a lot more interesting, a lot more functional, and a lot more convenient for him over the next seventy-two hours.

The old Mile High Stadium, where Bronco games were sold out every fall and winter, had a neighbor the television networks rarely ever mentioned: a hotel high enough that anyone on the upper floor could look out over the football games. The rooms were renowned for their football day parties, even though only a small fraction of the attendees ever actually watched the action in the stadium.

When the new stadium was built, he'd held the rights to some property north of the sports arena. The city and the Bronco organization had tried to push their agenda on him, making sure he could build only so many stories, but he had pushed back. Consequently, he'd been grandfathered and was now in the process of building a structure that would once again overlook the gridiron battles. His concession was to promise in writing and in perpetuity that the building, including the higher floors, would be used only for business purposes from nine-to-five on Monday through Friday. Absolutely no one, including cleaning staff, could ever occupy the upper floors during a Bronco game.

The frame of the building had been erected and the first two floors completed, and there were enclosed portions on each of the other floors to store equipment and supplies. He'd secured Jamie in one of them before he had flown back to Aspen Falls.

An expanded plan had more potential, and his plan had expanded significantly.

Jacqueline Taylor was a huge acquisition. He'd be able to play with their genuine emotions for a bit. He could try to experience what the death of a sibling meant to someone who really cared.

He drove around the back of his building to the loading dock where his construction crew received deliveries. He'd used a flatbed dolly from the dock to move Jamie, and it was still there. He grunted as he hoisted Jax's drugged body onto her wheeled chariot.

Everything was coming together, and with bonuses. His months—years really—of planning were about to pay off. He almost experienced some kind of genuine emotion. *Pride? Excitement?* He shook his head. *Not quite there.*

Teague Blanton dumped Jacqueline like a sack of potatoes in the storage shed next to her sister. He pulled out a roll of duct tape and secured her ankles and wrists. He ran it twice around her face to cover her mouth, then pushed her over. Her head thudded a little on the concrete, but it was nothing to be concerned about.

He still needed to move the equipment into place for his Sunday launch. He hadn't wanted to set up too early, but with each passing day, the risk of discovery lessened, especially since he'd given his entire crew a few days off with pay. It was hunting season, so no one questioned a thing.

The trailer he'd towed behind him three days ago from Aspen Falls held everything he required. He'd make as many of his preparations as possible now, then come back after dinner to have a little fun with the ladies. He had plenty of time.

Tonight, he'd have a special, late-night, pre-celebration dinner at Elway's. His luxury suite at the Ritz-Carlton, the big one this time, was secured. Sunday afternoon the entire city, even the nation, would be forever changed.

He wondered whether he would be changed as well.

CHAPTER FIFTY-EIGHT

Jamie worked at her duct tape restraints with a carpenters nail she'd found wedged between a supply box and the wall of the shed. After jabbing her wrist enough to draw blood, she finally figured out a kind of punch-saw motion that, at least in her imagination, seemed to be doing the trick.

She didn't want any more drugs pumped into her system, so she faked more drowsiness than she felt whenever Teague came around, but he'd been gone for quite a while.

Jamie figured she was somewhere in Denver. They hadn't been in the air long enough to be out of the state. She was in a large empty building or a warehouse of some kind. Nothing cushioned sounds and she smelled metal, like tools and grease.

There was loud traffic, then silence, then traffic again. *A busy city street with stoplights.* She didn't think it could be the Springs, either. The traffic never entirely let up here like it still did in Colorado Springs. At least it hadn't in the last several hours.

Who was this man she'd imagined might be the one? She remembered his smile and the charm and the respect she thought she'd read in him when they'd first met, as well as the flattering attention he'd lavished on her. *What a fool I am.*

Tears propelled out of her eyes and the cloth blindfold grew damp. She needed to blow her nose. Another strip of fabric was pressed against her mouth, stretching her lips into a painful shape. She'd at least been able to work the bit of cloth stuffed in her mouth to a place where she could breathe even though her nose was clogged.

Other than the obvious involvement Teague Blanton had in Ellen's torture and murder, there must be some reason he had taken her to hold her captive. *Why in Denver? And why didn't he just kill me?*

Finally freed, Jamie's hands fell to her sides. Pain shot up both arms to her shoulders. Her wrists throbbed and she brought them in front of her to rub some life back into them. Sweat trickled down her sides. Her coat felt bulky.

How long have I been tied up? Gray light filtered through the blindfold and she inched it up over her right eye just enough to see her surroundings. She closed her eye against the glare. Set her fingers to loosening the grip on the gag covering her mouth. She didn't want to over-loosen either of them unless she knew she could get away. She needed to either be gone when Blanton returned or have surprise on her side.

She heard someone approaching. Something thudded to the floor. A padlock unlatched, chains clanked, and the shed door pulled open.

Jamie lay in the corner, her back against the wall, her hands behind her. *Need to move a little. He'll know I can't still be out.* She moaned, then fell still. She forced herself to keep her body slack even as she focused on what she could hear.

There were no words, just his breathing and a small grunt as he hauled something across the floor, something new and heavy to join her. The hairs on the back of her neck and along her arms stiffened. The body of a person had settled next to her. Dead or alive, she couldn't tell.

The door to the shed closed and the padlock snapped closed. She pulled her hands from behind her and pushed her blindfold out of the way. *Oh, God, no! Jax! No, no, no, no!*

Jamie moved to undo the restraints that bound her sister. Her mouth. Her eyes. Finally, her hands and feet. It took a long time. She fought not to rip the restraints from Jax's body. Each one of them was an assault against Jamie for believing in the wrong man one more time and pulling her sister into something that might cost both of them their lives.

CHAPTER FIFTY-NINE

Only after she'd freed Jax of every bit of duct tape and the gag did Jamie concentrate on the rest of her own, her mind scrambling to consider their next step. *We have to get out of here.*

The first issue was to break the lock on the door holding them in. After she released the last of her own bindings, she tested the door. It gave a little, but not much. She pressed her back against the wall furthest away from the padlocked door. She closed her eyes, shot off a prayer and bolted for the barrier, digging deep with her right shoulder. The aftermath resulted in a rattling-thunder sound no one nearby could have missed. She hoped that Blanton was far enough away that he hadn't heard it.

Blood was dripping from her wrist to the floor of their cell.

Jamie backed against the wall one more time, then sprinted hard. The door warped. Enough room to work with. She brought out the carpenter's nail, and morphed into lock-pick mode. After a minute or two, Jamie checked Jax's pockets and pulled out the ME Security Card that allowed her access to the building and her lab. She began to work the two. Ten minutes later, she and Jax were still trapped. She had never felt so all alone, responsible and unequipped.

Jamie pushed herself. She cursed the movies she'd seen that had made this look easy. Jax's security card snapped in two, the larger piece flipping through the slotted opening. *Damn.* She pinched hard on the remaining small piece of the card in her left hand while she maneuvered the nail with her right.

Something clicked. The door bumped open with an enormous clang, then stopped. A chain link and lock had pulled tight.

Jamie focused on the next step. She'd gotten this far.

She pulled the door to get some slack in the chain and prayed hard the sound hadn't carried to wherever Blanton had gone. Her clenched heart pounded against her chest as she fingered the padlock to slip it from the chain. Twice she lost her hold on it and twice it came close to locking up again.

With the calmness of a surgeon, she pulled her hand away from the lock, swallowed and took a deep breath. She clenched then spread her fingers in a yoga move she'd heard about. *Starfish. Relax. Starfish. Do this.*

This time, her fingers moved through the opening like they'd been greased. Steady—her wrist remained limber. And she lifted the lock, palmed the chain, and carefully pulled it through. *Freedom.* Now to deal with her sad sack of a sister.

"Jax?" She knelt before the deadweight and turned her sister's face so she could see it. "Jax? C'mon, girl. Wake up."

Nothing.

Jamie put her hands under Jax's armpits and hauled. The first couple of seconds were hard, but she finally got both traction and momentum. She pulled her sister out of the shed and onto the open floor of a building under construction.

She laid her sister down, then went back to close the door and reattach both the chain and the lock, careful to pick up the larger part of the plastic card that had fallen through. Jamie could only hope she put it together the way Blanton had left it. *What if he counted the links or something? No telling with the kind of crazy we're up against.* The padlock snapped into place.

She dragged Jax behind a huge pile of drywall. She whispered, "Jax? Jacqueline Angelique Taylor, wake up!" She popped her sister's cheeks with her palms. "Wake up! You need to wake up!" Tears spilled from Jamie's eyes. "You need to wake up *now!*"

Jax moved her head, then slid back under whatever blanket the drug had covered her with.

Jamie pinched her sister's arm. "You cannot *do* this! Wake up, Jax! I need you to be *awake!*" *What the hell am I doing?* Jamie knew how to work with her dogs. She knew the secret of good risotto. She knew how to put a loan package together. She knew how to clear a clogged drain, change engine oil, and even replace roofing tiles. She had absolutely no idea how to get away from a mad man.

Jax stirred and opened her eyes.

Jamie started, then stared. "C'mon, Jax! We need to boogie!"

Jax laughed. "Boogie?"

"Cut it out. We need to go, and without making any noise."

"Go where?"

Okay. Between a drunk-acting sister or a dead-acting sister, I'll take the drunk. "Good question. Do you think you can walk? Run if we have to?"

"Yeah. Let's boogie."

Jax took off, heading back toward the storage shed.

Jamie caught her and grabbed her hand. "This way."

223

Jamie kept a tight hold of Jax's hand and they sprinted for what Jamie thought was the back of the building, looking for any kind of escape. The sunlight had shifted in the last few minutes. Darkness would not help them in a building that was under construction and that they knew nothing about. "There... a freight elevator." She pointed and Jax nodded. They ran between steel studs that marked where walls would one day be erected. Even in her haste, Jamie noticed the bird's-eye view of Sports Authority Field.

Twenty feet before the elevator, Jax stumbled and fell.

Jamie helped her up. "Are you okay?"

"Fine. Just banged my knee."

Jamie thought, *More trace evidence just in case.* They had to use whatever they had, and right now, skin cells just might be at the top of the list.

The freight elevator made a rattling sound as it roared to life.

CHAPTER SIXTY

"The stairs." Jamie pointed toward a corner of the building. "Quick."

The freight elevator rumbled, getting louder.

They slipped into a dark stairway and stood, fighting to control their breathing. Jamie wished they could see, but she didn't dare open the door even a crack. Instead, she tried to see with her ears, an old trick her dad taught her when they went camping. She closed her eyes and listened.

The elevator jerked to a stop and the doors slid open. She heard a loud tap, but the doors didn't close. Someone had pushed the button to hold them open.

Jax grabbed at Jamie in the darkness.

Jamie held her sister's arms and squeezed. "Shhh." She focused her concentration back to what was happening in front of the elevator.

Someone rolled out a four-wheel cart. It bumped over the space between the elevator and the building floor. She heard boxes being shifted, a low grunt, and what sounded like a dolly joined the cart. Finally, two soft *thunks*, like duffel bags landed, another loud tap, and she heard the doors slide closed.

It had to be Blanton, and he was alone. She listened as he hefted something, probably one of the duffels, and began to whistle as he walked away.

Jax began to pull her down the stairs, but Jamie wanted to wait a few seconds longer and try to get a look at whatever Blanton had felt necessary to haul up to this floor by himself.

She leaned close to her sister's ear. "Go slow. I'll catch up."

Jax nodded and for the first time since they'd gotten out of the shed, physical contact stopped. Jamie moved closer to the door of the stairwell and nudged it open. The sound of the Blanton's whistling grew louder.

Jamie scanned the items on the cart and tried to read the labels on the three boxes stacked on a dolly, not understanding what she saw, but feeling certain someone else would. She eased the door closed and moved down the stairs toward her sister.

"Jax?" Jamie whispered for her sister. "Jax?"

Jamie's eyes were either beginning to adjust to the pitch dark or she imagined they were when her foot hit something soft and she reached out, blind as a ghost fish.

Another body broke her impact on the landing. *Warm. Jax? Who else would it be?* Jamie knelt and ran her hands over the heap on the floor. *Sticky blood! Okay, okay. Calm down. Head wounds bleed a lot, and not all head wounds are fatal head wounds.* She felt Jax's head and couldn't feel any major cuts. "Jax, listen to me. I need you to stand up. Can you stand?" Jamie grasped under her sister's arms and pulled.

Jax moaned.

"C'mon girl. Up. Help me."

"How, um... "

Jax pulled her arms away and pushed herself to a kneeling position while Jamie steadied both of them.

"You've hit your head. I don't think it's bad, but Honey, we don't have time to deal with it now." Jamie held a firm arm while Jax stood and straightened.

With clarity and force, Jax said, "Let's go.".

Jamie had never loved her sister more.

After they'd hit a few more landings, Jax began to lag. "How many more floors do we have, do you think?"

Jamie figured they had been between fifteen and twenty stories up when they'd begun their descent, but she couldn't tell her sister. "One or two, I think. Maybe three. We can do this."

Less than three minutes later, Jamie had to support Jax and drag her down the steps. She had to rest at every floor landing and massage her arms. She pushed aside the temptation to check her sister's head wound at every stop. *Nothing I can do about it right now anyway.*

The darkness became a blanket. Security. Her steps stayed sure and regular, even as her arms quivered under the strain.

When they finally reached the ground floor, Jamie dropped to the cement and leaned her back against the concrete wall. Harsh breaths, spaghetti limbs and fear were the only things holding her up. She sat in the dark and tried to think. *If Blanton went back to the storage shed, he knows we escaped, but I haven't heard the freight elevator.* Maybe he'd been moving his supplies to a different location on the open floor of the building, and hadn't yet gone back to the small unit in which he'd held them captive.

She arched her neck to try to push out the tension. She forced her arms to stretch. *God, I want to cry... be with my dogs... light a fire... talk to Ellen.*

She tried to put together their next move. Once they got outside the building, then what? She didn't even know where they were.

Up the stairwell—how far she couldn't tell—Jamie heard a whistle.

CHAPTER SIXTY-ONE

Jamie cracked open the door leading outside to let in a little light. She looked around quickly, trying to determine where they were. A sign on a closed door about ten feet from theirs read *Fire Command Center. Must be in the back of the building.* She found a rock to wedge the door open, then turned her attention to Jax. "C'mon, now. Let's get this show back on the road." Tears were rolling down Jamie's cheeks. She had used up everything in her arsenal to get them this far. She didn't have anything left.

Somewhere out there, safety beckoned, or at least a chance at safety, but Jax remained unresponsive and Jamie would not leave her sister.

The whistling continued, but louder.

Jamie pushed the door open wide, moving the rock to hold the weight. She grasped Jax's hands and pulled, leaning backwards out the door. One step. Two. Another. Another. Almost cleared now.

How far could she hope to get this way, a few inches at a time, getting weaker with each step? Any minute now, Blanton would appear in the doorway and it would all be over.

Jax pulled her arms. "Stop."

Jamie kept tugging.

"Stop. You're hurting me!"

228

A scream began in Jamie's gut and unfurled like some gigantic sail inside her. She punched it back down to a manageable size and continued pulling her sister to safety.

"Jamie. Stop. Let me try to walk."

Jamie dropped her hold on Jax and fell to her knees. Jax faced her, mirroring her position. Jamie put her arms around her sister and hugged her, then checked her head wound.

"You're not bleeding very much anymore. Are you dizzy?"

Jax shook her head. "I'm leaving Phil."

"It's about time. But for right now, we're going to move. I know you can do this. There's nothing but houses on this side of the building, but I heard a lot of stop and go traffic, and where there's stop and go, there has to be a lot of people. We'll get help."

On their feet, arms around one another like marionettes in a macabre dance, they limped across the parking lot. They stayed away from the building and in the dark perimeter.

Twice, Jax went down. Twice, Jamie got her back up. Words of encouragement sugared the air each time. The traffic noise became louder, its promise of safety wrapped in the roar of engines and smell of exhaust. She saw a Denny's sign high in the sky, and the unmistakable outline of Sports Authority Field, the Bronco's home stadium.

Jamie squeezed Jax's arm and hissed, "Stop!"

The sisters froze, then stooped as if to burrow into the darkness.

Their breathing seemed explosive to Jamie, even against the sounds from the busy street, and she fought to calm hers. She strained to both listen and see into the distance.

Eyes stared in her direction with an otherworld glow. A cat decided the two humans weren't of much interest and moved on into the growing shadows.

Jamie sighed. "Sorry. A little jumpy, I guess."

"I'm good with jumpy."

Quiet giggles softened the night and they moved on, dodging around the odd car left overnight in the parking lot. Or maybe they belonged to construction workers who were working late. Jamie and Jax skirted past an Aston Martin DBS. Who would leave such an expensive car parked anywhere other than under a light? At the very least, Jamie would put out traffic cones to keep anyone from getting close to it.

Ten feet past the luxury sports car, a soft click sounded. Then a whistle. "Ladies, please. Don't leave on my account."

CHAPTER SIXTY-TWO

Blanton was leaning against the car door, but he was anything but relaxed. It was as if he were playing a role. What she noticed most was the gun pointed in their direction.

"Teague, just let us go. As far as we know, you haven't really done anything wrong."

"It all depends on your definition. I'm pretty sure most people would consider murder wrong."

Jamie had trouble catching her breath. *Will he shoot us out here? Now?* Probably not, but the traffic noise was so loud, people would just think a car had backfired. "Sure, Teague. I agree with you, but the only thing Jax and I know for a fact is that you kidnapped us. It could be some kind of prank... a joke."

"Well, so let's be clear. I'm responsible for a lot of deaths." He gestured with the gun, and when they didn't move right away, he said, "Including Ellen's. Now move."

Jamie's anger seemed to stretch her skin. She would gladly risk a bullet to attack Blanton and draw blood, but Jax was injured and still a little drugged.

Her jaw clenched, hands ready to fight, Jamie turned her back on the man she had been close to falling in love with and marched back to the high rise construction. She waited a split second to make sure her sister was following her.

Jamie's mind bumped wild with questions, and a flash of inspiration hit her as they walked back toward their prison. She tracked backward rather than her natural inclination to track forward. If someone pieced together anything at all in Aspen Falls, maybe found the scarf she'd left behind at Blanton's, they could be on their way to Denver, presumably with more than one potential target area where they could be found. She prayed they would bring some dogs.

Jamie tripped and fell, hard. She scraped both knees on the asphalt as well as an elbow and the palm of one hand. The sting and burn gave her hope. *Blood and skin... things dogs would understand.* It wasn't much, but it was the best she could come up with at the moment.

CHAPTER SIXTY-THREE

Nick directed a team around to the back of the house. The perimeter was in place, the only vulnerable area the rear exits that led to the national forest.

The process of elimination had led them to this house. After Scott Ortiz, the local vet, met with Jerry Coble regarding his findings, things kicked into high gear. A biological threat, especially one like saxitoxin, warranted swift action. Homeland Security had come through with all of the warrants they needed and had covered all four homes.

The three other homes had been cleared. One owned by a Hollywood celebrity turned up empty, literally. Another, owned by a European finance guy, was still sealed tight until ski season. He wasn't exactly happy to be contacted in his London office by the FBI, but a call to his caretaker enabled them to do a quick search of his property. Other than a weird proclivity toward enormous statues of men with erections large enough to lift small buildings, they found nothing. The third home turned up a New York Times bestselling author. She was so completely engaged in her manuscript that the team had entered her property, cleared it room by room, and finally found her working away at her computer, naked, noise canceling headphones clamped to her head. Nick guessed that the shock of finding three assault rifles trained on her would somehow find its way into one of her books.

So here they were, at house number four, prepared for battle. The HazMat team was on stand-by as they had been through the last three searches.

Nick readied his mike to give the signal to the sheriff's deputies behind the house, held his right hand high in the air and took a controlled breath.

"Now!" He slammed the hand down and all hell broke loose. Controlled hell, but still enough heat and energy to bring whomever might be inside to their knees, hopefully without any weapons in their hands.

Nick's back cried out with a phantom pain. *An oxy or six would be good right about now.* He pushed through the need and focused. Lives were at stake, including his own.

"Clear!" The word echoed through the main level of the home. Nick moved in, eyes cataloguing the expensive furniture, rare art and precise detail without any personal expression.

Rapid Spanish preceded a short, heavy-set woman into the room. The agents, gripping either arm, hauled her toward him.

"*No sé, no sé!*" The woman shouted over and over, intermixed with a jumble of words that included "*Madre de Dios*" and a few other selections.

Nick looked at the young FBI agents. "Escort her as gently as you would your grandmother to that chair right there, and nod your heads as you let her go after she sits."

Nick looked at the woman, dignity and fear warring on her face.

He all but knelt in front of her. "*Señora, por favor.* Please. You are in no danger. We are here to look for something your employer may have been using to hurt people. Something secret."

"Secreto? Clandestino?" Her eyes lit up with hope. Survival. Sometimes it makes the world go round. The proud woman looked at him like he was an idiot.

"Sígueme, por favor." She motioned for him to follow her. *"Aquí. Oprimes."*

Nick pushed the button the maid indicated and watched as the floor fell away. This was significant. They would have found it eventually, but this woman might have just cut hours off of their search.

"Gracias."

He glanced down at the steps winding down to a lower level and listened carefully, then descended the stairs. *Winding. Sterile. Unlike the rest of the house.* Everywhere he looked was stainless steel and white tile. Abutments and corners were curved to minimize any accumulation of human debris. The flooring provided a nonporous solid mass with drains spaced every twelve feet. *Efficient. Clean.* Glass cabinets held an array of equipment. Three high-powered microscopes stood like sentinels on the pristine countertop. Nick had been in a lot of labs in his time. This one had to be in the top five as far as apparatuses were concerned.

An enormous tank of water and algae commanded the attention of anyone who entered. A bio-suit hung on the wall next to the glass doors that sealed the tank off from the rest of the room.

Nick moved closer for a better view. *Looks like the vet was right.* Even before tests were run, Nick was certain the tank contained deadly saxitoxin.

He pulled out his cell to call for samples to be taken, but before the connection could be made someone cleared his throat behind him. With the phone in his hand, he couldn't go for his weapon.

"Don't move."

CHAPTER SIXTY-FOUR

"Hands on your head, slow."

Nick did as told, his cell phone still in his right hand.

"Drop the phone. Clasp your fingers."

This guy knows what he's doing. Nick loosened his grip on his phone and it clattered to the ground. He intertwined his fingers and stood perfectly still.

"Turn around. Slow."

Nick shuffled his feet in a circle and turned. The man was not Blanton. Older. All muscle with intensity.

"We need to talk, ASAC Grant." The words were civil, but the gun didn't waver.

"Who are you? How do you know my name?"

"We're after the same person, Agent." The man standing in front of him, filled with obvious intent, didn't give up any more information.

"How did you get in here?"

"I was with an international security company for a long time. I've kept up with the tools of the trade. It took you long enough to get here."

Nick figured that was as good an answer as he was going to get, at least for the moment. "You know I'm FBI. You must also know this entire property is crawling with law enforcement, federal and local."

"You're the only fed on site. But yes, I'm aware you've

put different pieces of the puzzle together to come to the same conclusion I have." The man squared his shoulders. "Teague Blanton is a murderer."

"He's more than that."

"Speak."

Nick looked at the man. Instinct told him he could be trusted. The situation told him different.

"Two things are making it hard for me to speak." Nick had the man's attention. "First, when a gun is pointed at me, it tends to consume my thoughts to the point of distraction."

Nick watched as the man lowered the gun to the ground, but he didn't move his trigger finger. *Nothing to lose by waiting him out.* Eventually, the man met Nick's eyes and moved his finger off the firing mechanism.

"The second thing?"

"I need to know who I'm talking to."

"Before I answer you, can we agree that Teague Blanton needs to be caught?"

Nick nodded. *Who the hell is this guy?*

"Can we agree that he's the bad guy, and that anyone looking for him must automatically be on the side of good?"

Nick squinted. "Depends."

The man pushed out a deep exhale. "Whatever you're after him for now, you can add at least one more count. The murder of my wife."

Nick relaxed. *The man isn't a killer.* "Your wife?" Even though he no longer felt threatened, he also felt the need to keep the guy talking, at least long enough to figure out what came next.

"Star. My wife's name was Star. Blanton took her to get back at me. He buried her alive." The words spread into the air without emotion, sorrow or hatred. The man had lived with those words and emotions for so long, thought about them for so long, that the agony had long since left his consciousness. He was acting out of rote, the kind of thing a soldier does after months in the war zone.

But it didn't make sense, considering what they'd uncovered. "Buried her alive? When?" *Could this man be connected with one of the bodies we just unearthed?* ID was coming together on all of them. Maybe the guy could help them with at least one.

"Ten years ago."

No way. Ten years ago was Bonzer, not Blanton. Any current identification was moot, but Nick suspected there might be more.

"Why do you think Teague Blanton killed your wife?"

"Because my security firm had been hired to look into some improprieties for an international bio-tech company almost twelve years ago. We discovered some questionable protocol in our investigation, and it implicated Blanton. Rather than face criminal prosecution, he elected to resign. No one else would touch him. He'd become a pariah in his own profession, and he blamed me. Teague Blanton kidnapped my wife and buried her alive to get back at me, or so it seemed at the time. Apparently, he had some other needs as well." The man gestured to some devices chained to a nearby wall, a drain in the floor near them.

Nick wanted to get the techs to that drain right away. But first, he had to deal with this guy. "And so, I go back to my earlier question. Who are you?"

"My name is Bryce Taylor."

Taylor? Crap. This is getting way too complicated. "You're related to Jamie and Jacqueline Taylor?"

Bryce nodded. "My daughters."

"Do they know you're here?"

"I left a message for both of them, but Jamie would be the one to eventually connect everything... and she and I have talked."

"Why Jamie?" Nick realized it wasn't pertinent to the moment, but he couldn't help himself.

Nick and Bryce Taylor locked eyes. A weird current of knowledge passed between them, and a kind of vague understanding Nick wasn't ready to examine too closely. To his surprise, the man had a lot to say on the subject.

"Jamie is both my dreamer and my investigator. It's why she's so good with her dogs, and why she brings closure to so many families. And, by the way, it's why she also finds so many people lost in the Rocky Mountains on a regular basis. Her sister, Jax, knows how to dig into bodies. She knows the science of death and is one of the smartest MEs working in the country today. Jamie knows how to dig deep into the psyches of both the two-legged and four-legged variety, except she's not so good with men in the romantic sense."

"And you're here now because...?"

"I'm here because I finally found the bastard, and I'm ready to kill him."

Nick's cell rang.

"May I?"

Bryce Taylor nodded, set the safety and slipped the gun into his waistband.

"Grant."

"Sheriff wants you upstairs. We might have a situation."

You don't know the half of it, Nick thought. "On my way. Send two crime scene techs down here to collect samples. I also need a deputy to search here and the rest of the house for lab notebooks." Maybe they'd get lucky and discover a clue as to what the ultimate target might be.

CHAPTER SIXTY-FIVE

Nick looked at Bryce Taylor. "Come with me."

The two men walked up the winding staircase without talking. A group of three people, two men and a woman, were waiting at the top. Nick noted with satisfaction that they were all booted and capped.

Sheriff Coble began to talk but stiffened when he saw another man with Nick.

"This is Bryce Taylor." Nick motioned toward Bryce and watched the sheriff's reaction.

"I know who he is." Not exactly cold, but a long way from warm.

Taylor nodded to the sheriff. "Coble."

"Mr. Taylor has apparently been tracking his wife's killer for—"

"Ten years. I know."

Nick realized the kidnapping and murder of Star Taylor happened on the sheriff's watch.

"Turns out Mrs. Taylor's killer is Teague Blanton."

Coble looked at Bryce Taylor. "You sure about that, Taylor?"

"Dead sure."

The sheriff looked at Nick. "A moment, Agent?" Jerry Coble turned and walked away. Nick followed him to the kitchen.

"We found something," Coble said when they were out of earshot. He handed a scarf to Nick.

"So? A scarf."

"It belongs to Jamie Taylor."

"How do you know?" Nick asked.

"Well, aside from the fact it's covered with dogs and has a label attached that says *Property of Jamie Taylor*, I know it's hers because I gave it to her at the Secret Santa gift exchange last Christmas."

"So?"

"We can't reach her. I sent a deputy to check out her house. Her car's there, but she's not around and neither are her dogs."

"Maybe she's on a walk?"

"Could be, but right after Ellen's murder? I don't think so."

"Maybe she went somewhere with her sister."

"Also could be, but we haven't been able to get hold of Dr. Taylor either. I don't like it."

"Is the deputy still at Jamie's house?"

"He is."

"Tell him to enter, see if he can find anything."

"But—"

"It's my ass," Nick promised.

Less than ten minutes later, Sheriff Coble approached Nick. "Jamie left a note for Jax. Said she was coming here. Said to not go to bed without them talking."

Nick shook his head. *Not good.* "We've gotta get something on this guy. Find out where he might be since he's not here. Are we into his computer yet?"

A deputy sitting behind the enormous desk said, "I'm in... but what am I looking for?"

"A calendar, a journal, a Facebook page—anything." Nick walked up behind the young woman. "Check for any online banking."

The deputy pulled up a credit card statement. There were multiple charges over a two-month period to Elway's and the Ritz-Carlton in Denver. "Here are records of some recent trades our subject made in the commodities markets."

Nick looked at the screen. "Print this out for me now, and then I want a copy of the credit card statement."

The sheriff waited for Nick to process the new information. It didn't take long.

"We need to get to Denver," Nick said. "But we need to do it without calling out all the troops. If we move too hard and too fast, we're likely to set him off, or worse, make him change his target. I'll contact Homeland Security and let them know we're moving on this. Sheriff, do you know who to call in Denver?"

"I've met the chief at a couple of conferences. I'll call him now."

"Make sure he understands we don't yet have a target, but his department needs to be on alert," Nick said. He turned to the deputy on the computer. "We need more information, and we need it fast. Keep looking. Tear this place up, and contact me the minute you find anything. I'm heading to Denver." He needed to be in the field, not phoning in from the sidelines.

Bryce Taylor moved into their tight communication circle. "I'm in, and we need Jamie's dogs."

"This operation—"

"*I'm in*, Agent. You're going to need those dogs, and you and I both know you need me to help handle them. Plus, I've been tracking Blanton for ten years. I know how he thinks."

Nick nodded and felt his guts twist. "Sheriff Coble, please have someone call the woman who has Jamie's dogs. Tell her to meet us at Jamie's house with the two dogs that know how to track."

CHAPTER SIXTY-SIX

A tear crawled down Jamie's cheek and she cursed her body's betrayal. The coarse rope that bound her raw wrists afforded no give, no hope. Raw fear vibrated in her head.

Blanton hadn't blindfolded her, but the gag cut deep into the corners of her mouth. She sucked in some oil-stained air and twisted to look at her sister. Jax was bound in similar style, her eyes wild. Jamie willed her sister to look at her, and in a moment, she did. Jamie forced herself to blink slow and measured. After a few seconds, she was rewarded with two purposeful blinks back. Jax was okay, at least as under control as one could expect given their current situation.

"I do have plans for you, you know." The voice was smooth, softer even than when she'd met him at E-lev 2.

Jamie arched an eyebrow. *What the hell?*

"Yes, yes, yes. The plans I have for you are rather new, but I've been able to ad lib my entire life, so this is nothing new to me. I had a choice to make. If you were free, you could derail my plans. If I killed you too soon, in the wrong place, there could be some nasty questions. My timing is carefully planned, so if there was even a chance you could achieve freedom, and then be able to convince someone of what most would consider lunatic ranting... well, I couldn't risk that. My ultimate goal is too powerful, too personal and filled with purpose. I can't risk discovery until I'm ready."

She cocked her head, trying to get him to continue. *Go on. Keep talking, you son of a bitch.*

Blanton bent to look closely at her. "I wonder which one of you loves the other one more? Do you know?" If she could, she would have spat on him. "No? I didn't think so. Maybe we'll find out. We'll learn which of you has the highest tolerance for pain. It should be interesting. I'm more interested in your emotional pain though. Is one preferable over the other, especially when someone you love is being tortured?"

He began to pry open some of the wooden crates. He removed the filler from one, and then pulled out a strange hunk of metal as if it were the Holy Grail. More pieces followed.

Jamie considered the steel configuration. Clearly, it was something meant to be airborne, a main body with wings extending from either side. But something told her it wasn't complete. More needed to be added. Blanton looked like he was waiting for something.

He also looked like a man who needed to talk. *Please God, let it happen now. Let him spill his guts. Information was her best and only hope.*

Without any preamble, Blanton approached Jamie.

Is this it? Am I going to die now? She closed her eyes and waited.

With a bite, the gag constricting her mouth tugged hard, then fell away. She slid her tongue to explore the corners of her mouth.

"You know, I really did enjoy our conversations. You're more intelligent than most of the idiot bitches out there. You think for yourself."

"What are you—"

"Don't disappoint me, Jamie. You know more than

244

that asinine question begs. Just pay attention."

Blanton laid out the pieces of metal with the touch of a lover. After a few minutes, he looked at her.

"Can you describe for me your feelings about Ellen? And her death?"

"Death? You bastard! You mean her torture!"

"If that's what trips it for you."

"Why the hell should I tell you anything?"

"Because if you don't, I'll look elsewhere for information, for interest. You're physically scarred, but your sister isn't."

Stall. Keep him talking. Learn things.

"What do you mean, my feelings? Of course I was sad."

"Sad? What does sad feel like?"

"Sad... sad feels like something came along and pinched a little bit of your heart."

"That's all?"

"When I found out about Ellen, it was like something pinched my heart, ripped a bit off, and squeezed."

"Could you breathe?"

"I don't remember."

"Did you hate her killer?"

"Not in the first seconds. The first seconds were for Ellen."

"And then?"

"And then I hated him."

He began working with the pieces of metal. He assembled the parts, focusing on their precise attachment. When he finished, he set his creation to the side, then stood up and stretched. What looked like a large model airplane sat on the cart.

"What are you going to do with a model airplane?"

"It's a drone."

"Okay, fine. What are you going to do with a drone?"

245

"Well, to most of the world, I'll make history. The infamous kind. But to me, *for* me, the plan is to experience personally the profound emotions of thousands."

What? Infamous? Emotions of thousands?

"Are you making a bomb?" If the people on Flight 93 could sacrifice their lives to prevent a terrorist from taking a plane into a building full of hundreds of people, she could do the same thing here, if she could come up with a plan.

He shook his head. "Not the kind of bomb you think. With a regular bomb, everything would happen too fast. And with all of the debris, it would be next to impossible to have a visual. I need the visual."

Blanton stopped and walked over to the open edge of the incomplete building.

What's he watching? The unmistakable sounds of a huge crowd of people drifted up to Jamie. *Today's Sunday. The Broncos are playing at home.*

Chapter Sixty-Seven

It was up to him—an FBI agent on leave because of an oxy habit—to save two women and who-knew-who-else from a madman. He was flying down I-70 with two canines and an aging security guy with a vendetta who refused to fly as passengers. Sheriff Coble, the third man in the team, would join them in Denver.

Nick wiped his hands on his jeans, hoping Bryce Taylor didn't notice.

"Don't worry, Son. I've dealt with my share of dogs."

"How could you tell?"

"There aren't a lot of things that will make a man sweat, especially an FBI field agent. Must be the dogs."

Nick focused on driving.

"You're attracted to my daughter, aren't you?"

"She's nice," he said noncommittally.

Bryce Taylor barked out a rusty laugh. "You mean, except for the dogs."

A chuckle burst from Nick's lips. "Yeah," he said. "Dogs bite." Suddenly he relaxed.

"Did you know Jamie didn't get her first dog until I retired and we moved to Aspen Falls?"

"To tell you the truth, we didn't talk much about her dogs... or her history."

"Ah... got it. Visceral. Sexual."

Nick chose not to respond to Bryce Taylor's assertion. The conversation was getting a little out of hand, and it was closer to the mark than Nick wanted to admit. He redirected the discussion. "Tell me about Blanton. Why were you after him?"

"I didn't have a name because he'd changed it but Blanton's been on my short list for the last seven years. Nothing dramatic—the list just kept getting shorter." Taylor visibly stretched.

"For killing your wife?"

"Why else would I be after him?"

Twenty-five minutes later, he had an entirely new appreciation for what motivated Jamie Taylor, and for that matter, her sister. Even the dogs lost a little of their threat. Any FBI agent worth his salt could understand that a mission is a mission, period. "So, Mr. Taylor, do you think you'll be able to handle confrontation with Teague Blanton without your personal mission getting involved? We're risking the lives of both of your daughters, not to mention the lives of many more people."

"I'm fine."

"Convince me. You've been after this guy for ten years. He took your wife, and she died an unspeakable death."

"I said I'm fine, Grant. Leave it alone."

"Look, the fact is, you and I don't know each other. We're about to enter into a situation where we'll have to rely on each other, so your advice to leave it alone pretty much sucks."

"Okay... you might be right, given any other set of circumstances, but he has my daughters. They are the best things I have left, and my only connection to the most amazing woman in my life."

"And yet you walked away from them." Nick thought about the daughter he hadn't even known about until recently. Would he end up abandoning her because of his inability to parent? How different would that be than just walking out?

"I didn't abandon them. They were grown and on their own. Politics being what they were, I had the best chance of bringing him to justice. My wife deserved that, and so did my daughters." He looked pointedly at Nick. "So yes, I left. I made a choice, and I've lived with it. Now, shouldn't we strategize a bit before we get to Denver? Let's talk."

CHAPTER SIXTY-EIGHT

Jamie glared at Teague Blanton. "You're planning on harming those people, aren't you?" She watched as he assembled the last bits of the drone. "Teague, what are you planning?"

He finally looked in her direction. "Oh, dear, sweet Jamie. I'm not planning on *harming* anyone."

Jamie sucked in a breath.

"I'm planning to kill them... within minutes... while I watch." He cocked his head. "What do you think they'll do when they realize they're dying? And that the person next to them is dying?" A dreamlike mask settled onto Blanton's face. "Will they reach out? Will they express their love? Their fear?" He looked at her. "What exactly will they do? How intensely will they feel?"

Jamie twitched with recognition. "You're sick! You're *evil!*"

"Oh, no, no, no. I'm simply committed to becoming more than I am, to increasing my experience."

Jamie was incredulous. "By killing people?"

"It's more than that. It's enabling them to push down to their deepest emotions. It's giving them the opportunity to connect to the things that really matter in their lives and to express what they find. They'll flood the air around them with raw emotion."

Jamie tried to digest that information. "And that will benefit you how?"

Teague Blanton pinched the upper part of his nose, then began to massage it, harder and harder. Tension spread into the air.

Shit. Jamie stumbled, clambered for a way to redirect the conversation. "Okay, how is the drone going to help you?"

The nose rubbing lessened, then stopped. Blanton dropped his hand to his side only to come up again in a weird, grandiose theatrical gesture. He dipped his head. "I have concentrated one of the most lethal natural toxins known to man in powder form: saxitoxin. It's nearly perfect on its own when conditions are right, and I know how to duplicate those conditions: create the toxin; distill it and increase its potency. In the history of man, no one else has been able to do this. I have changed history."

He looked at Jamie as if he expected applause.

Jamie forced herself to continue watching him. *Keep him talking.*

"Of course, I had a few trials and errors. The formula took a great deal of tweaking, and then I had to consider the method of delivery. I have the United States military to thank for their drone program. Without this wonderful airborne friend, my plan would require a much more complicated strategy."

He opened another crate and pulled out the pieces to build a second carrier of death.

"Two?"

"Probably overkill." He smiled. "But I've got one chance to pull this off, and a good plan always makes room for error."

Jamie wanted to ask where the saxitoxin was, but she didn't trust herself, or him, not to do something stupid. *I have to think... fast.*

Jax moaned and opened her eyes. Jamie made sure she was in Jax's line of vision. She watched her sister's eyes clear and then fill with panic. Relief swept over Jamie as the panic was replaced with control and intelligence.

CHAPTER SIXTY-NINE

"Okay. Wake up. We're in Denver." Nick didn't have to repeat himself. The man riding shotgun popped open one eye and then the other. Nick checked the GPS. They would arrive at their destination—the Ritz-Carlton unless they got better intel—in less than fourteen minutes. Sheriff Coble and the deputy would meet them there. DPD would stand by.

Bryce Taylor stretched as well as he could in the passenger seat. "Damn, would you look at the traffic?"

"Game day. It's going to get worse the closer we get to the stadium."

A dog barked in the back of the SUV. Nick tensed.

"Here's what you have to know about those dogs, Nick. Just as you know your job, they know theirs. It will be like a choreographed show. Don't get in their way, and they won't get in yours. They'll also follow your commands, so speak clearly."

"Commands?" Nick hadn't even considered that he'd have to talk to the dogs. He didn't know any commands other than sit and stay, and somehow those didn't feel appropriate given the circumstances.

"Jamie's dogs are trained to find people who want to be found. They're not DEA or ATF, so her commands won't be coded. She would have taught them basic words

253

to respond to when they hear them. Maybe a few hand signals as well."

"Hand signals?" Nick felt less and less able to deal with the situation. "Look, maybe you ought to go in with the dogs. I'll get there my own way."

"We're not even sure where *there* is, Cowboy." Taylor pulled two energy bars out of his pack and handed one to Nick.

"My daughter would never raise a mean dog. You have absolutely nothing to fear from them. Now, do you want to hear the commands I think Jamie has taught them or do you want to wing it?"

CHAPTER SEVENTY

Jamie watched as Blanton loaded each of the drones with their payload of saxitoxin. *These are the worst moments of my life.* She figured one way or another she was going to die. Once again, she thought of the heroes on 9/11 who had sacrificed their own lives to save thousands.

"Okay, girls. Time for us to move." Blanton gestured stiffly. "Get up."

Jamie flinched at his touch as he hauled her to her feet. She'd made her decision and was no longer afraid. All she wanted was an opportunity. Given any window, she'd take Teague Blanton out regardless of the cost. And she knew her sister would do the same, given the opportunity.

Jamie noted he left everything but them where it was. *The greater distance between him and his drones, the better.* She complied as he urged them toward the elevator.

During the ride down, Blanton kept a hand on her back, like a date. *What a complete bastard.* She looked for a chance, any chance, to swing the balance in her favor.

"We'll have a little time for some intimate experiments regarding human emotion," he said as the doors opened at the basement level.

It finally became clear to Jamie what Blanton was after, and logic told her that regardless of what he experienced or how many he killed, Teague Blanton would never get what he wanted.

But he didn't know that. As long as he didn't know, maybe she could figure out a way to leverage their position.

"You have certainly proven a lot more difficult than your mother did."

CHAPTER SEVENTY-ONE

"Agent Grant, I'm Deputy Linda Jane Roberts. I'm at the Blanton house and I've found something you need to know about."

"Speak to me, Deputy."

"Teague Blanton is a real estate developer, among other things. We're just beginning to uncover all of his holdings. One of them is a large apartment complex near I-25 and Colfax."

"I'm not familiar with the Denver area. Why is that piece of real estate important?"

"It's a stone's throw from Sports Authority Field, and I believe the Denver Broncos have a home game today."

"Good work."

Nick clicked off, pulled to the side of the road and input a new location. He called Coble and told him to alert the DPD but make sure they stood down until he knew for sure the apartment complex was the right place. It was too late to come up with any plausible reason to stop the game.

Five minutes later, Nick turned his SUV into the main parking lot of the Rocking Horse Apartment Community. Bryce pointed out the trademark curvature of the stadium and they drove slowly toward that end of the complex. The place was enormous. Three high-rise apartment buildings were connected by parking garages. A clubhouse doubled as a leasing office, and the landscaping incorporated xeriscape plants with just enough grass that it looked both interesting and lush.

"You've been tracking Blanton for ten years," Nick said. "Any ideas?"

"Let's park and see if the dogs can pick up anything." Bryce opened a paper bag and pulled out a pale yellow t-shirt.

"Where did you—"

"While you were worrying about Jamie's animals, I found her laundry hamper."

Nick backed into a parking place in the farthest row. No other cars were around them, and evergreens were dense on the driver's side and at the back of the vehicle.

Bryce hopped out of the passenger side like a twenty year old kid and pulled up the back door before Nick had his own closed.

"C'mon, Cowboy."

Bryce placed leashes on both dogs.

"I'll take Gretchen," Bryce said. "You take Socrates. We'll head off in different directions and see whether the dogs come up with scent. If either of them catches something, one short whistle. If either is a bust, two shorts." He handed a silver whistle on a chain to Nick and put a second one around his own neck.

"How do you know the names of the dogs?"

"Their collars, Cowboy—their names are on their collars."

Nick hadn't gotten close enough to look.

"Look at me," Bryce commanded.

Nick looked up.

"Can you do this? There's a lot at stake here." Bryce's gaze darkened and bored into Nick's. "If you can't do this, I'll do it by myself. I'll get it done, but it'll take longer."

Nick nodded. "I'm okay. Let's go."

Bryce held Jamie's shirt up to both dogs and their response was immediate. "Find Jamie."

Nick was barely aware that Bryce and Gretchen had hauled off. It was all he could do to keep up with Socrates.

Socrates moved at a good clip. He was excited and loving this game. Nick guessed he'd probably played Find Jamie before. Nick was also glad that the dog was at the end of the leash, pulling and not closer to Nick.

Within thirty seconds, Socrates began moving back and forth in a search pattern he probably used when looking for lost hikers, and he slowed down significantly. Nick was hopeful as they approached a side entry door to the building, but Socrates didn't seem to find anything there that smelled like Jamie. He couldn't help saying, "Find Jamie, Socrates. Find Jamie." Nick had never before talked to a dog, not even his old Queenie.

The dog backtracked, then walked in a circle. He whimpered.

What the hell did that mean? Bryce hadn't said anything about a whimper.

"Find Jamie."

Socrates moved off and sniffed but nothing got his attention.

This wasn't working. Nick jerked on the leash in exasperation, then froze when he realized what he'd done. He fully expected an attack from the dog. It didn't come.

Not quite willing to take his eyes off the big beast, Nick knelt. Socrates sat next to him, and lapped the side of his face. Then the dog whimpered.

Nick wiped his face. "I get it. We didn't find her."

Two short whistles sounded from the distance. Bryce hadn't found anything either. Nick shoved himself to his feet and the two, man and dog, walked back to the SUV together.

"What do you know? No bloody gouges in your skin or anything."

Bryce opened the back of the SUV and both dogs bounded inside. While Bryce secured their travel cages, Nick called the sheriff. "This isn't the place. Call DPD."

Then he searched his cell records and hit the Call button.

CHAPTER SEVENTY-TWO

"Deputy Roberts, anything else? The apartment complex was a bust." She spoke to someone else in the room for a moment, then said, "We have a long shot, Agent."

"I'll take it."

"Blanton has a new high-rise building. It's still under construction, but it's also near the football stadium."

Nick input the address at 16th and Federal into his GPS. He thought he could get there without help, but he couldn't afford to be wrong.

He looked at his watch. Two-thirty. The game started at two-fifteen. They didn't have much time. Nick figured the attack would come in either the second or third quarter to maximize the number of targets. Fans tend to arrive late, leave their seats at half time, and even in a close game, they'll often leave early to avoid traffic.

Ten minutes later he pulled in behind the high-rise. The parking lot was almost empty, the result of the Denver PD stepping up parking enforcement in the areas surrounding the football stadium during games. Nick pulled his credentials out of his wallet and placed it on the dash. Maybe if they saw that an FBI agent owned the vehicle, it wouldn't get ticketed and towed.

The two men walked behind the SUV, each of them

scouting the surrounding neighborhood. It was quiet, strange to hear a little traffic on Federal Boulevard and know there was a game going on right across the street with tens of thousands of fans, and yet the neighborhood just two blocks away remained still and peaceful. The warm afternoon sun gave the area a lazy feeling.

A muffled cheer surged out of the stadium, and Nick and Bryce looked at each other.

"Gretchen or Socrates?" Bryce asked.

Nick reached for the leash attached to Socrates and waited.

Bryce once more pulled out the yellow t-shirt and held it down for the dogs to sniff. "Find Jamie."

CHAPTER SEVENTY-THREE

Blanton knelt and bound Jax's legs, then moved to Jamie and did the same. "I got lucky with your mother. She was so unsuspecting. She began as a retribution, turned into an object of hope, and then ended with disappointment."

Jamie swayed. Teague Blanton had killed her mother. *No wonder he targeted us. No way will this monster win, not if I have anything to do with it.*

As Blanton stepped out, Jamie thought, *Now's my chance.* She looked around the basement. Some wooden forms for concrete were piled neatly in one corner, and a large number of boxes and crates that had contained building supplies had been flattened and stacked next to them. Jamie didn't know when she'd seen such neat construction crews. Some odd scraps of metal in a much messier pile were waiting to be carted out and dumped. There was a large double-doored metal storage unit against the far wall. *Maybe there's something in that cabinet I could use.*

Jamie inch-wormed over to the cabinet and considered how to get it open. She got to her knees, then tried to push the handle up with her head. It didn't move. *Locked.* The cabinet wasn't flush against the wall. Maybe she could tip it over somehow. She tried ramming it with her shoulder. The unit didn't budge. She closed her eyes in pain.

Something pushed on her sore shoulder. *Jax.* Her sister gestured toward the pile of scrap metal and the two sisters hurried to try and release their bonds.

Jamie applied her tightly wrapped hands to a large piece of sharp metal. Jax did the same. When their hands were finally freed, each sister unleashed her ankle wraps. Jax slowly pulled the tape off from her mouth, leaving it dangling in her hair.

Together, they pried open the cabinet. Flammables. More than a dozen bottles carried the warning labels on them, and most of them were full. As part of Jamie's job with Search and Rescue, they'd spent one weekend training with the fire department. Jamie tried to remember what she'd learned.

Fire moves up and out. She looked around for the ventilation shafts. There would be more than one. They'd make piles of wood and cardboard under the vents and create a trail with the flammable liquids between each pile so it would quickly spread. They needed a source to ignite them.

Jax caught Jamie's eye with a strange gleam. "Okay, baby sister. Phil is an ass, but I was always his enabler." She reached into her back pocket and pulled out a lighter.

"No shit!" Jamie sent a quick thank you to Phil Sussman for his proclivity toward cigars.

The sisters worked together to drag the heavy wooden forms and other objects into position under the vents Jamie had identified. She'd found four. They stripped the cardboard and poked it into the visible gaps in each pile. Jamie's fingers were bleeding and she was sure Jax's were too.

Finally, they poured the flammable liquids on the piles and laid a trail between each of them. Then Jamie reserved the last bit in one of the cans, and the two sisters backed toward the stairwell. They wouldn't have long to get to the first floor and in to the Fire Command Center before the fire spread.

Jamie didn't remember many of the details about the command center they'd toured, but she did remember it was like the mechanical heart of the building. She just hoped that Blanton hadn't skimped and that it was at least as state of the art as the one she'd seen, with clear directions for all of the equipment. She remembered that having prominent directions was a requirement. She prayed whoever was in charge of this center had followed the regulations.

Jamie took off her t-shirt and soaked it. "Give me the lighter and start up the stairs. We need to go up to the first floor and find the Fire Command Center."

"I'll wait for you."

"Go. I'll be right behind you."

Jax moved to go up the stairs.

Jamie waited two counts, then held her shirt out in front of her. She flicked the lighter and touched the flame to the soaked piece of cloth. When the flame caught, Jamie simply threw the lighter into the mix. Before pulling the stairwell door closed behind her, she watched the flames build in strength and move to the drywall, finally kissing the ceiling.

Chapter Seventy-Four

Halfway to the back of the building, both dogs suddenly pulled on their leashes and ran around the side of the structure. Once there, Socrates leapt in the air and then remained stationary, tail wagging. Gretchen fell to the ground.

"That's how they alert," Bryce explained. "Jamie's been here."

"Odds are, she still is." Nick bent to the asphalt and looked at the spot the dogs seemed interested in. He couldn't see anything significant on the surface, but he reached one finger and touched a small bit that was still sticky, then put it to his nose. *Blood.* He looked up and saw a side door. "Let's go." He stood and scratched Socrates lightly on the head.

Both men pulled their weapons. The door clicked open and they entered, closing it behind them as quickly and silently as they could.

The dogs seemed confused for a moment; then as one they moved to the elevator. No way Nick could push the button calling the unit to life. He thought about what little he'd read about airborne toxins. He looked at Bryce. "The main operations should be on the top floor." Roberts had told him the building specs called for thirty-seven floors. "Airborne biotoxins in powder form will sink unless carried on an air current. They settle. With a toxin as powerful as saxitoxin, every living thing in its path will be exposed and probably die. The only safe place for observation is above the release level. We need to find the stairs."

"We passed them. How many floors are we talking about?" Bryce didn't sound happy, but he wasn't giving up.

"Quite a few," Nick said. No need to utter the number. Saying it out loud would make it so. Maybe things had changed.

Nick thought his lungs would burst. His knees had been quaking for the last five flights, but if the dogs could keep going, so could he. Finally, they came to a stencil that said *ROOF* with an arrow pointing up. They were at the top floor.

Nick worked to settle his heart rate and calm his breathing.

Bryce, when he caught up, pulled out a water bottle, which he promptly offered to the dogs.

After the dogs had quenched their thirst, Nick placed his hand on the door handle and used his shoulder to nudge the door open. He was unable to see anything. He glanced at Bryce. "Ready?"

Bryce nodded.

Nick silently broadened the opening from the stairwell door. He and Socrates stepped through, with Bryce and Gretchen following tight. Both men had to hold the leashes and be prepared to shoot. Within seconds, both men realized they were alone. But it wasn't just a typical top floor of a high-rise building under construction.

The drones were there, sunlight glancing off their sides, ready. Not knowing what security precautions Blanton might have taken, they presumed the little planes were armed and ready, and they chose to leave everything exactly as they found it.

Quietly, Bryce said, "We need to move down... now."

Without another word, both men and their four-legged partners moved back to the stairwell. The downward trek was both easier and more difficult. Quivering leg muscles and the increased need for speed and stealth took their toll. He opened his cell. *Damn. No signal.* He needed to contact both Homeland Security and Coble.

Nick was grateful the dogs weren't barking. That would have been too much. He kept trying to remember they were professionals, but the fact that they were dogs kept encroaching. Then a thought occurred: *What if they weren't barking because Jamie and Jax are already dead?*

He'd gone down so many steps it surprised him when they stopped. They'd reached the bottom. The basement. Silently, the dogs expressed their excitement. Their Jamie was on the other side of the steel door, and they were ready to be heroes.

He opened his cell. "Sheriff Coble, this is it. Send everyone. Make sure they know we're dealing with saxitoxin."

Once again, Nick took hold of the door handle. The odds were against them this time. There was little doubt that beyond this door stood a mass murderer and two innocent victims.

Were they alive? Would the dog's excitement turn to dread and sorrow? Would his? Would there be a weapon aimed at his chest the moment the door opened wide enough? Could be whatever interest he had in Jamie Taylor wouldn't matter.

He smelled smoke.

268

CHAPTER SEVENTY-FIVE

The sound of the inferno took Jamie's breath away. They pounded up the stairs and pulled open the door for the first floor.

Jamie tried to orient herself but she couldn't remember which side of the building they'd been on when she saw the sign for the Fire Command Center, and right now, seconds counted. "Jax, you need to get out of here." Jamie gave her sister one of those looks that meant it didn't matter if she was the younger sister, Jax had better pay attention.

"What are you planning, Jamie?"

"I don't know yet, but you don't need to be involved in whatever it is." Jamie pictured the drones on the top floor of the building. She'd watched as Blanton had put in the payloads of saxitoxin, watched him connect wires to the canister lids containing the poison. There had to be a remote control somewhere. She hadn't seen it anywhere near the drones.

First she needed to find the command center. It would give her some protection from the fire—for how long she didn't know—and maybe give her an idea of what else she could do to keep Teague Blanton from killing tens of thousands of people.

"I'm not going anywhere without you." Jax looked like

she had when they were kids, braced for an argument, something they didn't have time for.

"Fine. You go that way, I'll go this way. We've got to find the command center. Whoever finds it first, yell!" Jamie had already taken off down the empty hallway. Either the heat was building faster than she had thought it would, or her imagination was running hot, because sweat covered her chest. Smoke was beginning to build up in the distance.

"Here!" Jax yelled. "Here!"

Jamie spun on her heels and raced back the way she'd come. Jax had opened a door and turned on the light by the time Jamie got there. She closed the door behind her and looked around.

Blanton had not spared anything. The center was more than state of the art. Video monitoring equipment showed every floor of the building from multiple angles, and two televisions were already turned on: one, some kind of remote camera shot of Sports Authority Field, and the other, the live broadcast of the football game.

The Broncos were ahead by three points less than five minutes into the second quarter. The Chiefs had the ball midfield on second down. No one in the stands would go anywhere until half-time. The game, as usual, was a sellout.

Jamie saw a flashing light and checked the label below it. The DFD had been notified of the fire. *Good.* But while she watched, the light quit blinking. *What does that mean?*

The door opened and Jax cried out.

Jamie turned around and froze.

Blanton closed the door quickly behind him. He did a quick survey of the room and apparently whatever he was looking for satisfied him. He focused on Jamie. "Well, isn't this cozy?"

"The fire department is on its way."

"No they're not. At least not right now. We have a few minutes, and that's all I'll need." He pulled a small handgun from his pocket. "Both of you. Over there. You can watch."

Blanton kept the gun pointed at them while he opened a cabinet behind the work area. Inside were two more monitors and controls.

He pursed his lips and cocked his head to the right. He squinted. "You thought a fire would work? Probably a good idea, really. Just too late. Good for me, bad for you."

He pressed a power button and the control panel began cycling through. Lights came on and blinked a few times before going solid.

"Let's have a look-see." Blanton turned to the large computer screen on the desk and keyed in a password. Within seconds there was an aerial view of Sports Authority Field. With a couple of clicks, a section of the stadium became crystal clear. A couple of more clicks, and what was obviously a family appeared on the screen, each clad in their favorite Bronco player's jersey.

Blanton fired up another, smaller monitor and found another section of the stands to zero in on. He keyed in on a young couple, both into the game and the crowd and the spice of the experience. "This is going to be an important day, but not for you or the city, and not even for them. This will be the day I finally crack through this god-awful clear shell I've lived in all my life. The chick will emerge. For the first time I will experience the emotions you take for granted. For the first time, I'll be truly alive. Even if I die seconds later, I will have won."

"You're crazy, Blanton," Jamie said.

"No. I've *been* crazy. I'm just about to become sane."

He turned his attention to the monitors, adjusting the cameras. Jamie shifted to get into a better position. She needed to find an opportunity soon.

"Don't. You won't make it. You'll be dead and so will that young couple and the family. You won't have changed anything."

Blanton put his finger on a switch.

The remote. Jamie lunged toward her target. *I have to stop—*

The exterior door flew open.

CHAPTER SEVENTY-SIX

Jamie squinted her eyes against the bright sunlight. Silhouettes grew inside the doorway and filled the space. Four silhouettes. Two of them were barking.

"What the hell?" Blanton reached for his gun and spun toward the light. As he raised his gun a blur of golden fur flew past Jamie and Gretchen took down Blanton.

Please, God, don't let her get shot!

The gun went off and one of the men behind her fell to the floor.

Two more figures joined them, one already calling for a medic. She recognized Sheriff Coble's voice. The sirens were getting closer. The DFD was on their way, and then some.

She looked back to Gretchen. Between the bared teeth of her retriever and the gun her father was aiming at Blanton, Jamie wasn't sure which image surprised her the most. She yelled, "Sheriff! Top floor. He's got drones up there loaded with—"

"We have it, Jamie. HazMat is on their way up now with DFD." He turned and spoke to someone else. "Get this son of bitch out of here. I assume one of those sirens is an ambulance? We have an injured federal agent."

At the mention of a federal agent, Jamie's gaze shifted

273

to the man lying on the floor, just inside the entrance to the small room. *Nick!*

She had started to go to him when Socrates jumped at her.

"I'm fine, Socks." A tear escaped and she wiped it away. The world exploded in uniforms and sirens. The cavalry had arrived.

CHAPTER SEVENTY-SEVEN

As Nick and Kylie sat on a bench in her favorite park, he had never in his life felt more uncomfortable. What was he supposed to say to this seven-year-old girl to put her at ease? She looked a little like him, in an entirely alien kind of way. He may have had a hand in making her, but the results—this little female human being—were beyond his understanding and totally out of his comfort zone.

"Did you love my mommy?"

How was he supposed to answer that? He wanted to be honest with her, but didn't want to scar her for life by being blunt. Maybe if he just pretended not to hear her question he could check with a child psychologist later and find out how to talk to little girls.

"Well, did you?"

He swallowed. "There was a time I thought I loved your mommy very much."

Kylie was quiet and Nick was afraid he'd blown ever having a father-daughter relationship. Then she nodded a little and Nick felt like Father of the Year.

He prayed she wouldn't ask any more questions.

"Did you know my other daddy?"

At least this was an easy one.

Nick had brought her pictures of his home in Aspen

Falls. A decorator was standing by to remake one of the guest suites into a welcoming place for Kylie. She would put her stamp on her own space, and he had told her so, but she was still anxious about leaving behind everything she'd ever known.

They were scheduled to fly back to Colorado in two days. He had two days to do his best to make her feel safe with him, and to make her want to give Colorado a try.

The two ate every meal together and spent as much time as possible with each other between Nick's visit with lawyers, child services and his employers at the FBI. He still hadn't been cleared for reinstatement, but it was only a matter of time. His drug dependency was behind him.

So here they were, on their last day in Virginia. As they sat on the bench together, her questions forced him to take a good look at his life. With each answer he gave her, he was making a commitment to her. She had charmed him beyond anything he could ever have imagined.

Maybe it was Kylie who was trying to make him feel safe.

As they were walking back to the hotel, Kylie grabbed his hand and looked up at him. "I think I look like you."

His heart was hers forever.

CHAPTER SEVENTY-EIGHT

Sitting at her kitchen table, Jax looked around. Some nice touches, but nothing she couldn't live without. Selling the little house should cover their debt. *At least the debt I know about.*

Phil hadn't come home last night, and for the first time, she didn't care. When he had finally walked in about ten-thirty this morning, he kissed her on the cheek and headed for the bedroom to change clothes. He left a few minutes later, saying he had some errands to run.

Jax had carefully rinsed out her coffee cup in the sink and placed it in the dishwasher. Then she had walked upstairs and pulled out two suitcases. Her marriage had been over for years. It seemed that everyone had known except for her. It was time to cut her losses and move on. She filled the suitcases and looked around to see whether there was anything else in the house she wanted to take with her. There wasn't.

Pulling the bags behind her, she stopped in the hallway outside the nursery she'd so carefully decorated. She walked into the pastel painted room and ran her gaze over all of the details she had so lovingly pulled together to remind her what was really important when Phil behaved like an ass. She ran her fingers over the rail on the crib and gently touched the Winnie-the-Pooh flannel

277

sheets.

The nightlight glowed softly in the shaded room, even though sunlight was filtering through the corner window. She wiped away a tear and closed the door behind her.

Jamie had a room ready for her in their old family home. It was the same one she'd had when they were kids. Jax hoped she wouldn't have to be here long. Having some place to go was good, but she needed to heal alone.

She put her clothes away and started down to the kitchen to see whether she could help Jamie with dinner. Her sister had been out all day searching for a missing ten-year-old boy who had wandered off without telling his parents. Jamie and Socks had found him trying to catch fish in a stream with a stick he'd sharpened into a spear. A good ending.

Jax's cell phone rang.

"Jax? It's Scott... Scott Ortiz."

"Hello, Doctor. What can I do for you?"

"I was wondering, actually... could I maybe buy you a cup of coffee tomorrow morning? I have an interesting theory I'd like to run past you related to bodies where there appears to have been cross-contamination with animal DNA."

She smiled.

Chapter Seventy-Nine

Kylie had fallen asleep within minutes after their plane left the tarmac. Nick was grateful for the quiet. Having an eight year old around all the time was wonderful, but exhausting.

He pulled out the novel he'd started to read on the trip to Virginia. As best he could figure, they were a few miles west of Denver when his eyelids got heavy. That's when Kylie woke up. Anxious. Fidgety.

"Tell me again about Aspen Falls. Are there a lot of kids there? Do you think they'll like me?"

Nick wanted to take her on his lap and hug her until she knew she would always be safe, but he knew she wasn't that comfortable with him yet. Instead, he told her once again about the little mountain town, the main park where all of the kids played, and the elementary school where he'd already enrolled her. She'd begin classes next week.

"Do you have a dog?" The question was hopeful.

"No, I don't," he said. "Do you want a pet?"

Kylie nodded. "I've always wanted a dog."

"Maybe we should start out with something smaller, like a goldfish." Nick watched as his daughter's face corkscrewed.

"I had a goldfish once. I'd rather have a dog."

Before Nick was forced to answer, the co-pilot approached them. "We'll be landing in about ten minutes. Please put everything away and buckle up until we're stopped."

Nick watched as Kylie pressed her face to the window, clearly wondering about her new home. She was scared and nervous, knowing her life would never be the same again.

When the plane came to a stop, the co-pilot came back out and put the stairs in place for them to deplane. "We'll have your luggage delivered directly to your home, Agent Grant."

"Thank you, and thanks for the smooth flight." Nick remembered a recent homecoming flight and felt a small twinge in his back. A moment later it was gone. He waited for Kylie and led her down the steep steps to the tarmac. He was worried she might fall, and he wanted to make sure he could catch her if she did. When they got to the ground, he finally looked around. What he saw took his breath away.

Jamie was standing there, all three of her dogs around her like a puddle, watching him with a smile tugging at her face. His world was suddenly more right than it had ever been.

Socrates and Gretchen began pulling on their leashes and McKenzie followed suit. Kylie let out a little squeal and ran to the dogs before Nick could stop her.

He watched as Jamie dropped the leashes, a delighted little girl spinning in their midst. Then the tall, trim, dog-loving woman stepped toward him, her lips ready for his.

Author Notes and Acknowledgements

The town of Aspen Falls is completely fictional. The same is true for Rocky Point and Kegger Point. I once lived in Limon and believe their law enforcement would never overlook the kind of thing hinted at in this work of fiction.

I learned early on that learning to write, getting better at it and moving toward a level of competency would require more than just my nose to the grindstone. There are a lot of people who helped me in one way or another create a story worth reading. You've heard the saying, "It takes a village"? For me, it took a small country.

It really began with The Writing Girls: Susan Lohrer, Kelly Irvin and Angela Mills. We've been together through thick and thin, literally. Their friendship and encouragement means a lot. Groups such as Sisters in Crime, Rocky Mountain Fiction Writers, American Christian Fiction Writers, Mystery Writers of America, Dorothy L, For Mystery Addicts, Crime Scene Writers and Murder Must Advertise have all had an impact on me at one time or another. Through these groups I've made some lifelong friends who love the written word.

L.J. Sellers has been an inspiration, a mentor and a friend. L.J. and Andrew E. Kaufman's complete and utter dedication to their readers rather than publishers helped me make the decision to step out in faith. To "trust the process" as Andrew taught me. My sister, Lala Corriere also helped me decide to go in an independent direction. We have reached a new and wonderful place in our relationship because of writing.

Harvey Stanbrough is a teacher at heart. He not only edited this manuscript, and made it better, he helped me learn enough today to be a better writer tomorrow. He is ridiculously talented. His spare use of "atta-girls" made me believe them (I got two), and I learned real fast that when he puts his foot down, I've crossed the line a little too far and too often. Thank you, Harvey. You took a Murphy Brown writer and showed her how to begin to sing on key. And Harvey, thank you from the bottom of my heart for helping me make this happen for what would have been my mom's seventy-ninth birthday. You're kind of a romantic, but don't worry—your secret's safe with me.

My cover designer, Patty G. Henderson at Boulevard Photografica is so creative and intuitive it's scary. She worked with me and tweaked with me to get a cover that made me smile every time I looked at it. In addition to the cover, she did the interior design for the paperback version. Patty, you are a treasure.

Lee Lofland and his Writer's Police Academy provided vast amounts of information and resources. A presentation by Dr. Jonathan Hayes at the WPA gave me autopsy detail, and the real life Jerry Coble is actually an Assistant Fire Marshall with the Guilford County Fire Marshal's office in North Carolina. Dr. Denene Lofland provided invaluable detail for the laboratory scene. Thank you.

Dr. Janice Larkin helped me formulate the psychology of the madman. My early search and rescue advice came from Rayanne Chamberlain, a first responder who is actively involved in using dogs to help find victims. Robin Burcell gave me direction and detail relating to the FBI, and I would be remiss if I didn't also thank Steven Brown, formerly with the FBI and now a private investigator for help in smoothing out the facts. Paramedic and firefighter,

Joe Collins also provided input.

Security expert, gun-guy and car-guy, Denny Moses, gave me perfect input for my plot. Cameron Bruns confirmed some ideas about Boston wildlife as well as local slang, and Fred X, involved with certain unmentionable military and civilian operations, solved my delivery problem in about three seconds.

For more information involving Human Remains Detection and Search and Rescue dogs: The Josephine County Search and Rescue Blog is top-notch (JoCoSAR Blog), as is Deb's Search and Rescue Stories. *No Stone Unturned* by Steve Jackson and *Buzzards and Butterflies* by J.C. Judah are full of stories and information.

If there are inaccuracies in this book, they are entirely my fault. My excuse is that this is fiction. I make things up.

To my tiny team of beta readers, who read before Harvey had a chance to begin grooming me, my profound thanks: L.J. Sellers, Lala Corriere and Andrew E. Kaufman. I subjected you to the manuscript pre-editing and you were wonderful and kind.

My encouragers are many. They include Kaye Barley, Kathleen Hickey, Leslie Pfeil, Sheila Moses, Jodie Renner, Joni Inman, Jason Corriere, Kim Sawyer, Sheila Lowe, Sheryl Reichenbach, Tim Hallinan, Beth Terrell-Hicks, Carol Myers, Amy Ortiz and Kel Darnell. If I've left someone out (and I'm sure I have) my apologies.

Mom, I wish I could tie this book up with a bow for you. Your love of reading made my desire to write a no-brainer. It just took me a while to grow in to the idea.

Frances, you are the next best thing in my world for a mom today. You're a reader and a writer in your own right. You raised up a son who knows how to live a good life and love a good woman. For that, I am eternally grateful. Thank you.

George, you are my hero every day. You are an exceptional man of integrity and intelligence. I love you. Thank you for wanting this for me.

I'm blessed.

About the Author

A Colorado native, Peg Brantley is a member of Rocky Mountain Fiction Writers and Sisters In Crime. She and her husband make their home southeast of Denver, and have shared it with the occasional pair of mallard ducks and their babies, snapping turtles, peacocks, assorted other birds, foxes, a deer named Cedric and a bichon named McKenzie. *Red Tide* is Peg's first novel. Her second will be released in late 2012.

You can find Peg online at:

http://www.suspensenovelist.blogspot.com, her one-person blog, with her crime fiction buddies at http://www.crimefictioncollective.blogspot.com or at her website, http://www.pegbrantley.com

12399544R00156

Made in the USA
Charleston, SC
02 May 2012